Stolen Innocence

By Joe B. Parr

First Edition

http://joebparr.com

My Girls Publishing Fort Worth, TX

Print ISBN: 978-0-9913947-2-2

eBook ISBN: 978-0-9913947-3-9

For anyone who has ever felt powerless in their situation and for all those who have come to their aid.

Also by Joe B Parr

The Victim

Chapter 1

Oh God… This isn't a dream!

Her sob was cut short by the searing pain that radiated throughout her being. It hurt so bad, she sucked in air which multiplied the pain, a vicious cycle that culminated a moment later with her vision going dark. She was gone again.

The next sound her consciousness registered was metal clanging. She fought to come up from the darkness. The pain was still there, but she pushed past it as her eyes focused in the dim light. The stench of urine, sweat and something industrial assaulted her nose. When she moved, her clothes stuck to her and her stomach quivered at the realization that the stench was coming from her.

She tried to raise her hand but when the restraints bit into her wrist, the quiver transformed into bile in the back of her throat. Blinking her eyes against the blurred images, she explored her surroundings. Shadows, metal, grime.

What is this place?

No windows. No external light. No way to know if it was night or day. In spite of the sweat popping on her forehead, she shivered. Her mind started to process, chasing memories of how she got here. Nothing but snippets of scenes; inside a van, a bowl of rice, that awful cologne. Nothing made sense. She lifted her head but only for a moment. The pain kicked in again and she had to lie back down.

The fear rose from deep within. Panic took hold of her as she felt her pulse race. Her breath became rapid, shallow and her chest lifted as the mental gears spun out of control.

Calm down. Think. What's happening?

Thinking was so hard, everything in her head was dull and

foggy. She wanted to sleep but knew she couldn't. She concentrated on her freshest memory, breakfast with Mom, Katie laughing when she spilled her cereal. A tear leaked down her face as she tried to smile when she thought of her little sister, Katie.

Was that this morning? No, it couldn't have been. It seemed so long ago. Where are you Mom? Where am I?

The metal clanged, louder, closer. Something else now.

Footsteps?

She struggled against the restraints, both arms and legs were trussed. It was useless. She was trapped.

As she continued to process the sounds, her mind fought against the haze. More slivers of memories; being grabbed, a sharp stab in her arm, darkness. She slowed her breathing, clinched her fist and felt the soreness in her arm. Rolling her head to the side, she could see the leather straps, the sores on her arm.

Are those needle marks? I've been drugged.

She counted the marks and started to sob. A tear rolled down her temple and into her ear. Her memory flashed on a hand with a syringe.

Eight needle marks. How long have I been here? What's happening?

Another clang. It was a door. Now muffled voices, movement beyond the wall to her right. She strained to hear the words but couldn't. The voices got louder, but stopped at the sound of a slap and a shriek. Her panic rushed back. She pulled and tugged as she heard rustling sounds, a thud against the wall, then silence.

The door opened and closed again. The next sound was a metal door opening right behind her head. Her whole body tensed as she gasped and jerked her arms against the bonds.

"Well now. Look who's bright eyed and wide awake today."

The voice twanged from behind her, just out of view. The smell of cologne made her whole body convulse. She thought her heart might explode as it tried to beat out of her chest. Her breathing was now so hard and fast, she was actually wheezing.

"Oh, Madi, relax. It's just me."

A man came into view and although she didn't think it was

possible, her heart rate ticked up another notch. Her eyes opened wide and stared at him. She wanted to remember, but couldn't. His dirty blond hair hung over his face like a greasy teenager but he was well into his forties. Maybe it was the lighting, but his skin seemed both tan and pale at the same time.

He smiled, highlighting the odd shape to his eyes and exposing a right front tooth that was angled and overlapped the left. "Oh, I bet you don't even remember me. You have been a little out of it over the past few days." He patted her arm sending a jolt through her brain. "That sleepy juice sure makes the time fly, doesn't it?" He laughed, ending with a hacking cough.

"I'm Jimmy Le James." He smiled, but it dissolved into anger. "Yeah, that's right. My old man thought it'd be real funny to have a kid with the same first and last name." He sneered. "I got the last laugh though. Blew that son of a bitch's brains out."

Her heart jackhammered now but she forced her mind to keep processing. Something was familiar about him.

Did he just say he killed his father? Why would he tell me that? Why would he tell me his name?

She began to sob and shake as the answers to those questions sank in.

"Now, now. Don't cry. Jimmy's gonna take care of you. After all, we've gotten to be good friends over the last few days." He reached up and gently caressed her cheek with the back of his hand. Her head jerked away and her whole body shuddered.

When he took his hand away, she forced herself to calm. She refused to consider what he meant and tried to analyze her situation. Thinking clearly in the midst of chaos had always been one of her strengths. He'd mentioned a few days and the sleepy juice. She'd seen the needle marks. She needed to know more.

"My parents…" Her voice was raspy and sounded foreign.

"What's that darlin'? Oh no… No, I'm afraid we haven't talked to your folks."

Now that she'd broken her silence, her words came more quickly. "They'll pay. They're not rich, but they'll pay what they can."

Jimmy patted her hand and smiled at her. "I'm sure they would honey, but that wouldn't make much sense, now, would it? After all, why would we sell something once when we can sell it over and over again?"

Terror ripped through her brain like a machete. Her breath caught in her throat and her vision tunneled. She fought to stay awake.

"What do you mean?" Her voice was shrill and shaking now.

"It's just business. Of course, you did throw us a little curve ball. You told your little friend you were a virgin." He made a tsk tsk sound. "We thought we'd hit the jackpot - A beautiful sixteen year old, blonde hair, blue eyed virgin. Do you have any idea what our towel head buddies will pay for that combo? Those sheiks do love the white girls."

His words were there but the meaning was too insane for her to grasp. Everything was a blur, his voice sounded hollow and distant. She fought to make sense of what she was hearing.

"Of course, they insist that we certify the merchandise as pure. We were surely disappointed when the doctor checked you out." He shook his head. "I bet your parents don't know, do they?" He was enjoying himself now. "Who was he? Captain of the football team? The boy next door?"

He waved his hand as if it was no big deal, turned toward the end of the table and continued his monologue. "Oh, don't worry. Sure the boss was pissed at first, losing out on that big payday stung a little but that's okay. You're young. You'll make up for it over time."

He turned back toward her, his eyes gleaming with delight. "Besides, since your purity was no longer a selling point, I got to try out the merchandise." His crooked teeth seemed to jump out at her as he laughed into a coughing fit.

The revulsion hit her and she retched her head to the side and spewed the little that remained in her stomach. She heard herself make a keening sound like that of a wounded animal. The understanding of her situation was starting to break through her fear.

Business... Merchandise... Selling point... Oh my God. This isn't about ransom.

Her mind started to race. She couldn't let this happen. She

wouldn't. She looked at this sleazebag, pushed the thought of him touching her out of her mind. This was about survival now. Her arms and legs jerked against the restraints as she flailed.

"Now, now. Calm down. We've got to get you cleaned up." He paused, scrunched up his face. "You do kind of smell." He went to work on the leg straps. "The boss wants to spend some special time with you soon so we're going to get you in a shower and some new clothes. You'll feel so much better."

She brightened at the thought of getting out of the restraints. He unhooked one leg and started on the next. "See there, it'll be so much easier if I don't have to use the needle. You're gonna be good for me, aren't you?"

She nodded her head as her eyes darted around, absorbing everything.

No visible weapon. He's not that big. This may be my only chance.

As he moved to her arms, he slid his hand up her thigh, across her midsection and casually brushed over her breast. His smile sickened her and firmed her resolve. He was mumbling something about a shower and scrubbing her down but she wasn't listening, she was thinking, planning.

Her mind was all over the place, scanning the room, wondering how she got here and playing scenes from home. She noticed the keychain clipped to his belt as a scene in the back of a van flashed. She lost focus as she remembered her last birthday, her Dad smiling through tears as he handed her the car keys for her first solo drive.

Her second wrist came free and she felt like she could fly. Her heart was pounding but not out of control. The adrenaline coursed through her veins, giving her courage, strength.

He reached his hand for her. "Okay, now sit up."

She took his hand and pulled. Her fingers went straight for his face raking across his eyes, drawing blood. Her arms and legs all flew at once, hitting, kicking, clawing and slashing. She heard him yelp. He stumbled back. She was off the table, a whirling dervish. She turned to the door, grabbed the handle and pulled. No movement. It was locked.

The keys.

She turned. There was a flash of movement. He was standing in front of her, blood streaming down his face, one eye shredded, the other furious. She felt a burning sensation and reached for her neck. Her hand was warm and wet. There was a gurgling sound. The last thing she saw as her legs gave way was the glistening red knife blade.

Chapter 2

The dust kicked up from the white Ford Explorer's tires, drifted north along the riverbank and across the freeway as Detective Jake Hunter pulled to a stop. May in Fort Worth, Texas was always windy, but it's also warm and bright, and winter is a distant memory. He absorbed the beauty of the day for a moment before climbing out of the SUV. As a homicide detective with the FWPD, if he was on location it usually meant that beautiful days like this were about to be spoiled by the ugly results of violence.

He stepped out onto what looked like an old, overgrown parking lot, stretched his lean, six foot two inch frame, looked east toward the Trinity River and scanned from south to north stopping at the highway overpass. He reached back into the console, retrieved his Glock G17 9mm, clipped the holster to his belt and straightened his sport coat. Feeling the concrete below his loafers, he looked down and realized what he thought was a parking lot was really an old concrete slab. He searched his memory banks and remembered years ago when a section of metal self-storage units used to be on this spot. He took a moment and pictured them in his mind.

Knee high weeds scraped against his Gap jeans as he edged down the slope to the river Squinting against the afternoon sun, he brushed off his pants and absorbed the scene. The taped off perimeter was roughly a hundred foot square shape starting about two hundred feet south of the bridge and stretching from the water's edge up the bank and overlapping the bike path. There was an offshoot area taped off that led up the bank, encompassed a trampled down area in the weeds and stopped at the concrete twenty feet from where he'd parked. In the middle of the square, down close to the water was a sight barrier made from blue tarp.

So far, it appeared to be only law enforcement and a few onlookers but as he sloped down toward the tape, his peripheral vision caught a satellite news truck crossing the bridge. He badged the uniform at the tape. "You need to move the perimeter out another fifty feet in each direction." He thumbed toward the approaching truck. "The circus is on its way." The officer nodded as Hunter slipped under.

"'Bout time you got here Cowboy." Billy Sanders smiled as he looked up from his notepad, his dark brown shaven head glistened in the sun.

"Lunch ran late." Hunter's face was placid with just a hint of a smile as he nodded to his young partner.

"Is that the same reason our lead CSI is still on her way?"

"I'll leave that to your finely honed detective skills." He looked toward the sight barrier. "What do we have?"

Billy exhaled, shook his head. "It's a bad one."

"Can't remember the last good one."

They moved toward the barrier as Billy referred to his notes. "White female, no I.D., between fifteen and twenty, throat slit, signs of abuse including ligature marks."

The body was located about ten feet from the water line. Hunter squatted next to her, lifted the tarp and was struck by the viciousness of the jagged gash, the contrast of the dark red wound against the pale skin and the hollowness of what he thought were once beautiful blue eyes. His stomach quivered and he realized that even after a decade of murder scenes, he was never prepared for the young ones.

"So now that you've given me the basics, tell me what you really see."

Sanders rolled his shoulder and pushed on it with his hand, a nervous habit Hunter had noticed since his return. Although he still looked as fit as his college playing days, he was just now getting his muscle tone back after the weight loss. "What I see are contradictions. There are multiple needle tracks in her arms but there are no signs of long term drug use. The marks are all fresh, no scars. She's filthy beyond just being dumped in a field. You can smell the urine and vomit on her clothes. But beneath that, she seems well cared for. She may look ragged but she has all the signs of being upper middle class. No tats, no extraneous body piercings. Manicured nails and perfectly straight teeth. Her hair's dirty and oily but the cut is high end. Hell, those jeans cost well over a bill."

Hunter gave him a raised eyebrow.

"So I take my lady shopping every once in a while."

Hunter smiled but made no comment.

"Speaking of those jeans, they're normally worn skin tight but hers are loose like she hasn't eaten in several days. Combine that with the signs of being restrained and this looks like something way beyond just somebody getting mad."

Hunter nodded. Sanders had joined the detective squad six months ago and had been teamed with Hunter over his objections. Their first case, a series of gangbanger murders carried out by a vigilante, was one that should have been a gimme but turned into a national media circus before they solved it. It had also led to Sanders getting shot in the shoulder and spending three months in physical therapy. Since his return, Hunter had used every case as a teaching opportunity and it was clear that his student was coming along. "You've been paying attention, haven't you?"

"He certainly has." A voice with an accent that sounded like a Texan who had spent his formative years in an English boarding school, boomed from behind them causing both to turn.

Hunter grinned at Doc's pretentiousness. "So what did he miss, Doc?"

"For a site examination of the body without moving it, not much. The only thing I'd add before we get her back to my place is that she clearly fought back based on the amount of tissue under her fingernails." Doc brushed off the sleeve of his tweed jacket, lowered his wire rimmed glasses on his nose and looked over the top at both of them. "We'll get DNA to test. May not help you find the guy but it will most definitely help you convict him."

"We'll take whatever you can give us at this point." Hunter replaced the tarp and stood. He looked back up the bank and noticed that their lead CSI, Stacy Morgan had arrived and was already taking control of the CSI team. She caught his eye and smiled. His eyes brightened as he continued. "What about time of death?"

Doc ran his hand through his already ruffled gray hair. "Based on rigor, best guess at this point is somewhere between eighteen and thirty-six hours. When you throw in general body condition and location..." He pointed toward the busy freeway. "My guess is she departed this world yesterday and was dumped here sometime during the wee hours."

Hunter nodded, once again surveying the area.

"We'll know more once I get her on the table."

"Timing on that?"

"Well Cowboy, barring an unforeseen killing spree, I should be able to get to her first thing in the morning." He looked down at the tarp covered shape as if he could picture her in life and shook his head. "What a pity."

"You should clear it with Stacy, but as far as I'm concerned, you can transport her anytime you're ready."

Doc nodded and waved to a bulky looking assistant standing by the medical examiner van.

Hunter and Sanders climbed up the bank to where Stacy Morgan was conferring with two assistants. She dispatched each in a different direction, looked over a handful of evidence bags and began writing in the evidence log.

As the two detectives got closer, Hunter's eyes fixated on Stacy. Their romantic involvement had become one of the worst kept secrets in department history. They did, after all, work with a bunch of detectives and Hunter's efforts at secrecy were halfhearted at best. He absorbed the sun as it reflected off her auburn hair and his eyes drifted down to hers, vibrant green and intense, with a faint scar underneath the left one.

She caught his stare, blushed and smiled. Her hand waved as if shooing a fly and she directed her attention to Billy. "How are my two favorite detectives?"

Sanders looked at the stack of evidence bags. "As usual, waiting to hear what you have to tell us."

Her face drooped and she shrugged. "I wish I had more. The team has collected a number of items but the chances that any are connected to our scene are slim. Most of it just looks like debris from the area." She paused. "I'm sure Doc caught you up on anything related to the body. My guess is we won't find much here. This clearly wasn't the kill site and based on location…" She nodded toward the freeway. "The body dump was very late and very quick." She pointed back up the embankment. "And whatever we get from that area won't do us much good since the first responders all trampled down the exact same path the killer used when he dumped the body."

Hunter followed her hand and smile. "They're just trying to make your job more interesting." He continued a panoramic view of the area. "Doc said there was no ID on the body."

"Nope, but we took prints. I've got one of my guys on the way to get them processed. He's also going to run her description against the various missing person databases. We should have something back on both before the end of the day."

Sanders shook his head. "Hope Doc finds something in the morning. As it is, not much to go on."

Hunter's eyes were fixated on the Freeway and the bridge spanning the river.

"What are you thinking Cowboy?"

Hunter broke off his stare. "Probably nothing. Just think this is an odd dump site. Even in the middle of the night, it's awfully public. Seems risky."

Sanders nodded. "They certainly weren't trying to hide the body. Maybe they wanted her found." He shrugged. "Maybe they were just in a hurry."

"Who found the body?"

"A jogger. Spoke with him and cut him loose. He was pretty shook up. Really couldn't tell us much. Saw her from the path and called it in. Never got closer than about fifteen feet."

Hunter nodded. He watched as Doc's assistants wrestled the gurney with the black body bag up the river bank. His mind drifted back to the woman, girl really. He pictured the jagged tear across her otherwise perfect neck, those beautiful blue eyes. Somewhere, a set of parent's hearts were aching now, wondering where their little girl was. They would soon know. That knowledge would shatter their hearts completely.

Chapter 3

"We have an issue."

The man behind the desk looked up, his eyes placid but fixed on his underling standing in the doorway. He exhaled and motioned for the underling to enter and sit. He did as he was directed.

"Issues are a part of business." The man behind the desk leaned back in his chair and steepled his fingers. "You seem more concerned than usual."

"There's been an incident."

The man behind the desk didn't react or speak.

"Our guy… Over in HC." The underling fidgeted. "He was prepping our premium package for your inspection." He stopped, searched for his words. "She… The package… There was a confrontation and our guy disabled the package."

"Disabled?"

"Permanently."

The man behind the desk exhaled, stood and stared out the window behind his desk, his hands clasped behind his back. "Where's the package now?"

"Disposed."

The man's head whipped around, his eyes like lasers. "Where?" He immediately shook his head and motioned for his underling not to answer. "Will the package be found?"

The underling squirmed in his chair. "I didn't know of the issue until earlier today. As soon as he informed me, I drove to the location. The authorities were already there."

Rage flashed across the man's face but he reeled it in, exhaled and leaned his hands on the back of his chair. "Why would he be so sloppy? Is he really that stupid?"

"He panicked. He normally doesn't do anything without direction."

The man's eyes searched his desk as if there might be an answer lying there. He sat back down and splayed his fingers on the desk. "This is unacceptable. This is going to bring unwanted visibility to our operations."

"There's no tie to us…"

"Bullshit! If he was dumb enough to pick a public disposal site, he's dumb enough to leave something that ties back to him or to our operation."

The underling had no response.

"He's a liability. Eliminate him."

"What?"

"Did I stutter? Eliminate him, permanently and do it now. Make sure there are no ties to you or to the operation." The man behind the desk looked up at his underling, noted the uneasy look on his face. "Do you have a problem with my order?"

The underling started to say something but thought better of it. "No. I'll take care of it tonight."

"Is there anything else?"

"No."

"Good." He waved his hand toward the door. "There may be other things we need to do to cover our tracks. I need some time to think."

Chapter 4

"Madison Janelle Harper, just turned sixteen. She was a sophomore at Eastern Hills High School over in the Meadowbrook area." Sanders slid a picture across the desk to Hunter. He picked it up and studied it. As he suspected, in life, she was beautiful. Those blues eyes he'd seen earlier in the day radiated in her picture, her hair straight and golden.

A lump hung in his throat and he had to compose himself before he commented. When he did, his voice was strained. "What else do we know about her?"

"Not much. We just got the ID back about thirty minutes ago. There's a missing persons report on her. I played some quick telephone tag with the lead investigator." He glanced at his notes. "A Detective Bennett Hodges. He's available to debrief if you've got time. We'll have to drive over to the East Lancaster Street station."

Hunter had continued to stare at the picture, almost in a trance, as he listened to Billy. The silence when Billy paused broke his focus. "What? Uh, yeah, let's go."

Most of the ride east on Lancaster was quiet with Hunter lost in thought. His eyes squinted as the late afternoon sun reflected in his rearview mirror.

Sanders finally broke the silence. "You okay, Cowboy?"

Hunter didn't speak immediately. He continued to search the road ahead as if it held the answer. Finally, he slowly shook his head. His voice seemed to creak out. "I just hate it when the victims are young."

Sanders opened his mouth to respond but closed it and looked out the window. For a moment, he seemed to take on the same stoic expression that had covered Hunter's face since they'd left the station.

Hunter glanced over. "What?"

Sanders waved his hand. "Nothing."

"Come on. Spit it out."

Sanders' brow furrowed and pushed his cheek out with his tongue. "Look, don't take this wrong but could it be that you're far more broken up about it when those young victims are pale?"

Hunter's head whipped around. "What? What the hell is that supposed to mean?"

"I get it. I'm not dogging you. I mean. You're a white guy. You see a young blond girl murdered, it has more impact on you."

Hunter's volume went up a notch. "Are you serious? You think I'm more broken up because she's white?" He started to say more but seemed at a loss for words and shook his head.

"I don't remember you getting all knotted up when it was a bunch of black gangbangers getting knocked off. Most of those guys weren't much older than this one."

"That's diff... Come on. You can't compare..." His voice trailed off, his face tightened and his eyes locked back onto the traffic ahead.

"Different? Why? Because they were black males and she was a white female? Because they were poor kids who ended up in a gang and she was a rich kid from a nice neighborhood?"

"That's not... You know I didn't mean it that way." Hunter steered the SUV into the parking lot of the station, slammed it into a parking spot and was out before Sanders had a chance to say anything else.

By the time Sanders caught up with him inside, Hunter had already identified himself to the desk sergeant and had gotten directions on how to find Detective Hodges. As they moved up the stairs to the second floor, Sanders slowed Hunter down. "I didn't mean to piss you off. It was just..."

"I'm fine. Don't worry about it." He stopped and looked at his partner. "You have a point. It wasn't intentional." He turned and continued to the landing, through the door and into the Missing Persons squad room.

They located Hodges, made quick introductions and found an empty conference room to talk. Hodges had a file folder and two small stapled packets of copies. When they sat, he handed each of them one of the packets.

Hodges cleared his throat. "I hate to hear it turned out this way. There was no indication of foul play. It really looked like a runaway."

Hunter was irritated. He wasn't sure if it was Sanders' comments or the fact that Hodges had missed this one so badly. "Why don't you walk us through what you know about her and her disappearance?"

The distress of having not played the case right showed on Hodges face as he went through the summary. "We got the call last Saturday morning." He looked at his planner. "So, four days ago. The parents informed us that she never came home from school on Friday and they had left multiple voicemails, emails and texts with no response. They had spoken with all of her friends and no one had any information on her whereabouts. As is usually the case, her parents claimed life was great at home, she was doing well in school and she'd have no reason to run away."

Hunter spoke without looking up from his notepad. "Did you search the residence?"

Hodges nodded. "Had full access. Didn't have the crime scene guys out but my partner and I searched her room and gave the whole house a once over. Nothing out of the ordinary." He held his palms up. "We got a full profile and pictures. Got a list of friend's names and numbers. We spent the rest of the weekend talking with her friends and school officials."

"Anything noteworthy in those conversations?"

Hodges raised a finger and flipped through his notes. "Most of the friends parroted the parents but there was one friend..." He ran his finger down the page. "Here you go. Her name is Valerie Bryant. She and Madison had only known each other for a few months but apparently had gotten close. She indicated that Madison wasn't happy with her parents. Something about them pushing her too hard to start thinking about college and where she might play."

Sanders looked up. "Play?"

"Yeah. Madison was an ace soccer player. One hell of an athlete and team leader. She was only a sophomore but already a starter on varsity and a team captain. She was being recruited by half the D-1 schools in the country."

Hunter and Sanders exchanged glances. Hunter motioned for Hodges to continue.

"Anyway, between there being no sign of foul play, no ransom note and at least some indication that there might have been some stress at home, it looked like a runaway. Besides, we really had nowhere else to go with the investigation." Hodges closed his file and leaned back. "I've been in touch with the parents every day this week but they had no new information and neither did we."

Hunter tapped his pen on the table. "I don't remember seeing anything about this on the news. Did the parents go to the media?"

"They tried but the news has been so dominated this week by the tornados up in Oklahoma that they couldn't get any traction." He looked down and shook his head. "Bet they will now."

The three detectives spent the next hour reviewing the details of the profile, double checking names and contact information for friends and speculating on what might have happened.

Hunter looked at his watch and started to pack up. "Thanks for your help. We need to get over to the Harper's house before it gets too late."

Hodges' face dropped. "Uhh…"

Hunter gave him a questioning look.

Hodges pointed to Sanders. "We only found out about her when he called shortly before you got here." He paused looking uncomfortable. "No one's had a chance to notify them yet."

Hunter looked down. "Shit."

Hodges just stood there, silent, and looked at Hunter.

Hunter glared for a moment and his shoulders sagged slightly as he pointed at Hodges. "All right, I'll do it. You owe me one."

Chapter 5

With the orange fingers of light stretching across the western sky behind the house and the finely manicured lawn in front, the Harper home looked warm and loving, an idyllic setting in which to raise a family. Hunter knew, as he and Sanders walked up the sidewalk, that he was about to destroy what was left of that ideal.

Hunter stepped up on the porch. "This is going to be pretty awful. Just let me do the talking until things calm down."

"Not a problem." Sanders fidgeted as he watched Hunter ring the doorbell.

He could see the resemblance in the eyes of the woman who answered the door. The hair was a similar color, just a little courser and with touches of gray. The face, though pretty, was tired and her blue eyes were streaked with red. "Can I help you?"

Hunter showed his badge. "I'm Detective Jake Hunter and this is Detective Billy Sanders with Hom… uh, with the Fort Worth PD. May we come in? It's regarding your daughter."

Her face was confused for a moment but she stepped back and opened the door further. "We met with Detective Hodges this afternoon. Are you working with him? Has something happened?"

Hunter stepped past her and into the entryway. "We've been brought in on the case, ma'am. Is your husband home?"

Anxiousness now mixed with confusion as she wrapped her arms around herself and chewed the inside of her lip. "Yes, he's here. Do you have news?"

Hunter's eyes met hers, his expression stoic. He hesitated, then pointed to a couch. "Maybe we should sit down. Can you please ask him to join us?"

Before she could call him, her face began to scrunch in anticipation. Her voice was strained but firm. "Brooks, I need you in here now." She sank onto the couch and her hand moved up to cover her mouth as if she hadn't recognized her own voice.

A man in his late forties, similar in height to Hunter but heavier around the middle stepped into the room, looked at Hunter, then at his wife. Reacting to her expression, he turned back to Hunter as if he were about to come to her defense. Hunter quickly displayed his badge and motioned for Mr. Harper to sit beside his wife. He complied, sat perched on the edge of the cushion and wrapped his arm around her shoulder.

Hunter didn't hesitate. "Mr. and Mrs. Harper, I regret to inform you…" His voice failed in mid-sentence as Mrs. Harper buried her head into her husband's chest and let out a guttural wail.

"No. Oh, God, No!" Brooks Harper looked dazed as his wife's voice started to rise. "It can't be. Please God, it can't be!" She pushed back from his chest, her eyes pleading to him and then to Hunter.

Hunter's mouth gaped a couple of times as he tried to continue. He felt something and turned to see that Sanders' hand was on his arm, concern etched on his face. He realized he'd stopped talking and tried again. He found his much weakened voice. "We identified her body late this afternoon. I'm so sorry for your loss."

He'd finished his statement but knew they had not heard a word. She had once again buried herself in her husband and now their bodies heaved as they sobbed and held each other. There was nothing Hunter could do at this moment other than wait. He reached over and gently placed his hand on Mr. Harper's shoulder as a sign of support. He turned and saw the pained look on Billy's face. It never gets easier but the first time's the worst.

Minutes that seemed like hours to Hunter ticked away. The violence of the sobbing melted into a conjoined moan. Mr. Harper was the first to compose himself enough to speak. "I want to see my little girl."

Hunter cleared his throat. "We can arrange for that tomorrow after the autopsy is complete."

Mrs. Harper recoiled. "Autopsy?" She looked at her husband,

eyes wide. "Brooks, you can't let them cut up my baby." She burst into another round of tears.

Mr. Harper looked at Hunter but Hunter spoke before he could. "Ma'am, an autopsy is required by law in a suspected homicide."

It was Mr. Harper's turn to react. "Homicide? You mean Madi was murdered?"

Hunter met his eyes with a look that indicated this wasn't the time to discuss the details. "Yes sir." He seized the opportunity to try to regain a level of control. "I know this is awful timing, but in light of events, there are a number of questions we need to ask."

With a nod from Mr. Harper, Hunter began with basic questions. He wanted to get their minds distracted away from her death so that he could get them through the moment. He knew the pain of loss and knew that the only way to keep it from consuming everything was to move forward.

At first, their answers were short, halting and interrupted with painful sobs. As he continued quietly walking them through the questions, the memories took over and their tears were mixed with distant smiles. They talked about how she danced around the living room squealing when she made the varsity soccer team and how she cried when a few weeks later she was voted captain.

As with most parents, in their eyes she was as close to perfect as anyone could be. Her grades were solid. She struggled a little with math but excelled in language arts. She was taking a debate class and her teacher had suggested that next year she should try out for the debate team.

Once Hunter got them talking, all he had to do was guide them while they relived the moments. He knew that most of what he was hearing was already in the file provided by Hodges but he also knew that getting them to tell the story of her life was important for them. With each topic, he confirmed what he knew and dug a little deeper.

He verified the list of friends that Hodges had interviewed and got a couple more names. The Harpers didn't think she had any enemies but there was a girl at school with whom she'd recently had an argument. Sanders and Hunter made notes of even the things they already knew or that didn't seem to matter.

Hunter looked up after an hour and saw the spent expressions on their faces. "Mr. and Mrs. Harper, thank you for your time tonight. Is there anyone I can call for you? It might be good to have friends or family around tonight."

Switching the conversation back to the present seemed to bring the pain back to their faces. Mr. Harper shook his head. "Thank you Detective but we have several calls we need to make." He paused and stared at the floor. "It's going to be a long night."

Hunter nodded. "Yes it will, sir."

He leaned over and gave Sanders some instructions. Sanders excused himself and left out the front door. Hunter turned back to the Harpers, provided them with his card and gave them the contact information for the morgue. He then explained that a CSI team would be there early in the morning to process Madi's bedroom and look through the house. "I'm sure you've already been in her room but I've asked Detective Sanders to bring in some tape. We're going to have to seal it between now and when the CSI team arrives. If you could make sure no one disturbs anything, that would be helpful."

It was dark as Hunter and Sanders walked down the walk to his SUV. They sat in his truck, neither speaking for several minutes. There was a slight breeze and they could hear leaves rustling and crickets chirping, all the normal nighttime sounds of a warm, loving neighborhood. Hunter knew that this one would never be the same.

Chapter 6

Sanders let out a slow whistle as he and Hunter walked toward the front of Eastern Hills High School. "They didn't make high school girls like this in my day." It was a Thursday morning in May and the kids were dressed for spring.

"Slow down tiger. They're children."

"I'm just sayin'."

Hunter smiled as he opened the door. "I got news for you partner. You're almost thirty. As far as these girls are concerned, you might as well be in a wheelchair at Happy Manor."

"If I'm ready for Happy Manor, what does that make you?"

Hunter laughed. "Hell, I'm partying with St. Peter."

They cleared through the security guard and made their way to the office. Hunter badged the lady at the counter. "Fort Worth PD. We need to speak with the Principal."

Her eyes grew wide for a moment then she put up one finger. "Um, just one moment." She spun on her heels and marched off. A moment later she reappeared. "Mr. Thompson will see you now. Please follow me."

Mr. Thompson, a lean man with wire rimmed glasses, was seated behind an immaculately kept rustic oak desk. Hunter appraised him as he walked through the door and thought his thinning gray hair looked as if it had once been long and likely worn in a ponytail. Thompson finished jotting a note and looked up as Hunter and Sanders were both displaying their badges.

"Mr. Thompson, I'm Detective Jake Hunter. This is Detective Billy Sanders." They put away their badges. "We have a short list of students we'd like to interview in regards to the Madison Harper case."

Hunter handed him a list of six names.

Mr. Thompson reached out and shook their hands. "Please call me Samuel." He motioned to the two leather chairs. "Everyone was shaken by Madi's disappearance. A Detective Hodges spoke with these kids earlier in the week. Was he not satisfied with the information they provided?"

"Mr. Thompson, I'm afraid there's been a development in the case. Madison Harper's body was found yesterday afternoon so…"

"Oh dear God." Thompson's face was stricken as he pushed back in his chair. "How awful. We hadn't been told."

"Her parents weren't notified until late last night." Hunter pointed to the list. "In light of the new situation, we need to re-interview her friends."

Thompson looked as if he were going to get ill. "Certainly." He tapped the list on the arm of his chair and looked out the window, blinking several times. "I'm sorry Detective. This is just a bit of a shock. We knew she was missing, but you never think…" He took a deep breath, blew it out, puffing his cheeks. "Madi was… Well, she was one of the good ones."

"Sir." Hunter nodded toward the list.

"Oh, yes." He leaned forward and reached for his desk phone. "We got releases from their parents for the interviews with Detective Hodges. Those are still in force. Do you want to speak with them as a group or individually?" His finger punched the intercom button eliciting a buzzing sound.

Hunter spoke before there was an answer. "One at a time would be preferable."

A female voice squawked on the speaker. "Yes Mr. Thompson."

"We need to set the Detectives up in a conference room and make arrangements to have some students speak with them one at a time. I've got a list for you."

"Yes sir. I'll be right in."

Thompson stood, extended his hand. "Detectives, you have our full cooperation. Let me know how I can help."

The assistant led Hunter and Sanders down the hall, set them up in a conference room and got them some coffee. "Mr. Thompson said you had a list of students?"

Hunter handed her the slip of paper. "If you could send them in one at a time. We'll need about twenty minutes with each."

She nodded, turned to leave but stopped and turned back. "I'm sorry Detective but Valerie Bryant was out sick yesterday and is still out today. I can give you her phone number if you need to contact her at home."

"That'd be great. Thanks."

After she left, Sanders stepped to the window, looked out and shook his head. "This ought to be fun. We get to break the news five more times."

Hunter shook his head. "Naw. Maybe not even once. My guess is that by the time the first one walks in the door, the whole school will know. A tsunami of text messages are burning through cyberspace as we speak. Everyone in the school already knows we're here. Someone will have a source in the office. Hell, I'm surprised you and I haven't already gotten texts, or tweets or pokes or whatever."

Sanders laughed. "For an old man, you got a little street tech savvy."

"Keeps me alive." Hunter smiled. "That, and my partner's good aim."

"Damn straight."

Hunter's phone rang. He looked at the caller ID, noticed it was Andre Kipton, the Police writer for the Star Telegram. He shook his head and let it go to voicemail.

A timid knock and the sound of a sniff drew their attention to the door. A petite brunette with big, brown, tear-filled eyes stood holding a back pack. "I'm Erin Perkins. Mrs. Brown said you needed to see me."

"Yes Miss Perkins, please come in a sit down."

As she stepped forward, she looked at Hunter, her eyes seeming to plead. "Is it true? Is Madi really..." A sob coughed out and her face contorted.

Hunter pulled out a chair and guided her by her arm. "Yes

ma'am, I'm afraid so." He circled around to the other side of the table and sat down. "We're hopeful you can help us in our investigation. We have a few questions."

Her head was bobbing up and down as she now started to cry harder.

This was the first of five nearly identical scenes. Jacqueline Lowery, McKenzie McBride, Sage Tyler and Trevor Carson followed Erin. Trevor put up a brave front but Hunter sensed his pain may have been the most genuine of the group.

They had finished up the interviews and it was closing in on noon. Hunter paused a moment from keying in notes and rubbed his neck. He and Sanders were still sitting in the EHHS conference room debriefing after almost four hours of listening to teenagers fight back tears and overuse the words 'like' and 'you know'.

Sanders got up and stretched. "That was painful and the worst part is I don't think we learned anything."

Hunter stopped clicking, pushed back in his chair and referenced his hand written notes. "We didn't get much but we might've gotten something." He flipped through several pages and looked at Sanders. "Did you hear a pattern to their answers when I asked them, 'when was the last time you and Madi hung out'?"

Sanders sat back down. "Let me see… Erin said, 'We really haven't in a while. She's been hanging out with Val'." He flipped a couple of pages. "Jacqueline said, 'I don't know, a couple of months or so. She and Val have been buddy-buddy'." He eyed Hunter while turning more pages. "McKenzie said, 'I can't remember. Lately her and Val have been kind of standoffish'." Sanders smiled.

Hunter nodded. "Yeah, you can go on, but Sage said basically the same thing and the one that sealed the pattern was Trevor. He clearly had the hots for Madi and was put off by the fact that she was dodging him to spend time with Valerie."

Sanders arched his eyebrows. "Sounds like we need to talk to Valerie. Guess we'll have to wait for her version since she's out sick."

Hunter tipped his head. "We'll get her address and phone number on the way out." He looked at his watch. "She's on our list but first we've got a date with Doc at the morgue." Hunter grinned at Sanders. "So, do we visit Doc before or after we eat lunch?"

Chapter 7

"Stop staring at the building like that. It's not going to bite." Hunter opened his door and got out. "You were twitchy all through lunch. Come on, let's go."

Sanders sat a moment longer, exhaled deeply and slid out of the passenger side. "It just gives me the creeps."

"You're a homicide detective for God's sake. You can't tell me you're freaked out by dead bodies."

"It's not the dead bodies that freak me out, it's what they do to them." Sanders shuddered. "Cut 'em up. Slice and dice them. Take out their innards. That's just not natural."

Hunter was still shaking his head and laughing when they pushed through the double doors into Autopsy Two. Doc was washing his hands as one of his techs was cleaning up the area. A white cotton sheet covered a body lying on the table. Hunter paused as he processed the size and shape. He knew it was Madi Harper and he also knew that the damage inflicted by the killer was mild compared to what Doc was required to do. It was an indignity no one should have to endure, especially someone so young.

"What a rare treat, being visited by two of Fort Worth's finest. How are we today gentlemen?" Doc smiled broadly, unaffected by his work.

Hunter didn't return the smile, his eyes taking a moment to turn from the sheet. "We'll be better if you can tell us something we don't already know about our victim."

"My, you do have high expectations."

"And?"

"I do hope you take a little more time warming up with your

favorite CSI."

Hunter just raised an eyebrow and stared.

"All right. As usual, I will exceed your expectations." Doc reached over and picked up a clipboard where he'd made notes and drawn pictures. "I don't think I'll surprise you with the cause of death or that other than that hideous gash across her throat, she was in perfect health." Doc held up one finger. "But, have you ever been in the middle of something and all of a sudden your mind drifts to a very vivid scene from way back in your past?"

Neither detective answered. They just exchanged confused looks.

Doc didn't wait. "Psychologists will tell you that those random memory bursts are usually triggered by something in your current environment, maybe a sound or a color or a smell." Doc paused, leaned back against the countertop and drifted off in thought.

Hunter cleared his throat.

Doc startled. "Oh, yes, sorry." He raised a finger for emphasis and continued. "So you can imagine my bewilderment when, in the middle of the autopsy, I found my thoughts drifting back to my days as a medic in Viet Nam."

Sanders cocked his head. "You were in Viet Nam? You don't look old enough."

Doc smiled. "I was only there for a short time right at the tail end in seventy-five and I was fresh out of high school, barely eighteen at the time." Doc waved his hand to get back to his story. "At first I didn't think anything of it but after a few moments, I began to wonder what had triggered my thoughts." He tapped his pen on the clipboard. "It finally dawned on me. It was a smell, specifically the smell of her stomach contents, what little there were."

Both detectives involuntarily curled their noses at the thought.

Doc didn't notice but circled something on the page and handed it to Hunter. "I found two spices. Two very distinct spices - Cinnamomum Loureiroi and Persicaria Odorata, better known as Saigon Cinnamon and Vietnamese Coriander." A big, self-satisfied smile broke across his face.

Hunter's expression didn't change. "I'm sure you're going to get to your point eventually."

"Don't you see? Clearly during her last few days, she had to have eaten a preponderance of Vietnamese food, and I don't mean some American version. I'm talking about real, authentic Vietnamese food."

Sanders shrugged. "So how does that help us?"

Hunter, now sharing Doc's smile, stopped Doc from answering by holding up his hand. "Think about it for a second."

Sanders rubbed his chin, rolled his shoulder and squinted his eyes as if he were trying to see the answer in the air. After a moment, he snapped his fingers and his eyes lit up. "There can't be very many real authentic Vietnamese restaurants in the area and if she was eating it every day, wherever they were keeping her had to be close by."

Hunter nodded. "Exactly. The only other alternative would be that her captors were cooking authentic Vietnamese food for her. That doesn't seem likely and even if that were the case, they'd still need the ingredients and I bet you can only buy that stuff at a Vietnamese grocery store."

Sanders continued the thought. "Which means we're looking for someplace close to Vietnamese restaurants and/or grocery stores. That's got to narrow down the possible areas."

Hunter had begun pacing, his hand on his chin and his eyes locked on the floor. "Well, it may make that haystack smaller but it's still pretty big and that needle is still damn small."

"Maybe I can help narrow it a little further." Doc flipped the pages on his clipboard while both detectives stopped and stared. "Here it is." Doc handed the clipboard to Hunter. "Tetrachoroethylene. I found traces of it on her skin and clothes."

Hunter looked confused. "In English Doc?"

"It's a chemical solvent used predominantly in the dry cleaning industry."

"You think she was held at a dry cleaner?" Sanders furrowed his brow.

Hunter had stopped pacing, his eyes were lit up. "No. That wouldn't make sense. Too public. Too much traffic. But..." He was talking with his hands now. "There are a lot of dry cleaners that are really just store fronts. They don't actually do the cleaning at the store. The clothes are only there when they're dropped off and when they're ready for pick up. The actual dry cleaning itself is done offsite, usually in a warehouse of some nature. Some of those are near sweatshop level"

"Even so. If you've got a bunch of employees running around all day, how do you store a prisoner without someone noticing?"

Doc raised a finger. "Keep in mind, I said traces. It's a rather nasty chemical that would tend to permeate a building and might leave residue for quite some time, even if the facility was no longer in use."

"No longer in use..." Hunter reached for his keys and moved toward the door. "Billy, let's roll. We need to get Nguyen and Reyes. We've got a building to find."

Billy was on his heels. "That'd be an empty building, formerly used as a dry cleaning facility that just happens to be close to an authentic Vietnamese restaurant?"

Chapter 8

Hunter hadn't slowed down since leaving Autopsy Two. On the drive, he'd called Pete Nguyen, a detective from the gang unit who specialized in the Vietnamese groups, as well as Jimmy Reyes, one of his fellow homicide detectives in Central Division. Both were available and agreed to meet him within the hour at the FWPD Central Division station.

Sanders followed Hunter into the conference room on the second floor of the Central Division Station, walked directly over to the whiteboard and started erasing it. Hunter, full of nervous energy, walked to the windows facing the Performing Arts Center and started adjusting the blinds.

When Sanders was satisfied with the whiteboard, he turned to Hunter. "How do you want things set up, Cowboy?"

Hunter spoke while continuing to stare out the window. "Call Tech Support. We'll need three laptops and a printer set up on one of the tables." He spun toward the front of the room and pointed. "Find the area map that's covered in Plexiglas and wheel it in here. We're going to have to mark possible locations. Make sure we have plenty of markers" He stepped toward a table. "Grab the other end, let's put these tables in a U shape."

Sanders was already moving. He and Hunter rearranged the room to fit the team they had assembled. Just as they were setting the last table in place, the door opened Jimmy Reyes' voice rang out. "Looks like they finally found something to fit your qualifications Cowboy." He laughed at his own joke. Hunter rolled his eyes.

Reyes, a short, stocky Hispanic with streaks of gray highlighting his jet black hair, was followed into the room by a techie from the IT team who looked to be barely out of high school. Hunter debriefed Reyes on the case while Sanders worked with the techie and directed where the laptops and printer should be placed.

Just as the techie was running a test print from the second laptop, Pete Nguyen walked into the room. While Pete had been on the force longer than anyone in the room, his physical fitness, easy smile and wrinkle free face allowed him to pass for much younger, a necessity when the specialty was gangs.

Hunter nodded. "Pete, thanks for coming so quickly."

"Glad to be here." He looked around the room, smiled. "Looks like we're getting the band back together."

After quick handshakes between the detectives, Hunter stepped to the front of the room and looked at his watch. "Let's get moving. It looks like we've got a warm trail and I don't want to let it get cold."

He spent the next twenty minutes detailing everything Hunter and Sanders knew about the case from the original disappearance through the new information learned earlier that day. "To sum up, we need to find where our victim was held between her disappearance and when her body was found. We think she was in a building that is or was used as a dry cleaning shop and is located very close to authentic Vietnamese restaurants or grocery stores." He twirled a dry erase marker in his hand and looked at the team. "Our job today is to find that building."

Hunter tossed the marker to Nguyen. "Your turn."

Pete caught the marker as he rose from his chair. "I can help with the Vietnamese criteria." He walked over to the area map and drew a rectangle. "There are pockets of Vietnamese communities throughout the city but there are two that are significant in size and density. The reason is that when the refugees landed from South Vietnam in the mid-seventies, local churches were the major facilitators for helping them get settled."

He pointed to an area in the southeast corner of the map. "Although it didn't exist back then, today, the Vietnamese Martyrs Catholic Church in Arlington is the center of one of those two major pockets." He came back to the rectangle. "The other one is St. George's

Catholic Church over in the Riverside area. That's where I think we should focus based on where the body was found and on other socioeconomic factors… Crime rate, industrialization, etc.

"This rectangle represents the most densely populated Vietnamese community in Tarrant County. It basically runs southwest to northeast along Belknap Street starting just west of Beach Street and stretching to Haltom Road. That's about a mile and a half stretch of Belknap. Include three blocks north and go south to Airport Freeway and you've got your rectangle."

He put down the marker. "Even though the area isn't that big, the bad news is, there are a ton of places a person could be hidden in that box."

Sanders had been quiet to that point but now perked up. "That's where the dry cleaning angle comes in. How many can there be in that small an area?"

Nguyen grinned. "You might be surprised, especially if we're talking about a place that used to be a dry cleaner. That part of the world is littered with industrial buildings, many that have been there forever and have been used for just about everything at some point in their lifecycle."

Reyes grinned, pointed to the map. "Guess we've identified our haystack." He thumbed over his shoulder at the laptops. "We've got access to Building Permits, Usage Permits and Building Inspections along with Mapquest and Google Earth. Let's go find our needle."

They spent a few minutes defining their criteria for what the needle might look like and working through a process of elimination for how to narrow their list. With that, Sanders, Reyes and Hunter started working the laptops with Nguyen scribing on the white board, making his own notes on the map and giving his personal intel on the possible buildings.

The afternoon dragged on with a familiar cadence of identifying a building, determining its current and past usage, finding it on the map, applying Nguyen's thoughts and some basic logic and in almost every case, eliminating it from the list.

By four, the team was in dire need of caffeine and Hunter made a run to Starbucks to visit Bernard, his favorite barista. By six, the map was full of crossed out circles and the white board filled with scratched through addresses. Sanders' eyes were bloodshot and Hunter had run his hands through his hair so many times, it was spiked straight up.

Reyes pushed back in his chair. "Guys, all the lists I've got are done."

Sanders looked up from his notes. "Same for me."

Hunter had been pacing with his fingers interlocked on top of his head. He stopped and stretched. "So, Pete, where does that leave us?"

Pete scanned the map for a moment, then walked to the board and circled two addresses. "These are the only two we haven't eliminated. They are both on Higgins, about three blocks from each other. One's at the corner of Higgins and Earl, the other is at Higgins and Goldie. Both appear to have no current usage permit and both were once used for dry cleaning."

Reyes, Sanders and Nguyen all turned toward Hunter in unison.

"Okay. We need to plan to hit both places in the morning which means we need to get eyes on both of them tonight and we need paper for the search."

Pete chimed in. "I can check them out this evening. My partner and I already have some business over in that area. We can swing by a few times to see if there's any sign of life and to scope out obstacles for the morning."

"Perfect. Jimmy, can you and Billy get warrants drawn up for each building. We can reevaluate in the morning based on Pete's drive-by's. We'll make a call on whether to hit one or both and then get the necessary docs signed." He paused, his eyes distant. "I hope we're right."

Before he could comment further, his phone buzzed. He held up a finger asking them to hold and read the text message. "Hmm. That's interesting. Looks like my job will be to follow up with CSI on something they found at the Harpers."

All three of the other detectives started laughing. Hunter looked up with a genuine look of confusion. "What?"

Sanders rolled his eyes. "Let me get this straight. Jimmy and I get to write up a bunch of paperwork, Pete gets to spend the evening reconnoitering a couple of warehouses and you *have to* have dinner with your girlfriend."

Hunter slid his phone down the table. "This is pure business. Stacy says she found something strange when they processed the girl's room and says I need to see it tonight." A sly grin crept across his face. "Of course, now that you gave me the idea, dinner sounds nice."

Chapter 9

Stacy Morgan had spent the early morning hours at the Harper's home and then the rest of the day working with her team at the Tarrant County Forensic Labs, which shares a facility with the Medical Examiner. Her team's preliminary findings had prompted her to drive over to Central Division so she could confer with Hunter.

Hunter had suggested dinner but had been lost in thought and had barely spoken since they left the station. He hadn't even bothered to ask Stacy about her day or if she had a preference about where to eat.

Since she wasn't up to speed on Hunter's afternoon session, she was confused as to why they had left downtown and were now in the Riverside area. With overt sarcasm, she enacted a two sided conversation. She started in a mock deep voice. "So Stacy, where would you like to eat tonight?" She switched back to her normal voice. "Oh, I don't know Cowboy, how about we go over to Riverside since there are so many great dining options."

Before she continued, Hunter broke out of his fog. "What? Oh, um, sorry. There's a new Fuzzy's Tacos just around the corner on Race Street. You like Fuzzy's don't you?"

She eyed him for a moment as they turned onto Race. "Fuzzy's is great, but you're missing my point."

Hunter steered his Explorer into the parking lot and found a spot. "Sorry Stace, just processing a little too much information at once." He nodded to the restaurant. "Let's go have some tacos and a beer."

As they walked toward the restaurant, Stacy caught up to Hunter and stopped him with a gentle tug on his arm. When he turned to her, her green eyes glowed with concern. "Are you okay?"

He tried to look away but she reached up and softly turned his face toward hers. He finally relented. "I'm fine. It's just this case... The victim... It's getting to me. That's all."

She pulled his face toward her and kissed him gently on the lips. "Now, let's go have some tacos and let me tell you what I found. Maybe that will help."

After ordering their food and getting their beers, they sat down to wait for their orders. The Rangers game was playing on several of the big screens so Hunter was a bit distracted until their number was called and he'd retrieved their food. She smiled when Hunter took a bite of his tempura fish tacos and made a 'mmm' sound. After a moment, he took a sip of beer and tipped his bottle toward Stacy. "So, fill me in on everything."

She wiped her mouth with a napkin. "Hodges had collected her laptop and diary during his first visit. I had one of my guys run over to Lancaster to pick them up even though he said they'd looked through both and had found nothing of interest. I'll make sure you get those tomorrow so you or Billy can look at them."

"What about her phone, wallet or driver's license?"

"Nope. Hodges said she had them with her when she left for school that morning. They checked on the GPS but haven't gotten any signal." She took a small bite and continued. "The rest of my team hit the house a little after eight." She paused, hung her head and blinked away tears. "Those poor parents. They looked like they hadn't even tried to go to bed. God, that must be awful."

Hunter nodded without making eye contact and took a long swig of beer. He waited for her to continue.

"We really weren't out there long. There wasn't much ground to cover. We used Luminol to check for any blood or semen. No surprise, negative on both. It didn't seem to make sense to worry about DNA samples, so the rest of the time was spent dusting for prints."

"Anything in particular?"

Stacy shook her head. "We hit all the main surfaces and any objects that were out. Really figured it was a long shot, but we wanted to see who had been in her room. By midmorning, we were back at the lab."

Hunter cocked an eyebrow. "And?"

"That's where it gets weird. The bulk of what we had were prints, most of which I assumed were from her family and friends. We collected prints from the parents and the sister and set those up in the system. That eliminated about half of the prints taken right off the bat. I figured any prints left would end up being friends so we just grouped them and narrowed them down to about five distinct sets." She took a drink and stared for a minute as if she wasn't sure she should continue. "Just on a whim, since there were only five sets and I had some time, I decided to run them through AFIS." She looked across the table at Hunter. "I got a hit."

"In AFIS? Are you sure?"

"Ran them twice and then checked them manually under a magnifying glass."

Hunter leaned forward, eyes wide. "Does that mean we have a suspect?"

"Not exactly. The prints matched a missing girl from Amarillo named Caitlin Ann Gardner."

"A missing girl? What the hell?"

"Exactly my reaction. How in the world do prints from a teenager who went missing eighteen months ago, end up in Madison Harper's bedroom?"

They both sat in silence. Hunter took a swig of beer, his eyes absently drifting up to the game but his mind clearly processing what he'd just heard. He picked up a chip, dipped it in the queso and swirled it around, apparently more for something to do with his hands than for eating. "What do we know about this missing girl?"

"At this point, not much, just her name, that she was a suspected runaway and that she was fourteen at the time."

"So that would make her right around sixteen now." He cocked his head. "Same age as Madi Harper."

"Coincidence?"

Hunter leaned back in his chair. "Not a big believer in those. Do you know where in the bedroom you found those prints?"

"According to my notes, they were on the box for a new iPad.

Madi had gotten it as a present recently, but hadn't had time to start using it."

"Do we know who gave her the present?"

Stacy shook her head. "We'll have to ask."

Hunter shrugged. "The iPad was recently bought. The Amarillo kid could have been the store clerk or just another shopper who happened to pick it up off the shelf. There are a number of ways her prints could have gotten on that box."

Stacy furrowed her brow incredulously. "The fingerprints of a missing sixteen year old from Amarillo just happen to show up in the bedroom of a missing sixteen year old from Fort Worth. Coincidence. Right."

"Looks like tomorrow's going to be a busy day."

Chapter 10

"I come bearing gifts." Anytime he asked the guys to get in especially early, Hunter knew it was wise to bring Starbucks coffee and pastries. It was 7:30 and Reyes, Billy, Nguyen and Nguyen's partner Jay Tran were already getting settled but were easily distracted with the goodies.

"Jay, good to see you." Hunter shook his hand. "Thanks for coming out this morning."

"Wouldn't miss it, Cowboy." He filled his cup. "Looked like a couple of prime targets last night." He breathed in the scent of the coffee. "Besides, I knew you'd bring the good stuff."

After the troops were fed and well caffeinated, Hunter looked to Pete. "Catch us up on what you guys saw."

Pete had already drawn a rudimentary map of Higgins Street on the white board. "Jay and I scoped both locations last night. One at the corner of Higgins and Earl." He drew an X in a square. "Here." He moved to his right. "And one at the corner of Higgins and Goldie." He drew another X in another square.

He turned to the team. "We cruised both locations multiple times between eight and midnight. No activity, lights or sign of life at either. Once it got late and the traffic died down, we did a quick perimeter search on each, but found no clear windows, no view inside." Hunter stiffened. "No worries, Cowboy. It was dark and we were careful not to be seen."

Reyes smirked. "Yeah, just like ninja's."

Jay rolled his eyes. "Dude, ninja's are Japanese. We're Vietnamese. Get your Asians straight."

That brought a round of laughter from the team. Hunter quieted them and motioned for Nguyen to continue. He pointed to his first x. "Both have potential to be our location, but between the two, my money's on Earl. It's bigger. It sits on the corner with vehicle access from both streets. It's got a parking area in the rear with an iron fence and gate. On the Earl Street side, it's got three rollup garage doors which would allow someone to pull a vehicle inside where they could load or unload without being seen. Also, the walk-through doors are steel with deadbolts and no windows. Very secure."

He moved to the second x. "Goldie is smaller. The only real access is in the front in plain view of the traffic light at Higgins and 28th. Behind the building is cluttered with junk." He paused. "Still wouldn't discount it, just think we have better odds with Earl."

Hunter stood with his arms crossed, staring at the board. He could feel the momentum building. One of these buildings is it. After a moment, he nodded. "Reyes, let's get signatures on both. We'll hit Earl first and Goldie second. Can you get that moving while we sketch out a plan?"

"You got it, Cowboy." With that, he was up with the documents in his hand and out the door.

Hunter looked at Pete. "What else have you got?"

"We took photos of both buildings from multiple angles. I printed eight by tens. I also printed out a map of Higgins Street." He laid out two stacks with five pictures in each and the map. "Let's take a look at target one, Earl."

Hunter, Billy, Pete and Jay gathered around the table and walked through each photo and reviewed the map. They spent the next hour talking through a number of scenarios including approach points, cover points, resource locations and the sequence of actions to get into each of the buildings.

When they had a plan defined, Hunter looked at the team. "What should we be prepared to find once we're in the buildings?"

Nguyen shrugged. "Chances are we find an empty building."

Jay leaned back. "Worst case, we meet a bunch of bad guys with guns." He pointed to the map. "Think our plan covers that possibility. Best case, we find an empty building with enough evidence to lead us right to the killer."

"What about other victims?" Everyone turned to Billy. He put out his hands, palms up. "Well, it's possible."

"Good catch. We need to make sure we've got a wagon on call in the area." Hunter gave Sanders a thumbs-up.

"Here we go boys!" Reyes burst through the door with the search warrants clutched in his hands. "It's rock and roll time."

Hunter nodded, turned back to the team. "Let's get ready."

The mood shifted, smiles disappeared. All five detectives began what looked like choreographed movements. Each one donned their vest, inspected their magazines, chambered a round and holstered their weapons. Hunter passed out hand held radios and made sure cell phones were on silent. They left the rear of the building and loaded into two vehicles, Hunter and Sanders in his SUV and Reyes, Nguyen and Tran in Reyes' sedan.

There was minimal conversation on the short ride east on Airport Freeway. Hunter's eyes drifted to the right as they passed the location where the body had been found. He thought about how the dump location made more sense if one of these buildings was the murder scene. It was close, the first open area someone would stumble on, and technically, since the buildings were located in Haltom City, it was in a different jurisdiction. Hunter wasn't sure he would give them that much credit.

As the vehicles exited the freeway and neared the area, the landscape changed dramatically. Strip centers lined both sides of the street with shops, stores and restaurants that had names like Phuong, Phat Dat and Pho Nam. Hunter nodded to himself as he thought about Doc's findings. You can definitely find authentic Vietnamese food here.

Hunter had coordinated with the Haltom City Police Department so that they'd have support from a HCPD patrol car. They drove past Higgins on down to Layton and circled back so they could meet the HCPD at Higgins and Creech. This would allow them to approach from the north, block the garage doors with Reyes' sedan while parking Hunter's SUV on Higgins directly in front of the door.

The patrol car was waiting for them. Hunter got out and spoke with the officers, providing a quick briefing. At that point, Nguyen joined Hunter in his vehicle. The plan called for Nguyen to enter with Hunter and Sanders so that he could bark commands in Vietnamese just in case this was tied to the local gangs. When they were set, Hunter walked to each car. "Get ready boys. We're live on this one."

You could almost smell the excitement as they pulled out to caravan the three short blocks south to Higgins and Earl. Moving fast but without lights or sirens, Reyes led with Hunter next and HCPD following. The trip lasted thirty seconds. Reyes took a hard right on Earl, moved diagonally into the driveway. He and Tran were out and moving as Hunter squealed to a stop on Higgins with the HCPD car pulling in tight behind him.

In seconds, the teams were in position: Reyes and one officer were on the north side of the building pushed up against the white brick between the windows and the three rollup doors. Both had their weapons drawn. Similarly, Tran and the second officer were at the southeast corner of the building by the iron gate. Hunter's heart pounded as Sanders and Nguyen took their positions by the front door. He ticked through his moves in his head as Sanders kneeled by the doorknob with a powered lock pick gun. If this was the place, they had to be perfect.

Hunter nodded to him. He inserted the needle and went to work. Hunter banged on the door with his fist. "Fort Worth Police. We have a warrant. We're coming in."

Sanders had made quick work of the two locks. By the time Hunter looked back at him, Sanders had tossed the pick gun, drawn his pistol and pushed the door open. The three men moved in unison, Sanders first, low and moving right, Hunter next, high and moving left, Nguyen followed. With all three men yelling at once and with Nguyen yelling in Vietnamese, the cacophony of voices was loud and jumbled.

In seconds, Sanders had moved into one small office. "Clear!"

Hunter hit the next room. "Clear."

Nguyen bolted down the short hall, through an open door into the garage area. He stopped two steps into the space, his gun held out in front of him, moving from side to side. Hunter and Sanders took up similar positions on each side of him.

For a moment, nobody spoke. You could hear all three breathing heavy as the adrenaline coursed through their veins. Sanders lowered his arms, his face jumbled in disbelief, his voice low and hoarse. "Sweet Jesus."

Hunter unclipped the hand held from his belt, clicked the mic. "Reyes, we're clear in here. This is definitely our place. Have the HCPD set up a perimeter and call in CSI." He clicked off the radio, continued to stare forward, eyes blinking as if trying to adjust.

What he saw roiled his gut. To his left, a caged-in area stretched thirty feet along the south wall, about ten feet deep. Chains hung from the walls. The floor of the caged area was littered with dirty blankets and thin mats. There were no toilets, just five gallon buckets. The third garage bay had been replaced by two small rooms. Their doors were open with most of their contents visible. The other two garage bays were open space and available for vehicles.

"Guys, I'm going to step over to those rooms to make sure there aren't any surprises. I want you two to step out of the building. Be careful to keep contamination to a minimum. This whole place will have to be processed."

Both men nodded, holstered their weapons, took one last look around and started to leave. Hunter stopped Sanders. "Nobody comes in here without my say so. Got it?"

"No problem Cowboy." His voice raspy.

Left alone, Hunter stood in the silence and surveyed the room. He could smell the human odors, sweat, urine, feces. It was clear that people had been held here. Hunter wondered how many and for how long. His mouth went dry as his mind processed the likely answers.

His thoughts were interrupted with the sounds of approaching sirens. Rays of dim light from the frosted windows streaked across the room. He moved forward to the two small rooms, careful where he placed his feet.When he peered into the first room, his stomach lurched. His eyes scanned the metal table, the built in leather restraints, the makeshift cabinets with their doors open and the floor littered with hypodermic syringes, empty medicine bottles and cotton swabs.

What kind of hell is this place?

He moved to the second room. It looked the same. Now he could hear cars stopping, doors slamming and voices. He knew he should leave but his head was swirling and his thoughts were slow and confused.

"Hunter!" Sanders' booming voice cleared his mind. "You okay in there?"

"I'm good. On my way." Hunter retraced his steps across the garage area, down the hall and out the front door.

What had been a quiet side street fifteen minutes ago now looked like a circus. Hunter looked around at the growing chaos. "Holy crap."

Sanders grinned. "Yeah, I think half the HCPD is here and the other half is on its way. This is the biggest thing that's…"

"Are you Hunter?" The gravelly voice cut through the noise and cut off Sanders.

"Yes." He turned to see a barrel chested HCPD officer who appeared to have no neck. He looked to the officer's shoulder to see his rank. "How can I help you Sergeant?"

He poked his finger in the air at Hunter. "You can help me by taking me inside and telling me what we've got so I can debrief my crime scene guys when they get here."

"Like hell." Hunter's jaw was set and he was glaring at the officer. Now it was his turn to poke the air with his finger. "This is my crime scene and my CSI team will process it and if anyone, including you, sets one foot inside that door, I will personally arrest him."

The sergeant bowed up and was now nose to nose with Hunter. "This is Haltom City, not Fort Worth. You are out of your jurisdiction…"

Hunter cut him off. "I'm perfectly in my jurisdiction. This is the result of an ongoing investigation and I followed protocol by clearing through your head of detectives before we arrived." He leaned forward, their noses almost touching. "I'd suggest you get your facts straight before you make an ass out of yourself any further."

The sergeant glared. Hunter didn't budge an inch. The sergeant huffed. "We'll see about this." He wheeled around and stomped off.

Before Hunter could make a comment, Reyes walked up. "Looks like we found our needle. Guess we won't need that second search warrant."

Hunter shook his head. "I think we're going to be busy here for quite some time." He started to say something else but his phone rang. "Hunter."

"I hope I caught you at a good time Cowboy."

Hunter looked back over his shoulder at the building, exhaled as if to expel the evil he'd seen. "I'm good Doc. What's up?"

"It seems I've solved your murder for you… Well, sort of."

Hunter continued to stare at the building absorbing all the chaos. "You certainly know how to get a guy's attention Doc. Who did it?"

"When can you come see me? I think you need to see what I've got."

Hunter scanned the scene, saw Stacy and her team in the CSI truck following a white van as they weaved their way north on Higgins. "I'm at a scene Doc, but Stacy just pulled up and Reyes can manage the scene. I'll get her team going, grab Billy and head over."

Sanders heard him and scrunched his face. He shook his head and mouthed, "no".

Hunter hung up. "If I have to go, I'm taking you with me." He nodded toward Stacy. "I'll get her debriefed. Get with the guys. Tell Reyes, he owns the scene until we get back. Make sure they know to look out for our blow-gut sergeant."

"You got it." Sanders headed off.

"What's so important that you make me come all the way to Haltom City?"

Hunter turned to see Stacy's smile beaming at him. He caught her eyes with his, but didn't return the smile. "I hope you brought Kevlar for your soul." He looked over his shoulder at the building. "You're gonna need it for this one."

Chapter 11

The stench hit her first, even before she'd made it past the small office area. Dressed in her coveralls with her booties, latex gloves and drop down plastic face shield, Stacy was making a first pass while her team geared up. She needed to understand the scene so that she could make the proper assignments and ready any special equipment.

As she stepped through the doorway into the garage area, it felt as if she had stepped through the looking glass into another world. She looked to her left and her heart sank as her mind grasp what her eyes saw. A cage for humans. Her feet felt glued to the floor. Thin pads, like something you'd use for a dog, lay across the floor for bedding. They were filthy and scattered around, overlapping each other in places.

My God, how many people did they have in here?

There were a handful of thin blankets waded up in balls, but not nearly enough to match the number of mats. She walked to the cage, reached out and placed her fingers through the thick wire mesh. It seemed as if a shock ran through her. She felt them, the prisoners. It was as if she could see them, their pleading eyes, their hopeless faces.

Butterflies flew through her stomach as she continued to survey the cage. She saw the five gallon bucket in the corner. Realizing its purpose, she thought of the indignity they must have suffered, maybe were still suffering in some other location.

Her hand let go of the cage as she walked to her right and stepped through the single door. The walls seemed to surround her, stealing her freedom, her humanity. She looked back through the mesh at the door to the office. The doorway to freedom had been so close, just twenty feet. It might as well have been twenty miles.

The smell was now overwhelming. The afternoon sun baked the

building, intensifying the odor. She hadn't remembered it being that hot outside, but sweat had already drenched her T-shirt and pants. So much for her hair, it was falling and sticking to her neck. She closed her eyes and chastised herself. How could she be thinking about her hair? How frivolous.

Looking around the cage again, she noticed a few pieces of clothing scattered about. She walked over and picked up a shirt. At one time, it had been white, with lace around the collar. And the size... Her eyes burned before the realization had fully formed in her mind.

Oh my God, this belonged to a child. They had children here.

Stacy had been with the FWPD CSI team for almost ten years. She thought she had seen it all. Like most veterans, she was tough and never cried at a crime scene. Now, a single tear crawled down her face and a sob caught in her throat. In her mind, she could hear a little girl crying, the silence of her mother's heart breaking.

What kind of evil could do this to another person? To a child?

It took a moment to compose herself. She pulled up the plastic shield and wiped her face on her coveralls, the tear and sweat left a damp pattern on the sleeve. Her hand slowly dropped to her side. Exhaustion seemed to overtake her and her arms felt too heavy to lift. She dropped the shirt back on the floor where she'd found it. The team would bag it later. Her neck muscles had tightened up like steel cables from the tension. She took a moment to massage them with little relief.

She straightened her shoulders, shook her head and got her mind back into investigation mode by making mental notes of specific pieces of evidence. Samples of DNA could be collected from the mats, blankets, clothes and of course, the bucket. Every surface needed to be printed. Thinking and planning helped. Her mind was working now.

Moving back to the door of the cage, she continued to process. She looked at the cage and wondered where you could buy this material and what kind of skills would you need to install it. Maybe they could track who did the work.

Back at the door, she looked to her left and noticed the two small rooms. The doors were open and she could see in but couldn't really discern what was inside. She left the cage and with it, the visions and sounds of the prisoners her mind had created. Her heartache seemed to ease as she moved across the open garage.

When she stepped into the door of the first room, her breath caught in her throat. Her hand instinctively reached out and grabbed the doorframe. She knew she shouldn't be touching it, but her hand was gloved and without her hold, she wouldn't be standing. As her eyes scanned the room, she saw the metal table, the restraints. Without realizing it, she had moved her hand from the doorframe and she was now rubbing her wrist.

She looked more closely at the room, the articles strewn about the floor, the way the table was constructed. This was set up like a doctor's office, more specifically, a gynecologists. She had blinked away more possible tears. She thought about the victim, Madison, and her parents.

What did they do to that poor girl? What will we tell her parents?

Once again, she had to steady herself. She had to force herself to think like an investigator. Traces of blood spatter marred the walls and stained the floor. Someone had made a halfhearted attempt to clean it up. She could see the residue of fluids on the table. They'd need to test the DNA, but she knew they'd match Madison.

This was where she died, alone, terrified.

Stacy backed out of the room, her hands shaking and her knees on the verge of buckling. She wanted to run. She found herself moving across the garage and into the hall, not stopping until she felt warm, fresh air.

She stepped out into the cloudless afternoon heat, tore off her plastic face shield and latex gloves and threw them on the ground. She bent over, hands on her knees sucking in air, her lungs hurting. Her face felt flush and her head spun.

A hand touched her arm. The voice sounded like it was in a well. "Stacy, are you okay?" Jimmy Reyes.

She heard another voice. It was hers, mumbling, almost a whisper. "No, I'm not."

Chapter 12

Hunter had managed to compartmentalize the evil he'd seen at the crime scene by spending most of the ride taunting Sanders about his dislike of the morgue. By the time they walked through the double doors into Autopsy Two, Hunter's normal smile was back.

Doc looked up from his papers. "You're in quite a good mood Cowboy."

"Just having some fun at my partner's expense."

Sanders gave him a playful shove. "When are you not?"

Doc smiled. "Well, I hope I can keep the frivolity flowing."

"Show me what you've got Doc. We're working on a tight schedule. It looks like we found where our victim was held."

"Sounds like my information was helpful. Splendid. Glad to hear it." Doc snapped his finger. "That reminds me. You ran out of here so fast yesterday, I didn't get a chance to tell what else I had found. With today's events, it might not be relevant but I do think it's quite interesting."

Both Hunter and Sanders looked curious.

Doc put down the clipboard in his hand and walked over to a laptop. After a few quick taps, he leaned back and pointed to the screen. "Yes, here we go." He turned to the detectives. "We did an initial tox screen and found that your victim had traces of Propofol in her system."

This elicited blank stares from both detectives.

Raising his finger as if he realized he'd lost them, Doc continued. "Propofol is a hospital grade intravenous anesthetic. The significance is two-fold. First, this is not a street drug and unless you are a doctor or work in the medical field, it would be very difficult to get. Second, it's used purely to induce general anesthesia or to knock someone out. It's not a pain killer, it doesn't get you high and it's not addictive."

Hunter nodded but still looked a little confused.

"Cowboy, what this suggests is that whoever was holding her wasn't trying to get her high or addicted, they were just trying to keep her sedated, almost like an induced coma. That's not exactly the M.O. for your average kidnapper. I keep wondering why someone would do that."

Hunter was now pacing. "Doc, based on what we found this morning, we are definitely not dealing with your average kidnapper. This just adds to it but I'm going to have to digest this a bit." He stopped and nodded his head as if he was filing the information. He looked back to Doc. "Now, you said something about solving the murder."

Doc's eyes lit up. "Ah, yes. Follow me." He walked over to the autopsy table and pulled the sheet back revealing the head and shoulders of the male corpse. "Meet James Le James. At least that's what it said on his driver's license. He was brought in late last night. He was found over in Oakland Lake Park. As you can see, the cause of death was a single gunshot to the middle of the forehead. Rather effective bullet placement."

Hunter leaned forward for a closer inspection. He found himself looking at man in his early forties with greasy dishwater blonde hair, patchy facial hair and light olive complexion. One of his almond shaped hazel eyes stared blankly into space. The other appeared to have been shredded by fingernails. "Let me guess. Some of his missing eyeball was found under the fingernails of our victim."

"Precisely. You can add a few more evidentiary points. First, I ran a preliminary DNA match to semen found on her skin and it's an exact match. Second, there was dried blood on his right hand. It matched your victim's. Third and finally, he appears to be at least partially of Vietnamese decent. Note his eyes and complexion. Combine that with the fact that his middle name uses the Asian spelling of Le, not the American spelling of Lee." He nodded toward the body. "Pity we didn't find him alive. With this much evidence, the great state of Texas would surely have stuck a needle in his arm."

Hunter smiled at Doc's thinly veiled political commentary.

"Looks like somebody beat us to it. Clean entry wound."

"Yes, well, I can't say the same for the exit wound. I'm guessing it was a forty-five with hollow points. The whole back of his head is gone. Whoever did this didn't want there to be any questions about the outcome."

Doc reached down and held up the man's wrist showing deep bruising and several small cuts. "Although they didn't find any at the scene, it's clear his hands were cuffed and based on body position and the angle of the shot, it appears he was on his knees."

Sanders whistled. "Full on execution."

Doc nodded. "That's how I see it as well." He looked at Hunter. "So, as I said on the phone. I think I solved your murder, kind of. I think there's little doubt that James here was the animal that raped and murdered your teenage victim, but his manner of death would lead one to the conclusion that he did not act alone."

"Close one investigation, open another." Hunter leaned back against the countertop and folded his arms. "With what we found this morning, I think we may be looking at something a whole lot bigger than just our friend here."

Doc looked a question to Hunter, so Hunter spent the next twenty minutes catching him up on what they had found at the Haltom City building, how it connected with the information he'd provided from Madison's autopsy and how it now connected with the body of James Le James. By the time he'd finished, Doc's forehead was furrowed and his jaw was tight. "Why do I get the sense that you may get to visit me a few more times before this is resolved?"

Hunter looked up, his face grave. "I hope not, Doc."

As Hunter backed the SUV out of the parking space, Sanders cast a grim glance back at the building. "Any idea what the hell we've got ourselves into?"

Hunter shook his head, paused before shifting into drive. "No idea. Whatever it is, it's big, evil and organized."

Chapter 13

"I need to tell you something."

The man behind the desk looked up to see his underling standing in the doorway. His jaw clinched as he noted the expression on his underling's face. He motioned for the man to come in and sit. "More bad news? This is becoming an undesirable pattern."

Nodding his head, the underling spoke quickly. "One of our guys was driving past our primary HC location. He had some merchandise to drop at the secondary site. It was on his way." The underling paused. "The cops were there."

"The cops were where?"

"At our HC location. He said they were swarming the place and searching inside." He instinctively lowered his head.

The man behind the desk shot out of his chair. "What the fuck?" He leaned across the desk and glared. "How could they have possibly found it? What kind of trail did that idiot leave?"

The underling looked down, avoiding eye contact and shrugged. "No idea."

"You need to find an idea." The man pushed away from the desk and started pacing. "Speaking of the idiot, did you eliminate him?"

"Yesterday, and I made sure there were no links connecting him to us or the operation."

"Really?" He cocked his head. "Where was he disposed?"

"At a park. We staged it to look like a gang shooting."

"Then how the hell could they have found my holding site?"

Sweat glistened from the underling's forehead. "Must have been something to do with them finding the package. It couldn't be tied to him. They may not have even found him yet."

The man behind the desk sat back down hard, drummed his fingers on the desk and stared at the bookshelf.

"The one good note..." The underling face was hopeful. "Is that we had moved all the merchandise like you had suggested. Had they hit there a day earlier, we would have lost over fifty units and two of our guys."

The man behind the desk rubbed his forehead. "I guess that's why I'm sitting here and you're sitting there."

The underling looked uncomfortable again. "The only problem is that while we got the merchandise out, we didn't have time to sanitize the place." Reacting to the man's glare, the underling added. "But there shouldn't be anything linking to us or the bigger operation. We've always been careful about that."

"Yes. Just like there shouldn't have been anything linking the package to the HC location." The man behind the desk frowned and shook his head. "This is too close. We need to start making provisions." His mind was racing through his contingency needs.

"Is the girl under wraps?"

"Yes. I'm tracking that personally. We have our best guy on it."

The man behind the desk sneered. "I bet you are." He thought for another moment. "We need to know how they found that location and what else they know."

The underling looked confused. "How?"

The man waved the question away. "I'll handle that. In the meantime, I want you to get everything that's public. Is the investigation being run by HC or FW? Who's the lead detective? Who else is on the team? I want names and backgrounds on all of them." He paused, his eyes cold. "Go! Why are you still in my office?"

Chapter 14

"Paige, this is Hunter, I need to speak with the Lieutenant." Hunter had pulled onto I-35N heading back to the building in Haltom City.

Paige answered without a pause but with plenty of whine. "Sorry, Cowboy. Lieutenant Sprabary is unavailable."

Hunter rolled his eyes at Sanders. "Paige, my teenage homicide just turned into a multiple homicide and based on the crime scene, the number may get a lot bigger. Let him know I need to speak with him as soon as he gets this." He clicked off without waiting for her to respond.

Looking at his watch, Hunter pressed the accelerator and started weaving in and out of the midafternoon traffic. A moment later, he ran his fingers through his hair and then drummed them on the steering wheel.

Sanders looked over at him. "Cowboy, are you…"

Hunter answered his phone before the first ring had finished. "Hunter."

"Multiple homicide?" Sprabary didn't bother with small talk. "Talk to me Hunter."

"Well, the good news is we've found Madison Harper's killer and we found where she was held before her death. The bad news is that our killer has been executed and where she was held is apparently some kind of… Uh… House of horrors."

Hunter spent the next few miles giving Sprabary the details of James Le James's death, the house of horrors they found in Haltom City and the fingerprint of the missing girl from Amarillo. When Hunter finished, he could hear Sprabary chewing his gum hard. "Sounds like a hell of a mess. Sounds like human trafficking."

"Yes sir. That thought crossed my mind. Don't know that much about it."

"That's because at the local level we usually just deal with the end results, prostitution, overdoses, burglary, petty theft, illegal immigrants. The real crime spans cities, states and sometimes countries. In Texas, most true trafficking cases are handled by the Rangers."

Hunter was now exiting at Beach Street. "Wouldn't hurt my feelings if we got some help on this one. Based on what I've seen, we've just scratched the surface."

"All right, let me make some calls." Sprabary paused. "If you have a chance and want to give Charlie a call, couldn't hurt."

"I'll do that Lieutenant." He said goodbye and click off as they were turning onto Higgins.

Hunter parked on Higgins, a half block south of the scene. Much of the chaos had died down. There were still several HCPD cars parked along the street with officers directing traffic and manning the perimeter. His phone rang. It was Andre Kipton with the Star Telegram again. He signaled for Sanders to go ahead without him and punched the accept button. "Hunter."

"You're not avoiding me, are you?" Kipton's voice dripped with sarcasm.

"You're always at the top of my list."

Kipton laughed. "I won't ask about which list that is… Anyway, wanted to get your input on the body you guys found Wednesday, a teenage girl named Madison Harper."

"Your timing is amazing since we just solved that murder. The perp was a guy named James Le James. That's Le as in L-E, not L-E-E." Hunter paused, smirked to himself. "The FWPD has already taken him off the streets."

"What else can you give me?"

Hunter spoke with Kipton for a few minutes providing minimal information, broad statements and letting Andre make a number of assumptions. He was careful not to give Kipton anything that would lead him to what was going on in Haltom City. Until they knew what they had, he wanted to keep the media out of the picture. He hung up satisfied that he hadn't let anything slip.

As he walked from his SUV, Hunter shielded his eyes from the sun and surveyed the scene to see CSI team members carrying large bags of evidence out of the building while Stacy stood at the truck marking and logging evidence and directing her team. Hunter and Sanders badged the HCPD officer, stepped under the tape and walked over to Reyes, who appeared to have the scene under control.

"How's the scene? Anything we didn't expect?"

Reyes shook his head, looked toward the building. "As long as we expected a living hell, then no, I think we're seeing exactly what we expected. I released Nguyen and Tran. They had some gang business to deal with and they weren't really needed for processing the scene." He nodded down the street to the HCPD Sergeant talking to one of his men. "I did get to fight off Sarge and his Lieutenant one more time."

"No kidding? Persistent bastard."

"Yeah. I just told him if he wanted to get past me he was going to have to talk to Sprabary." Reyes raised an eyebrow. "Apparently, he's met Sprabary before." Reyes subtly stepped toward Hunter, turned his back toward the CSI truck and lowered his voice. "You didn't hear this from me, but Stacy was really shook up when she walked the scene. You may want to make sure she's okay."

Hunter looked toward the building as if Reyes was giving him a scene detail. "Will do. Thanks for the heads up and thanks for running the show here today."

"No problem. What was so urgent over at the morgue?"

"Oh, you're gonna love this." Hunter spent the next ten minutes updating Reyes on James Le James.

Reyes shook his head and kicked at the dirt. "So what do you think it all means?"

"Means that you've been assigned to team with Sanders and me on the case and we aren't going to get much of a weekend."

Reyes exhaled loudly, rubbed his forehead. "Cowboy, if my wife didn't like you so much, she'd kick your ass." Reyes looked at his watch. "I'll check in with everyone and see how we're doing. If we're going to be working all weekend, least we can do is get out of here at a reasonable hour." He gave a mock salute and walked away.

Sanders reached into his pocket, pulled out a handkerchief and wiped it across his shaved head. "So, what's our game plan?"

"No idea yet. We've got a ton of stuff to chase. I've got a feeling when we get with the Rangers, they'll have some new angles as well." He paused. "Speaking of stuff to chase, have you ever gotten in touch with Madison Harper's friend? You know, the one that was out sick."

"Not yet. I've left her several messages but just goes to a generic voicemail."

"Hmm. That's not good. If we haven't heard back from her tomorrow, we'll swing by her house in person."

"Works for me."

Hunter looked over his shoulder to catch a glimpse of Stacy, her face was stoic. "Give me a minute. I'm going to see how she's doing."

"No problem. I'll go try Valerie Bryant again."

Hunter stepped over to the back of the CSI truck and touched Stacy on the arm. "How're you doing?"

Without flinching or looking up, her tone was curt. "Fine."

"How close are you guys to wrapping up for the day?"

"Not close. I have to process a lot of this back at the lab."

"Stace." Hunter reached over and touched her hand and spoke softly. "Look. It's been a really long day. Why don't we get something to eat?"

Stacy pulled her hand away and started writing in her log. "Can't. Too much to do. Like I said, I'm going to the lab and start processing."

"Stace, you're beat. Doing this tonight isn't going to help Madison Harper."

"It's not for her." She looked up at him, her eyes glistening. "It's for the others.

Hunter's mind flashed to the inside of the building, the cage, the rooms, the leather restraints. He folded his arms, leaned against the back of the CSI truck and stared at the ground. "So, Chinese or Mexican?"

"Didn't you hear me?" Her voice raised and her eyes flashed at him. "I'm not going out to eat tonight."

"Neither am I. I'm ordering take out and bringing it to the lab. It's going to be a long night and we're going to get hungry."

"We?" Stacy's anger melted into a soft smile.

"Yeah… We."

Chapter 15

"The bodies must be piling up this week." Bernard brushed his black bangs away. His pale, Goth look was right at home behind the Starbucks counter. "I haven't seen you all week and now you're visiting me on a Saturday morning?"

Hunter shrugged. "What? I can't come visit my favorite barista on a weekend without a reason?"

"You can't fool me. I could be a detective you know." Bernard put his finger up beside his cheek, eyed Hunter up and down in mock appraisal. "Hmm. Let me see Cowboy. Bags under your eyes, you're moving kind of slow and your hair is spikier than usual." He pointed at Hunter. "You were up very late last night working." He smiled. "I rest my case. Now, I'll get your usual order going."

"You might want to add a couple of jugs of fully leaded and an assortment of pastries to go."

"Aha. A team meeting on a Saturday!" He turned to start working the order. "Like I said, the bodies must be piling up."

Hunter just shook his head and snickered. *Maybe I should enlist Bernard on the case?* He waited for his order and left to walk the one block to the station.

It was almost 10:30 by the time Hunter carried the team fuel into the conference room. Sanders and Reyes were just getting settled. "Gentlemen." He saluted as he started to get set up for the meeting.

Reyes looked over at him, cocked an eyebrow. "Don't take this wrong, Cowboy, but you look a little ragged."

Without expression, Hunter continued booting up his laptop. "Stacy and I were up late last night."

Snickers and mischievous looks broke out between Reyes and

Sanders. Hunter looked confused, finally got the joke and shook his head. "Get your minds out of the gutter boys. Unlike you slackers, we were working late. I helped her sort and log evidence from the scene."

Reyes, still stifling a smile. "Are we going to see some of that evidence today?"

"I'm sure we will, but there's a ton of stuff to be processed. Our first order of business today is to get synched with the detective from the Rangers." He looked at his watch. "He should be here anytime."

Sanders cleared off the whiteboard. "Do you know this guy?"

Hunter shook his head. "No, but I did talk with Charlie last night and he says the guy's got a strong reputation." He paused, his face quizzical. "When I asked for a description, Charlie just laughed and said, 'you'll know him when you see him'. Not sure what that means."

A knock on the door drew their attention. "I'm Detective Colt Barkley with the Texas Rangers. I'm looking for Detective Jake 'Cowboy' Hunter."

Reyes grinned and pointed to Hunter.

Barkley had a lopsided, confident grin that was somehow overshadowed by the overt cockiness that gleamed from his brown eyes. At six foot five and barely two hundred pounds, he risked looking gangly, but his tailor's skill made the angles flow naturally from his short, spiky dark hair to his size thirteen custom black Lucchese boots. His presence was made even more imposing with his white felt Stetson and a Lone Star badge.

Barkley looked at Hunter, confusion on his face. "Your nickname is Cowboy?"

Hunter just shook his head. "Long story."

Barkley grinned. "All right... I understand you're Charlie Hunter's son. He's pretty close to legendary in Rangers' circles." The men shook hands. "I guess you've heard that before."

"Yes." Without further comment, Hunter turned to Sanders and Reyes and introduced them.

"For those of you who might be wondering..." Barkley cocked his head and grinned. "No, I'm not related to Charles Barkley. I'm taller with better hair and he's got a better tan."

Sanders shot him a look. "Taller?"

"Well, if I'm wearing my boots and hat." That brought chuckles from the team

Hunter just grinned. "Thanks for driving up on such short notice."

"No problem. Austin's not far, and based on the little I know, I should be thanking you. I've been focused on human trafficking for over two years and I can count on one hand the number of holding centers we've found." His cockiness waned for a moment. "I don't even need two fingers to count the number of real major players we've nailed."

Hunter nodded. "We were just solving a murder. I'm not sure exactly what we have beyond two dead bodies."

"Hopefully I can help with that. Give me an overview of what you've got and we can go from there."

Hunter tossed a marker to Sanders. "Billy, you drive. Reyes and I will add color commentary."

Sanders went to the whiteboard and spent the next thirty minutes going through everything they knew about the eight days since Madison Harper's disappearance. He detailed out the original assumption that she'd run away, finding her body, interviewing her friends, the autopsy findings, how they led to the building, finding James Le James' body and the fact that they'd found the unexplained fingerprint of Caitlin Ann Gardner in the Harper's home.

"Damn." Barkley's eyes were wide when he looked at Hunter. "Detective, you've definitely stepped right in the middle of a human trafficking ring."

"Okay. So, what exactly does that mean? I've heard the term, but I'm not well versed in the subject. My last decade has been pretty focused on dead people."

Barkley stood and strutted to the white board. "First things first, gentlemen. I'm a killer whale hunter. Orca's are the meanest, nastiest predators in the ocean. Your young victim was killed by a barracuda. That barracuda was in turn eaten by a bull shark and now you guys are hunting that bull shark." He paused and with dramatic flair took his hat off and hung it on the edge of the white board. "I don't give a damn about that bull shark. I want the killer whale that owns him." His eyes gleam as he made that statement. "The good news is that helping you catch your bull shark is the fastest and easiest way for me to catch the orca."

The team swapped glances as if they didn't really know what kind of fish they had landed in Barkley.

He turned to the white board. "So let's go fishing." He started to write on the board. "The first thing you need to know about modern day slavery…"

"Slavery?" Sanders bristled.

"Yes, slavery. While it may not be in the same form as it was a hundred and sixty years ago, it is absolutely slavery. Instead of being chained and beaten and forced to pick cotton, people are coerced, lured, manipulated, drugged and intimidated into working in any number of dangerous or degrading jobs with little or no pay." He tossed the marker up and caught it. "And if those methods don't work, chaining and beating someone isn't out of the ordinary."

He looked at Sanders. "What would you do detective if you were a woman, poor or illiterate and you were kidnapped, drugged and taken to a country where you weren't a citizen, you didn't know anyone, you didn't speak the language and every day someone told you they'd kill your family back home if you didn't do what they said?"

Sanders didn't answer but his expression was solemn.

"That's right." He paused to let that sink in. "There may be as many as twenty-seven million slaves worldwide right now, over a million of those are children. And don't think this doesn't happen in the U.S.. Close to twenty thousand people are trafficked into the U.S. from other countries and at least that many U.S. citizens are new victims each year." He turned to the white board and wrote the word sold. "Let's get past the politically correct bullshit term 'trafficking'. You need to understand these people are being sold, just like you'd sell a used car."

All three detectives shifted uncomfortably in their seats.

He continued. "Guys, this is a thirty billion dollar a year industry." He raised his hand and ticked off his fingers one at a time. "That's bigger than Starbucks, Nike and Google combined. A single prostitute can generate as much as two hundred thousand dollars a year for a trafficker. A forced laborer generates anywhere from ten to fifty thousand."

Reyes raised his hand to get Barkley's attention. "What do you mean by 'forced laborer'?"

"Good question. One of the big misconceptions about human trafficking is that it is only related to the sex industry - prostitution, strip clubs, massage parlors. While that's certainly a big part of the picture, domestic help, maids, construction workers and restaurant workers are also very common."

Barkley stepped over, sat on one of the tables and paused. "Guys, we sit back in our everyday suburban lives and think we have nothing to do with slavery. We've never 'bought' someone. We don't go to strip clubs or use prostitutes. We aren't involved." He locked them with his gaze. "That's just not the case. That maid or gardener that you found through a friend of a friend, who's really cheap, who doesn't speak good English and who always gets dropped off and picked up by someone, may very well be a victim. That hotel maid or restaurant busboy or construction worker you don't make eye contact with, could be one too."

Sanders leaned back in his chair. "I get the whole prostitute angle but maids and gardeners? Those folks are barely making minimum wage. How does that work?"

"Volume." Barkley stood, went back to the board. "It's basic math. They may only make ten grand a year off of a maid but if you own the rights to a hundred maids, that's a million dollars. And just like any criminal enterprise, all of it's off the books."

Hunter had started to digest this information and was now slowly pacing in the back of the room while listening. "Why don't we hear or see more about trafficking?"

"I call it the evolution of awareness. Slavery was theoretically abolished in the U.S. at the end of the Civil War. It stopped being legal, but it never completely stopped. And it's never stopped at all in many places around the world. Technology has made it easier and more profitable here. Because the end results aren't always related to trafficking, it's very hard to distinguish when it's happening. Not all prostitutes are slaves and certainly not all maids or laborers are. So it's taken an evolutionary process over a couple of decades for the awareness of law enforcement and social scientists to catch up."

Hunter had worked his way up to the front of the room with Barkley. "This is all interesting, but our girl doesn't seem to fit anything that you've described."

"No she doesn't." Barkley smiled again at the questions being asked. "Just like most industries, there are different markets. While most of the human trafficking related sex trade is built around street corner prostitutes and massage parlors, there is the rare, but incredibly high end world of the true sex slave. That would be someone who is kidnapped and physically sold to someone else for them to own and use however they want. In most cases, that is an overseas market and there is an extraordinary premium paid for young, white, blonde, virgin females."

"Virgin?" Sanders looked up from his notepad. "How the hell would they know?"

"I'm not a gynecologist, but supposedly that can be determined through a medical examination. These are sophisticated organizations which employ doctors to certify virginity and to ensure the health of their inventory."

Hunter shook his head as if to clear that thought out of his mind. "You mean she was literally going to be shipped off to another country and sold?"

"Yes. Probably to some Sheik in the Middle East for a price anywhere between half a million to a million dollars for a one shot transaction."

Hunter picked up his thought stream. "So, if she hadn't fought back and wound up dead, she would have just vanished without a trace."

"Exactly. And she would have spent the next decade being passed around as a sex toy for the Sheik and his friends. At some point, she'd outlive her sex toy usefulness and either be killed or used as a servant."

The room fell silent for several minutes. Hunter absorbed the impact of the conversation, thought about the beautiful teenage girl who Madison Harper had been and thought about the life that would have awaited her if she hadn't been killed. He finally spoke, more to himself than the others. "My God, she may be better off dead."

Chapter 16

"How does a guy that cocky not come off as a complete ass?"

Hunter slipped into a bad Chinese accent. "Because young grasshopper, there is a difference between confidence and arrogance." He dropped the accent. "Based on my sources, Barkley is the real deal. He may not have busted many of the real kingpins, or orcas, yet, but he's gotten a couple and he's disrupted their operations and he's arrested several of the bull sharks along the way."

The team had worked through lunch and continued their education about human trafficking and its effects.

Sanders tapped the screen on his laptop. "According to this, because of their borders with Mexico, Texas and California are the two states with the highest rates of human trafficking and the DFW area is the equivalent of a supply chain hub for the industry." He frowned, but continued. "A recent study estimated that seven hundred and forty American girls were sold over the internet in a single month, two hundred and fifty of those were in the DFW area."

"Damn." Reyes shook his head.

Later in the afternoon, they had made a list of action items. Barkley had agreed earlier to get a file on Caitlin Ann Gardner and to see if he could find any human trafficking connections to the Haltom City area. Reyes was to get background information on the building owner, find him and interview him. That left Sanders and Hunter to track down Valerie Bryant, get background on James Le James and search his home, assuming they could find it.

After rolling his eyes at Hunter's comments, Sanders tried calling Valerie Bryant's number once more. He hung the phone up. "Generic voicemail again."

Hunter looked at his watch. "I know it's getting late for a Saturday but why don't we take a drive by her place?"

"I'm good to go."

Twenty minutes later, the sun was deep in the rearview mirror and they were on Meadowbrook Drive near the golf course, looking for Green Hill Circle. Sanders looked at a Mapquest printout and compared street names as they passed blocks. "So, why didn't you join the Rangers?"

Hunter cut his eyes toward Sanders and frowned. "It gets cold living in a shadow."

"Your dad must have been hot shit in his day."

Hunter laughed. "I wouldn't assume he's over the hill even now." He pointed to a street sign. "Is that it?"

Sanders nodded and they turned into a neighborhood with large, old oak trees, lush landscaping and houses backed up to the golf course. The homes weren't overbearing but the neighborhood was clean, the yards were spacious and the cars in the driveways were expensive. "It's two houses up on your right."

As Hunter pulled to the curb, he surveyed the area. Much like the Harpers, the house and neighborhood seemed warm and homey. "Nice place."

Sanders nodded. "Lights are on. Cars are in the drive. Maybe they just don't answer their phone."

A few steps down a brick-covered sidewalk and they were on the porch ringing the bell. The door was answered by a man in his late fifties dressed for a casual evening at home. He smiled through the glass door. "Can I help you?"

Both detectives displayed their badges. "I'm Detective Jake Hunter sir. Do you have a moment?"

The man's face went wary, his voice hesitant. "Sure. What's this about?"

"We need to speak with your daughter."

Confusion flashed in his eyes and he cocked his head. "My daughter?"

"Yes sir. Valerie."

"Detectives, you must have the wrong house. I don't have a daughter." He shrugged. "I don't think I even know anyone named Valerie."

Hunter looked at Sanders. Billy opened the file in his hand, looked at the printouts from the school and verified the address with the man. After some additional confirmation, they started to turn and leave. Before the door closed, a woman joined the man at the door. He looked at her and shrugged. "Honey, these are Fort Worth Detectives. They're looking for our daughter." Her reaction was as confused as his but her interest made them stop.

The detectives went back through the same conversation again with her. When they mentioned the name, the woman's expression alerted and she looked at Sanders. "Valerie? Valerie who?"

"Valerie Bryant, ma'am."

"How odd. About six months ago, we started receiving mail in that name. I don't know a Valerie Bryant and I'd never heard the name before then, but it caught my attention because it wasn't just junk mail. There were letters from the high school and other stuff that looked official."

The detectives spoke with the couple long enough to determine they had no connection to Madison Harper or anyone at Eastern Hills High School. The woman was able to provide them with a few items that had shown up in the last few days.

Hunter was on his phone as he stepped up into his truck. "Mr. Thompson, this is Detective Hunter. I'm sorry to bother you on the weekend, but is there any way you can find out if Valerie Bryant has returned to school since our visit."

The Principal indicated he had access to the system from his home and after a few minutes came back on the line with the answer Hunter expected. She had not.

His next call was to Barkley. "How soon will you have the Caitlin Gardner file?"

"Already on its way. Should be on your desk within the hour."

"Is there any way you can email me a photo?"

"No problem. What's up?" Barkley's voice quickened.

"I think I know how her fingerprint got in Madison's room."

Hunter put him on speaker so Sanders could hear and explained to Barkley that Valerie Bryant had disappeared and in fact, never seemed to really exist. "My guess is that Valerie Bryant and Caitlin Gardner are the same girl, but I'm not sure how that makes sense."

"Amazing. I've read about this but I've never actually run across a case." Barkley paused. "They're using her as bait. They've either got her brainwashed or intimidated to the point that she's now part of the scheme."

Sanders looked at Hunter, then back to the phone. "How does that work?"

"For the high end trade, these guys don't typically just snatch girls off the streets. They know the exact type of girl they want - blonde, fourteen to seventeen, blue eyes, perfect smile, virgin, etc. The bait girl's job is to enroll in a school with likely targets, integrate with the kids, isolate one that fits the profile and become friends. When she's gotten close enough to get personal details such as the likelihood of virginity, then she sets her up to disappear. In the more elaborate versions, the bait girl creates enough drama that friends and family might actually buy into a runaway scenario."

"Why wouldn't the bait girl just alert the authorities?"

"Could be Stockholm Syndrome or just plain intimidation. These people are ruthless. They probably convinced her that they had someone watching her family, ready to kill them at any time."

Hunter was driving fast now. "Get me that photo. I'm almost at the Harpers. I want to get this confirmed so we can start working it." He clicked off and ninety seconds later his phone chimed with a new email.

As they stood on the Harper's porch, Hunter's foot tapped and his eyes absorbed his surroundings. Maybe it was his imagination but the house and yard that looked so warm and loving just three days ago now seemed worn and tired.

Mrs. Harper looked ten years older than she had on Thursday. She robotically stepped back to let them in as she nodded. "Detectives." She directed them to the same couch and they sat. "Have there been developments in Madi's case?"

Hunter looked up at her. "There have, but we've still got an awful lot to figure out. I know we owe you a complete update and I'll be glad to sit down at length with you tomorrow and do that. In the meantime, we stopped by to ask a specific question." He picked up his phone and tapped on the screen a few times. When the picture came up, he turned it toward Mrs. Harper. "Ma'am, do you know this girl?"

Her recognition was immediate and her eyes widened. "That's Valerie Bryant. Oh, please don't tell me… Is there something wrong with Valerie? Madi and her had become so close. Is she okay?"

Hunter took the phone back and slid it in his jacket, paused. "Right now we're just trying to figure out exactly who she is and how she's connected. Was she the one who gave Madi the iPad we found in her room?"

Mrs. Harper's cocked her head. "Yes. Why is that important?"

Hunter stood, wanting to cut the conversation off and avoid going into further detail. "Ma'am, will you and your husband be home tomorrow afternoon?" She nodded. "Can I come by and provide you with a full update then?" She nodded again but he had already stood and moved to the door.

Once in his Explorer, Hunter sat for a moment before hitting the ignition. He shook his head. "What the hell have we gotten ourselves into?"

Chapter 17

The sunrise cast an orange glow through the blinds as Panther jumped up on the bed, let out a long mew and kneaded the sheets. Hunter rolled over and reached out expecting to find Stacy's shoulder. Instead, his hand landed on a cold pillow. He lifted his head, saw it was six-thirty and reached out to his extremely large black cat. "Where'd she go buddy? Too early for a Sunday morning." Panther purred and head butted Hunter's hand.

Hunter saw Stacy as he stepped into the kitchen. "To bed late and up early?" He walked over and rubbed her shoulders as she sat at the table keying into her laptop. "You know what they say about all work and no play." He leaned over, kissed her neck and then stopped. "Hey, aren't you usually the one saying that to me?"

She pointed back over her shoulder but her eyes never shifted from her work. "I made coffee but we need to go out for breakfast."

Hunter glanced at the pot, breathed in the aroma, but reached for the refrigerator door. "Am I out of food?"

"No idea." She stopped and looked up at him, her eyes tired but determined. "When we started this thing…" She gestured between the two of them and almost smiled. "We made a pact not to discuss cases when we were at home and we need to discuss this case. I spent all day yesterday fruitlessly processing DNA and fingerprints from the scene and you were already asleep when I got here last night. I need an update."

Hunter folded his arms across his chest and leaned back against the countertop. "If we go out for breakfast and I catch you up, will you promise to take the afternoon off and get some rest?"

"No." She got up, grabbed her keys and started for the door. "I'll drive. I'm parked behind you."

She was gone before he could respond. Panther strutted figure eights between his ankles and he looked down. "Sorry buddy, gotta go."

It only took five minutes to get from Hunter's to the Denny's on I-35 but Stacy was lost in thought the entire drive. Hunter waited until they were seated and had placed their orders before he reached over and took her hand. "Are you okay?"

She was silent for a moment as she stared down at their intertwined fingers. "No." Her voice was hard to hear over the cacophony of conversations, silverware and dishes. "We need to find who did this."

"I didn't know you cared so much about finding James Le James' killer." He smiled at his lame attempt to lighten the mood.

Stacy didn't smile. "Cowboy… That building… Those people… What they did to those victims." She took her hand back, hugged herself and shuddered. "What they're still doing."

"Stace." Hunter stood, stepped around the table and slid into the booth to wrap his arm around her shoulders. "We've got Reyes assigned and we're teamed with the Rangers." He touched her chin and turned her face toward his. "Between all of us, we'll get these bastards." He kissed her on the forehead. "But you can't kill yourself in the process."

She buried her face in his shoulder and he pulled her to him. He breathed in her hair and felt her shoulders shake as her warm tears dropped onto his shirt. He thought about what he saw in the building but tried to keep the emotions contained. Over the years, he'd found it hard to be effective if he let the true suffering of the victims sink in during the investigation. His struggles usually came after a case was closed.

Stacy had composed herself when their food arrived. In spite of the scent of eggs and bacon, they only nibbled and pushed food around on their plates in silence. It was clear that eating wasn't a priority. Hunter pushed his plate away. "Let me catch you up."

He told her about Colt Barkley and gave her a high level overview of human trafficking sparing her some of the sadder details. He also told her about how they figured out that Valerie Bryant and

Caitlin Gardner were the same person, and Valerie was bait.

"My God, that poor girl." Stacy blinked hard a few times.

"We wouldn't have gotten that if it hadn't been for you and your team." Hunter reached over and squeezed her hand. "Now we've got Barkley running a background on the name Valerie Bryant to see where else that name might have been used. They're searching every form of social media out there. If they find her on something, they'll get a warrant and see if they can track her via the information she provided when she signed up."

Stacy flashed a faint smile but remained silent.

"I expect to hear back from Barkley later today. We'll see where it goes." Hunter waived to the waitress for the check and continued. "Billy's digging up information on James Le James. His DMV information was old so we haven't found his home yet. When we do, we'll get a search warrant and see what treasures we can find."

The waitress dropped off the check and Stacy grabbed it. "This one's on me. Payment for your counseling session."

A sly smile crossed Hunter's face. "Oh, my rates are much higher than this." He nodded for them to leave. As they stood, his phone rang. He looked at the ID. "What do you got for me Jimmy?"

"I got a good way to spend your Sunday afternoon Cowboy. Oh, and good morning to you, too."

"Friendship means never having to say good morning. So what am I doing this afternoon?"

"Interviewing the building owner. It took some effort to find the sleazebag but I found him. Got him sweating in a room right now. When can you get here?"

Stacy smiled when she saw Hunter look as his watch. "Go have fun. I'm going to the lab anyway."

"I'll be there in an hour, Jimmy." He hung up as they were getting into Stacy's Ford Escape. "Jimmy found the owner of the building. He and I are going to have a chat."

She paused and gripped the steering wheel before pulling out of the parking lot. "Fry the bastard."

Chapter 18

"Have you ever heard of House Bill 3000, Mr. Bell?"

Hunter's voice sounded like a lion's roar as it bounced off the hard walls in the small white room. The man jumped and stammered when Hunter slammed a folder down on the table. "What? I don't even know why I'm here."

"HB 3000, Mr. Bell, makes human trafficking a first degree felony. Do you know what the penalty is for a first degree felony?" Hunter leaned over the table and towered above the man inches from his face.

The man, paunchy with a bad comb over and three days of beard growth, flinched and whined. "Huh? What?"

"Twenty-five to life, Mr. Bell!"

"Human what?" His face crunched up, sweat beaded on his brow. "What are you talking about?"

"Don't play dumb with me." Hunter whipped open the folder and pointed at a picture of the building. "You're the owner of this building, correct?"

The man's hand shook so hard when he reached for the picture, he almost knocked it off the table. "Yes, but..."

Hunter cut him off and looked at Reyes. "Jimmy, book this piece of shit on human trafficking charges. By the time he sees daylight again, he'll be receiving social security."

Reyes stood but the man pushed back from the table and jutted his hands out. "Wait! Wait! What are you talking about?" His voice was shrill. "I haven't been in that building in months."

Hunter signaled Reyes to sit back down. They decided to play it tough anyway just to make sure. He could smell the man's anxiety. He had learned from Jimmy before the interrogation had started that the man truly seemed clueless as to why they wanted to talk to him and there was a possibility that he hadn't been involved.

He turned to the man. "Mr. Bell, sit down." The man complied, eyes wide, panting. "You are in serious trouble. Before we go any further, I need to read you your rights." Hunter pulled out a card, carefully read the Miranda rights word for word and verified the man understood them.

"Mr. Bell, you have a choice. I've got enough evidence to book you right now or you can answer my questions and maybe if you help me enough, I'll be willing to help you." Hunter leaned back, folded his arms and glared at him. "How are we going to play this, Mr. Bell?"

The man, eyes wide with shock, leaned forward in his chair and ran both hands through his hair. "I'll answer any questions you want. I don't have any idea what this is all about."

Hunter opened the folder, pulled out three eight by ten photos of the interior of the building showing the cages, beds and straps. He slapped them down on the table in sequence. "Tell me about these photos, Mr. Bell."

The man reached to touch the pictures but when his eyes registered the images, his hand recoiled as if he'd almost touched a snake. "What the hell?" His head was shaking and his eyes had grown even wider. "What is this?"

"That's what's in your building at Higgins and Earl. We've got fingerprints and DNA from over one hundred people who were locked up in these cages, at least one of which we know was murdered. Now I need to know where those people are and how you're involved."

The man's face contorted, he grabbed his head with both hands and started rocking in his chair. "I knew it. I knew it." He stopped rocking, put his hand to his mouth and bit down on his knuckles. "I knew that guy was bad news."

As if he realized he'd been talking more to himself, he looked at Hunter and leaned forward. "I didn't have anything to do with this. I had no idea. There was a guy, said his name was Jimmy, paid in cash for a year's rent. Paid top dollar. Told me not to go in the building." He looked at Hunter, his eyes pleading. "I didn't. You gotta believe me. I never went there. I didn't even have a key."

Hunter started to speak but his phone rang. He glanced, saw it was Barkley and looked at Reyes. "Take over Jimmy. I want to know everything." He held up his phone. "I've got to talk to Barkley."

He pushed through the door, punched the green button on his phone. "Hey Barkley. How's your Sunday?"

"Probably as busy as yours."

"I hope you're making more progress than me. We found the building owner but it looks like a dead end."

"No surprise. That would've been too easy. Maybe I can brighten your day. It seems our Valerie Bryant has a trail. I had my team combing through anything tied to that name. I'll give you the big news first." He paused and Hunter could hear him shifting the phone around. "Valerie Bryant has been registered at two other high schools since Caitlin Garner's disappearance. She was at each for only a few months and here's the kicker... A girl went missing at each school during the time Valerie was there."

"You definitely have my attention." Hunter started pacing in the hall outside the interrogation room.

"Thought I might. Kyrsti Quinn, fifteen, disappeared a little over a year ago at Stephen F. Austin High School in Sugarland, and Hallie Boyer, also fifteen, disappeared about six months ago at Westlake High School in Austin. Both share similar physical descriptions to Madison Harper."

"No doubt about a pattern there."

"Both were profiled as runaways so the cops weren't sold on kidnapping. No signs of foul play in either case and no trace of either has been found since. I've left messages for both lead investigators but don't expect to hear anything back until tomorrow."

Hunter had stopped pacing and was now leaning against one wall in the narrow hall. "So this confirms we're dealing with an organization, it shows that Valerie was the bait and it establishes a pattern. But how does it help us bust the ring, or in my case, catch James Le James' killer?"

"Not sure that it will, but our best shot is to find Valerie. Unlike the other girls, we know that at least as of last week, she was still alive and had not been sold out of the country. We've found an active FaceBook account for her and by tomorrow, we'll have all the account information for her and for everyone who has 'friended' her."

"Okay?" Hunter wasn't following.

"We hope to be able to reach her or find someone who knows how to reach her. Other than the dead guy, we don't have any other connections"

The two detectives speculated on how to use the Valerie information to penetrate the organization and Hunter caught him up on the apparently clueless building owner and the lack of immediate leads from the Haltom City building.

After planning to connect on Monday, Hunter signed off, opened the door to the interrogation room and signaled to Jimmy to join him outside. Reyes must not have made much progress. The man was still shaking his head, sweat pouring off his face. He looked about to cry. Reyes picked up the photos and the file. "You need to think harder Mr. Bell. So far you haven't helped yourself at all." Reyes left Bell distraught and rubbing his temples.

Hunter grinned at Reyes. "So what did Mr. Clueless have to say after I left?"

"Nothing new. Described James Le James to a tee. Says that James approached him about nine months ago, paid more than market rate, in cash for twelve months and told him he was working on secret designs for Lockheed Martin and that he needed privacy."

Hunter chuckled. "He bought that story from a guy that looked like James?"

"Money talks." Reyes shrugged, then smiled and held up a piece of paper. "I did get a phone number for James."

"Look at you go. Get that to Sanders, I know he's been struggling trying to work up a background on James." He jutted his chin toward the interrogation room. "Finish up with dumbass. Cut him loose but put the fear of God into him about leaving town."

"You got it." Reyes stepped back into the room.

Hunter leaned against the wall and let all the pieces flow through his mind. Four teenage girls. How did no one see it? After a moment, he looked at his watch, realized he was late for his appointment with the Harpers and headed for the door.

Chapter 19

Barkley's towering frame was silhouetted against blue sky through the west facing windows on Monday morning when Hunter walked into the conference room. It was only seven-thirty but he seemed impatient as he turned and nodded to Hunter.

Hunter smiled and looked at his watch. "Colt, you're a man after my own heart. The rest of the team should be here any minute."

"Sorry. You'll have to forgive my overbearing sense of urgency." He seemed to purposely try to relax his body language as he moved from the window and sat down, but his tapping foot betrayed him.

"No apology needed. This case is a little different for my team. The pace of a murder investigation is usually driven because someone might get away. That's important, but when you have live victims who are still being harmed, that's a whole other level."

Barkley nodded and started to comment but was interrupted when Jimmy and Billy pushed through the door laughing and bantering. Hunter looked over and smirked. "Glad you could join us."

Reyes smiled and elbowed Sanders. "Looks like we have two Energizer Bunnies to contend with now."

Hunter let everyone settle in for a moment before he stepped up to the front on the room. "Hope what little weekend you had was good. We've made some progress, but nobody's behind bars yet. Let's get everyone caught up and then we can figure out our next steps." He looked over at Barkley. "Can you start?"

"Happy to." He stood and took two giant strides to the white board. He caught Sanders and Reyes up on the connections between Valerie Bryant's school history and the disappearances of the two other girls. "At this point, Valerie seems to be our best connection to the traffickers. I've got teams working on two different tracks. First, local teams in Austin and Sugarland are re-interviewing friends and family of the missing girls to see what else they can tell us about Valerie and to see if any of them have been in contact with her since she left their school." He looked over at Hunter. "Can we have someone do that here as well?"

"Consider it done." Hunter made a note.

Barkley continued. "Second, we have our Social Media team tracking anyone who has friended her on FaceBook. Their objective is the same. We were able to subpoena the account profile information and found an active email address for her. We're monitoring the traffic and also plan to use it to contact her directly."

Sanders perked up. "Isn't that kind of risky?"

"Very. All of our teams are moving with caution. We're working under the assumption that the traffickers are monitoring her communications. All the witnesses we've spoken with have been told not to contact her. Our contact with her will be incognito. We will reach out to her under the guise of a marketing company telling her she's won a prize. Determining what city she's in is our top priority, so we'll ask her which prize center is easiest for her to visit. If she responds and answers the question, we'll know she's alive and we'll have a good sense of where she is."

"What happens then?"

"If we get that far, we'll try to set up a time and location for her to claim her prize. If she shows, we'll take her into custody."

Sanders leaned forward. "You mean protection, right?"

"Unfortunately, things get a little murky at this point. Our laws haven't really caught up with the criminals. Legally speaking, she's part of the trafficking ring and is an accomplice in a number of crimes including kidnapping and murder." He reacted to their looks by putting his hands out to calm them. "Guys, we're going to protect this girl, get her home and get her help, it just takes some effort. We also need her cooperation to move up the food chain to the next fish."

Hunter, as usual, was pacing along the windows. "What're the odds?"

Barkley shrugged. "No idea. Probably long, but finding her is critical, both for her and the case."

Reyes, quiet to this point, now he shifted in his seat as if he wasn't comfortable. "What happens if they find out we're onto her?"

Barkley stood, stared at the marker in his hand, his jaw rigid, his cocky veneer faded. "We have three risks." He ticked off three fingers. "Someone we speak with could reach out to her and tank the whole thing. The traffickers could figure out our ruse. The media could get wind that we've made a connection between Valerie and Caitlin and other missing girls." He paused. "If any of those things happen, she'll disappear immediately."

Reyes looked down and played with his pen. "You mean they'll kill her."

"Or sell her out of the country if they have that option." He exhaled, pursed his lips. "These guys are businessmen and they see her as nothing but a product. Killing her is faster and less risky at the end of the day."

The gravity of the conversation seemed to weigh on everyone in the room. No one looked up while Barkley remained quiet at the white board for another sixty seconds. Then he just set the marker down and took his seat.

Hunter cleared his throat. "On that happy note, Billy, you're up. Tell us about James Le James."

"You mean 'the phantom'?" Sanders got up and went to the board. "This guy fell off the grid about five years ago and on paper, hasn't existed since." He started writing on the board and ticking off bullet points. "No tax returns. No known employment. No credit cards. No checking account." He paused. "We did find a savings account at Woodhaven National Bank over on Riverside Drive. It has a balance of two hundred dollars and has had no transactions during that same five year period."

"Not surprising." Everyone turned toward Barkley's voice, his demeanor back. "The big bosses are insulated through dummy corporations and a couple of layers of underlings who, like James, don't exist. These guys work in cash with nothing that can be traced back to them or the boss."

Reyes frowned. "So is this guy a dead end?"

Barkley answered before Sanders. "Not at all. Other than Valerie, he's our next best link. There's a connection there. We just have to find it." He looked at Sanders. "Where was he before he became a phantom?"

"Let's start from the beginning. James Le James, forty-three years old, born in Shreveport, LA. He managed to graduate high school in spite of starting his criminal career early. I'd list all his offenses but we don't have the time or board space. He finally got caught when he was twenty-six during an armed robbery gone wrong and spent five years in the Eastham Unit near Houston."

"That could be the connection." It was Barkley again. "Our prisons are like grad school for criminals. If you haven't gotten information on his cellmates and prison record, I'll take that action item."

"I haven't. That would be great." Sanders continued. "He got out roughly twelve years ago and has stayed off law enforcement's radar. I've got a call into his parole officer but don't expect any revelations there."

Hunter leaned forward in his chair. "What about work history for the seven years between prison and phantom?"

"Unspectacular. According to his tax returns, he worked in a number of menial jobs for several companies. The last three years before he went dark were spent with Sledge Properties. He listed his job as laborer, but he must have been a little more than that. He made forty-five thousand his last year."

Berkley looked up. "What do we know about Sledge Properties?"

Sanders grinned. "You've heard of Lance Sledge, haven't you?"

"Heard the name, but not much more."

"Big Fort Worth money. He owns hotels and restaurants all over the state and has a massive ranch south of I-20."

"Interesting." Barkley rubbed his chin. "There may be a reason this was James' last employer before he disappeared. A company like that uses a ton of low end labor, maids, janitors, busboys, cooks, dishwashers. Hotels are a natural connection to prostitution. We need to dig into Sledge. He may be our trafficker. He's certainly a big potential customer for a trafficker."

The room fell silent, incredulous looks were passed between Hunter, Reyes and Sanders. Barkley glanced around the room. "What?"

"You're clearly not from Fort Worth." Hunter smiled. "You might as well suggest we dig into the Pope."

"No kidding." Reyes chimed in. "He's connected all the way to the Governor's office. Hell, the Mayor's probably on his payroll."

Barkley's eyes gleamed. "Sounds like my kind of challenge. I'll get my team digging." He turned to Sanders. "Good stuff. What else do you have on James?"

"Well, if it hadn't been for Reyes getting that phone number yesterday, I would've been stuck. His DMV records weren't up to date and we had no address. The phone number tied back to a cell phone which gave us an address for an apartment near 28th and Sylvania. I've already got the paperwork done. I'll have a signature on a warrant before lunch."

Hunter stood and stretched. "How convenient." He smiled. "We can grab lunch at Risky's and then go see what treasures James Le James left behind for us."

Chapter 20

Hunter gripped his Glock 17 with both hands pointing it toward the floor. His finger rested against the cold steel of the trigger guard, his shoulder pressed against the wall outside of James' apartment. Sanders held a similar position on the other side, Reyes was just behind Sanders. They had posted patrolmen at each end of the walkway leading to the door and had the key from the manager. They didn't expect anyone to be in the apartment, but they weren't taking any chances.

Hunter banged on the wood. "Fort Worth Police, we have a search warrant." He nodded to Sanders who slipped in the key, turned it and opened the door in one swift motion. "Police, we're coming in." The three moved as a single force as they swept through the one bedroom apartment in seconds.

Sanders had bolted into the bedroom, checked it and the closet. "Clear."

Reyes had done the same with the kitchen and bathroom. "Clear."

Hunter holstered his weapon and stood in the middle of the small living room already surveying his surroundings. Not many clues jumped out at him. The room was small with basic furnishings, little color and the dust of vacancy. The only obvious object of any real value was sixty inch flat screen with surround sound speakers that dominated one wall. "Even scumbags need to have their own man cave."

"Guess that'd be called a scumbag cave." Reyes snorted.

Still looking around, Hunter barely registered Reyes' comment. Something wasn't right. After a moment, the little anomalies started popping like the image in a 3D painting. He smiled and called to Sanders. "Billy, look around. What's wrong with this picture?"

Sanders, who stood in the bedroom doorway, began surveying the room, his face taut. His eyes glided from one end to the other, his head slowly shaking back and forth.

"What do you smell? What doesn't look quite right?"

Sanders took a deep breath, cocked his head. "Smells like sweat and body odor. I bet the windows haven't been opened in years." He crinkled his nose. "Something else." He stepped around the couch and bent down. "Chemicals?" He looked down at the carpet and pointed. "This area is more course than the rest. Recently cleaned." He touched the arm of the couch. "This has been moved."

"What does that tell you?"

A smile crept across Billy's face. "My guess is, this is where he was shot."

"Exactly. They did a half assed job of cleaning up." He pulled out his phone and tapped two times, waited for an answer. "CSI Morgan, I believe we've found our crime scene. How soon can you get here?" He listened and grinned. "See you then. We'll gear up and make sure not to contaminate anything."

Hunter hung up and pointed toward the door. "Let's step out, get gloves and booties and continue our search."

They left the two patrolmen to set up a perimeter and guard the door. Hunter popped the tailgate on the back of his SUV and was dishing out protective gear when his phone rang. "Hunter."

"This is Barkley. I've got some information for the team. Are you with them?"

"Hang on." Hunter set the phone down in the bed of the SUV and switched on the speaker. "I've got Sanders and Reyes with me. We just entered James' apartment and are about to begin our detailed search. What'd you have for us?"

"Hey guys. Got some details on James' stint in Eastham. Pretty uneventful, minor disciplinary things but nothing to write home about. I checked on his cellmates. He had three in his five years. One got crossways with the Aryan Brotherhood and never made it out alive."

Reyes snickered. "I'm guessing we can take him off the list."

"Yep." Barkley continued. "The second one, a guy named Paul

Raymond, seems to have gone straight. No legal issues since his release six years ago and has been working for Camelot Oil and Gas. Not too promising but worth checking out. The third one was very interesting. His name is Mark Cooper. Similar to James, kind of a general lowlife. He had a few issues shortly after his release but not anything in several years. Here's the kicker... Last known employer was Freemont Hotels, owned by Sledge Properties."

The three detectives sat in dumbfounded silence. Reyes finally whistled through his teeth and grinned. "Holy shit boys, looks like we're going big game hunting on this one."

The next few minutes were rambling free-for-all on the phone speculating on the possibilities of connecting the dots all the way back to Lance Sledge. Barkley had already put together a team to research Sledge and his companies. Hunter offered to have Sanders assist as needed.

"I should have known I'd find you roosters standing around crowing." All three detectives turned to see Stacy smiling at them.

Hunter pointed to the phone. "Barkley was just filling us in on James' prison time."

"Great. You can fill me in later." Sanders and Reye chuckled and slapped hands. Stacy rolled her eyes. "Would you two act your age?" She shook her head and turned to Hunter. "I've got some information to add to the mix if you're interested."

Barkley's voice rang out. "Do tell."

"We spent four days sorting through fingerprints and DNA from the building in Haltom City. Out of sixty-two unique DNA profiles and forty-five unique prints or partials and beyond the hits for Madison, we got one single hit in a criminal data base on a partial print. The rest of the samples are assumed to be victims." She stopped, her face went solemn, clearly thinking about the people still suffering.

Hunter cleared his throat.

"Sorry." Her voice was not nearly as strong. "A loser named Warrick Turner. His prints were in the system due to a number of small time arrests, but I didn't find anything big." She smiled. "I'll leave that to the he-man detectives."

Hunter nodded to Sanders. "Billy, sounds like you've got some homework."

"Like always."

Hunter picked up the phone. "Now that our crime scene boss is here, we need to sign off and get to work. Great job on the prison connections. We'll work with you to dig into them."

He clicked the phone and pointed back to the building. "Hi Ho, Hi Ho…"

Chapter 21

"Let me guess." Hunter looked up at Reyes when he appeared in the doorway of James' apartment. "No one heard or saw anything."

"I told you." Reyes frowned. "You could have saved me knocking on all those doors."

"Had to be done." Hunter shrugged. "At least I didn't send you back to the station to do a background check on Warrick Turner."

Reyes laughed. "Yeah, Billy didn't seem too pleased." He looked around the room. "Find anything here?"

Hunter looked toward Stacy. "She's been focused on the fun stuff like blood and brain matter."

"Found traces of both." Stacy spoke, face intense, without looking up.

"I've looked around the living room and kitchen." Hunter stood with his hands on his hips. "It's more remarkable for what we're not finding than for what we are. It's like the guy barely lived here. No phone, keys, wallet or glasses. No pictures, very little food or trash. I did find a couple of phone numbers on a scratch pad in a drawer." He arched his eyebrows. "Who knows? Could be something." He nodded his head toward the bedroom. "Put your gloves on and we'll see what we can find in there."

Hunter stood in the doorway absorbing the scene, an unmade bed, a small desk, a night stand, some clothes, blue jeans and T-shirts, hanging on the back of a chair. With the shades closed, it was dark and musty even in the middle of the afternoon. He noted again there were no pictures, books or mementoes, nothing personal. Who was this guy?

Reyes' voice came from directly behind. "What a miserable existence. You're whole life revolves around abusing other human beings and living alone in this depressing shithole." He shook his head and stepped past Hunter into the room and moved toward the closet.

"The world is full of sick assholes." Hunter stepped to the desk. "That's why we're here."

His gloved hands worked through the items lying on the desk, a pencil holder, a stapler, an unused notepad. He picked up the loose end of a cable, turned toward Reyes. "Check it out." Jimmy poked his head out of the closet. Hunter held it up, arched an eyebrow. "A computer power supply, but no computer."

"So maybe we're not the first ones to search the place?"

"That'd certainly explain why this place is so barren." Hunter turned back to the desk and started working through the three drawers on the left side, one at a time, rummaging through the contents but finding nothing of interest. He did the same with the one large drawer on the right. When he closed the drawer, it caught on something but he was able to close it by lifting slightly.

He turned, looked at the nightstand and took a step toward it but stopped. He went back to the desk and opened and closed the large drawer again. Again, it caught on something. He opened it once more, emptied the contents, an assortment of office supplies and crap. When it was empty, he took the drawer completely out of the desk and turned it over. "Well now, what do we have here?"

Reyes had just finished his fruitless search of the closet. "What do you got?"

Hunter pointed to the bottom of the drawer and a key that was taped there.

Reyes looked over his shoulder. "A safety deposit box key?"

"Looks like it to me. Maybe our friend has left us a present." He pulled the key off and examined it. "No bank name. We'll have to do some digging." He put it in an evidence bag and tagged it.

After finishing in the bedroom, Hunter and Reyes rejoined Stacy in the living room. By then, she had just finished her fingerprinting and was packing up her kit. Hunter was just about to say something to her when Sanders appeared in the doorway. He looked instead to Sanders. "You're back soon."

"Yeah, it doesn't take long to run a background check on another phantom."

Hunter cocked his head.

Sanders continued. "Just like James, Warrick Turner fell off the grid about five years ago and hasn't existed since. No tax records. No job history. No arrests. Not even a parking ticket. Checked the DMV, this guy didn't even bother to renew his driver's license last year. Made a quick call to the manager of the apartments for his last known DMV address, their records show him moving out five years ago with no forwarding address."

"What about his record?"

"As Stacy mentioned, he was in the system but it was for a number of near misses. He was brought in for questioning on a number of things and actually booked for possession once but he never served time."

Hunter leaned against the kitchen counter, arms folded across his chest. "Alright, get an APB out on him…"

"Already done." Sanders looked around the room and back at Hunter. "Find anything interesting?"

Hunter held up the evidence bag with the key in it. "Don't know the bank, but there's a box out there somewhere that matches this."

Sanders reached out for the bag and examined the key. "Probably Woodhaven National Bank. That's why he had that savings account with no activity. Most banks won't lease you a box if you don't have an account."

Hunter grinned, looked at Reyes who was chuckling and back at Sanders. "I knew I kept you around for a reason."

Sanders smiled and rubbed his shoulder.

Hunter looked at his watch. "It's too late to get to the bank today. We'll need a warrant anyway." He tapped his fingers on the counter. "Barkley said he was going to be up this afternoon. Said he had a meeting. Why don't I buy everyone a cold one? I'll call him on the way to see if wants to join us. We can debrief on the discoveries of the day."

Chapter 22

The Swamp Donkey Saloon on Belknap had only been in business for a little less than a year, but seemed to be doing a brisk business. It was a good old fashioned bar with neon beer signs, pool tables and the occasional strumming troubadour. Classic Fort Worth - a good dose of comfort with a tinge of redneck. The menu featured cold beer, good hamburgers and they had the Rangers game on the big screen. Since they were in the neighborhood, it seemed like a logical choice.

Hunter and team had already commandeered a table in the back and were halfway through their first round when Barkley swaggered in and turned heads with a red haired woman in a business suit.

Reyes got the tables attention and gestured with his longneck. "Now that's an interesting pair."

While she was attractive and fit for her age, she was at least ten years Barkley's senior. He spotted the team and ambled in their direction while he and his companion remained engaged in an animated discussion. When he got to the table, he gestured to the team. "These are the guys I've been telling you about."

She looked up and flashed a confident smile. "I'm so excited to meet you all, I'm Anne Robinson."

There was a momentary pause as they shared confused looks. Out of basic courtesy, Hunter broke the silence and extended his hand. "Nice to meet you, I'm Jake Hunter."

Barkley burst into laughter. "My apologies everyone. I forgot to tell you I was bringing Anne." He quickly introduced the rest of the team. "I thought Anne could add to the conversation. She is the founder of Emancipation Texas. They are a local organization dedicated to fighting human trafficking in Texas."

Looks of relieved clarity swept around the table. Stacy pulled up an extra stool and gestured for Anne to sit. "Here you go Anne. I'll help you fend off these wolves."

Anne eyed the team. "They look pretty harmless to me."

Barkley smirked. "She's dealt with a lot worse than this group in her work with ETX." He settled in and signaled to the waitress for another round plus two. "Anne's why I was in town. We meet every so often to compare notes and see if we're following any of the same names. Since you guys have now been baptized into the world of trafficking, an introduction seemed appropriate."

Stacy turned to Anne. "So what is Emancipation Texas?"

Anne sat up and looked around the table. She had told this story more than once. "We are a local organization dedicated to eliminating human trafficking worldwide."

Hunter cocked his head. "Based on what Barkley's told us about trafficking, that's a pretty big goal."

Her eyes locked onto Hunter. "It's a pretty big problem, Detective." She paused to get her beer from the waitress. "Fortunately, we're not in it alone. There are a number of organizations." She ticked off her fingers as she named them. "Traffick911, Polaris Project, World Vision, Global Freedom… They're all working toward the same goal."

Stacy was hanging on every word. "What exactly do these organizations do?"

"We all work a little differently. Some focus on fund raising and awareness. You'll occasionally see their television ads. Others like us, are more hands on. We work mostly at the local and state level and focus on education, recovery and repair. We do seminars to educate everyone from civic groups to teachers to politicians, even the police. It's stunning how many people truly don't know it's happening."

Hunter nodded sheepishly. "I certainly didn't understand it at any real level until Colt educated us the other day."

"Don't feel bad. That's pretty normal." She shrugged like she'd heard it before. "Beyond education, working through outreach programs and hotlines, we help victims escape their situations and through counseling and training, we help them put their lives back together." Her eyes cast down to her beer bottle as her fingers picked at the edges of the label. When she looked up, conviction etched her face. "The damage inflicted can be quite devastating. Unless you've seen it firsthand, you really can't imagine."

The conversation paused for a moment. The void was filled with sounds of country music, the clack of pool balls and ambient conversations. The team members absorbed her comments.

Sanders looked at Barkley. "How did you two get connected?"

Barkley looked down, took a swig from his beer and cleared his throat. "On a case."

He didn't elaborate further and took another drink. Anne looked over at him as his eyes tried to bore a hole in his bottle. She reached over and squeezed his hand, then turned to Sanders. "Her name was Casandra. Some would have referred to her as an illegal alien. She was sixteen, had been kidnapped in Juarez and smuggled across the border by a trafficker based in El Paso. She spoke only broken English. When one of our volunteers found her, she was working in a massage parlor over off Industrial in Dallas. We eventually realized that she was servicing anywhere from twenty-five to thirty men a day."

Barkley cut in, his voice hoarse and his eyes still staring at his beer. "My team had been working a number of leads pertaining to the owner of the business, but we needed that one last piece of the puzzle." His voice trailed off.

"We had blanketed the area with pamphlets advertising our hotline as well as phone numbers for the police. She somehow got ahold of one and called into the police line." Anne's consoling eyes peered at Barkley. "Colt's team made contact with her undercover and with the information she provided, they were able to raid the establishment the next day and rescue fifteen other victims."

Hunter looked back and forth between Anne and Barkley, instinctively knowing the answer to his next question. "And Casandra?"

Barkley's face contorted. "We were about an hour too late. The bastard found the pamphlet and used her as a teaching tool for the rest of the girls."

This time it was Anne's voice that struggled. "We've changed our methods since then."

"We've all changed our methods since then." A strange distant smirk moved across Barkley's face. "My only consolation is that the son of a bitch was stupid enough to draw down on me during the raid. I saved the taxpayers some money by putting a round into the middle of his forehead."

Reyes raised his beer. "Here's to using taxpayer's money wisely."

Barkley raised his bottle as some of the pain left his face. "May we be even more efficient on this case." Bottles clinked around the table as heads nodded. He looked at Hunter. "Speaking of this case, you mind catching Anne up on the background and bringing me up to speed on anything new?"

"Happy to." Over the next thirty minutes, the team ordered burgers and Hunter facilitated a conversation that brought Anne up to speed on the case details.

Anne looked at Barkley. "I see what you mean. This is a rare one." She turned back toward the team, her expression solemn. "Sadly, one of the main reasons human trafficking has managed to stay off the radar is that victims like Madison are extremely rare. The reality is the majority of the victims are poor, undereducated minorities, many are either runaways or in this country illegally. They aren't the blonde haired suburban princesses." She stopped. "I'm sorry. I didn't mean that the way it came out. It's just that I get very frustrated when I see CNN trucks parked in a wealthy suburb because one blonde girl went missing when I know that for every one suburban princess, there were a thousand Casandra's that no one even noticed."

Hunter leaned forward, pushed his half eaten meal away and picked up his beer. He thought about the conversation that he and Billy had when they first landed this case. He once again searched his soul. *Did I do that? Am I just as bad?*

As if reading his mind, Sanders looked over at him. "It's human, nature Cowboy."

"It's bullshit is what it is." He looked at Anne. "My gut tells me that when we break this one, we're going to find plenty of victims and my bet is they're going to come in all varieties."

Hunter was all business now. He briefed Barkley on the evidence from James' apartment and on finding Warrick Turner's fingerprint in the building. They talked further about James' cellmate Mark Cooper and his connection to Fremont Hotels and Freemont Hotels' connection to Sledge Properties.

It was late before they left the bar and even though they'd all switched to sodas long before they left, Hunter was still beat. Even so, his mind wouldn't stop. This case was different. Murder made sense. It was an event. Someone got mad or did something stupid and someone else died. Cause and effect. As a detective, you start with the effect and follow the evidence back to the cause. Trafficking wasn't an event, it was a process, an evil, sadistic process that robbed the victim of not only their life, but their soul.

His mind drifted as he walked Stacy to her car. "Hey." Stacy's voice pierced his thoughts.

Before she had a chance to say anything, he looked at her. "I'm seeing this one through to the end."

"Don't you always?"

He smiled. "What I mean is, our case is to find James' killer." Stacy's face went dark at the mention of his name. Hunter continued. "I'm going to do that, but I'm not stopping there. Whether Barkley wants me or not, I'm going to find the bastard at the top of this sadistic food chain."

Stacy smiled. "About time you caught up with me."

Chapter 23

"Can I help you?"

"We need to speak with the manager." Hunter flashed his badge which sent the teller scurrying off in search of her boss. Hunter and Sanders had been waiting at the door when Woodhaven National Bank opened.

"Officers? I'm Chip Richards. How may I help you?" A thin man with wide eyes and a sheen of sweat forming on his forehead stood before them when they turned. He looked younger than Sanders and was fidgeting with his tie.

They made their quick introductions and Hunter held up the folded paper. "We have a search warrant for one of your safety deposit boxes. Can you escort us to the vault?"

"Um, uh, well, yes." He seemed to twitch for a moment like a machine slipping a gear. He started toward the vault, abruptly stopped and turned the other direction, held up a finger. "Key." He stepped over to a cabinet and retrieved the master box key and walked them to the vault.

"What box number?"

Hunter looked at the key and read the stamped number. "Seven fifty-two."

He escorted them to the vault and then to a box that appeared to be ten inches wide and ten inches deep. It was on the bottom row and he had to lean over to insert the master key. "Detective, may I have your key?" When Hunter provided it, Mr. Richards inserted it in the slot beside the master, turned both keys and opened the door. He stood and took a step toward the door. "Just let me know when you're finished."

"Hold on Mr. Richards. We'll need you to stay with us. You'll need to witness our search and sign off on the inventory of the box." The man looked stricken but nodded.

Sanders reached down with his gloved hands, extracted the box from the drawer and carried it to a table at the end of the aisle. It took some effort for him to heave it on the table. "One thing's for sure, it's not empty." He reached up and opened the lid.

"Oh my!" Hunter and Sanders both turned to see Chip Richards' raised eyebrows. When they turned back, they were looking at a box full of neatly stacked and tightly packed bundles of money. "I've been working for this bank for three years and I've rarely seen that much money in one spot."

Hunter looked at Sanders. "When Barkley said they dealt in a cash only world, he wasn't kidding." He grinned. "How much do you think it is?"

"Over a half million, easy." Chip Richards' voice seemed about to pop. Hunter and Sanders looked back again. "Those are one hundred dollar bills, the bundles are fifty per, they're stacked... Let's see... Twenty across, three deep top to bottom and front to back." He stopped and stared up in space for a moment. "Closer to six hundred thousand." His head was about to nod off his shoulders.

Sanders smiled. "Oh my is right."

"This is a hell of lot more than I was expecting." Hunter stood and stared at the box. "All right, here's the deal. I've got to call in some additional resources. There needs to be two people..." He stopped and pointed at the two of them. "With this money at all times. No one touches anything until I get back."

By the time he'd walked across the lobby, he'd already called Reyes and told him to get there immediately and to have Stacy come as well. He hadn't wasted time with explanations. As he pushed through the door to the parking lot, he punched his phone again.

"Lieutenant Sprabary's office."

"Paige, this is Hunter. I need the Lieutenant." She started to balk but he cut her off. "Tell him I'm staring at a safety deposit box with over a half million dollars in it and I need someone at his level or higher on site immediately."

The next sound he heard was the lieutenant. "Hunter, if you're bullshitting I'm going to kick your ass."

"According to the bank manager, it's actually closer to six hundred grand. How soon can you get here?"

"I'm leaving now. Secure the area."

Hunter hung up, took a deep breath of warm spring air, stepped to his SUV and retrieved a large evidence box. He had started back toward the bank when his phone rang. He punched the button. "Hunter."

"Where are you?" It was Barkley, his voice excited and Hunter could hear his siren in the background.

"At the bank. You won't belie..."

"We got a hit on the email ruse. She's still in the Fort Worth area." He was talking fast and barely taking breaths. "I just made a U-turn on I-35. I was almost to Waco when I got the call. I'm lit up and northbound with my foot on the floor. I'm less than an hour out. My guys are narrowing down the location and said they'll have specifics by the time I get there."

"Where do you want to meet?" Hunter had turned and started toward his truck before remembering he couldn't leave yet.

"I'll call you when I hit I-20." Barkley clicked off leaving Hunter holding his phone in one hand and the evidence box in the other. He looked around the parking lot as if his reinforcements would have had time to get there by now. Shaking his head at the thought, he headed back into the bank.

Methodically, Sanders took each bundle of bills one at a time, counted out loud and placed it in the plastic lined cardboard box as Hunter filmed the process with a small video camera and Chip Richards made notes for his inventory. They were twenty minutes in and close to finishing the first count when Reyes and Stacy were escorted into the vault by an assistant manager.

Hunter looked up, motioned Reyes to take over with the camera. "Sprabary's on his way. I've got to go connect with Barkley. He's got a lead on the girl." He smiled at Stacy as he moved toward the door. "Make sure they do this by the book."

Sprabary was pulling into the parking lot as Hunter pulled out onto Bridge Street. He was reaching for his phone to call Barkley when it rang. He looked at the ID, smiled and punched the button. "If you're already to I-20, you are flying."

"Lights and sirens have a tendency to get people out of your way." Barkley chuckled. "Just heard from my guys, they pinpointed the IP address to a Wi-Fi hotspot in A-1 Food Mart at the corner of Riverside Drive and East Lancaster. How fast can you get there?"

Hunter looked around to get his bearings. "I'm ten minutes out."

"I'm twenty out. Meet you there. Don't wait for me. Find her!"

Hunter punched it and hooked a right on Belknap heading west.

When he pulled into the parking lot of the A-1 Food Mart, he looked at the store and shook his head. *The internet truly has gone everywhere.*

He was out of the SUV, in the store and badging the clerk before the dust had settled in the parking lot. "Do you have public internet access in this building?"

The clerk thumbed toward the back of the store. "In the café in back."

Hunter nodded, headed in that direction and smiled. Café? Right.

The café was a grungy sandwich counter with four dilapidated tables, random worn out chairs and the heavy smell of grease hanging in the air. A woman who looked as grungy and dilapidated as her surroundings stood behind the counter watching Oprah on an ancient TV.

Hunter had his badge out and announced himself as he stepped to the counter. "Ma'am, were you working here this morning?"

Her tangled grin was incredulous. "Every damn day of my life."

He pulled out his phone, brought up a photo of Valerie Bryant. "Have you seen this girl before? This picture is a couple of years old so she might look a little different."

The woman took the phone and digested the photo while Hunter twitched. "Yeah, I'm pretty sure. She's come in a few times."

"Alone or with someone else?"

She searched the ceiling with her eyes. "I don't remember seeing her with anyone."

"Was she in this morning?"

Her head was nodding as her brain seemed to struggle finishing the process. Her response was drowned out by the sound of the store's front door bursting open. Hunter turned to see Barkley repeating his steps and striding through the store to the café.

"What do we have?" Barkley was wound up.

Hunter nodded to the woman. "She's confirmed Valerie has been here before and was here this morning."

Barkley turned to the woman. "Do you know where she is now?"

She made a face like he was insane and shook her head as her eyes toggled between the men.

"Thank you." Barkley turned to Hunter who was tapping away on his phone. "Thoughts?"

Hunter showed him the map displayed on his phone. "If she's come in more than once and she was by herself, she's staying close by. There are only three hotels within walking distance. She's got to be at one of them."

"Let's hit them, closest one first." Barkley had already turned and was halfway out of the store.

Hunter nodded to the woman and tried to catch up.

The Great Western Inn made the A-1 Café look chic. It was your typical low-end two-story motel with the room doors exiting directly to the parking lot, peeling paint and an assortment of weeds growing anywhere not covered by concrete. Barkley slid to a stop after driving the half block around the corner from the food mart. Both men bolted from the truck and quick stepped up the walk into the dank lobby. Barkley almost took the door off its hinges as he pushed through.

With his badge held out, his voice bellowed as he crossed the lobby to the counter. "Texas Ranger, where's your manager?"

The startled clerk fumbled with his magazine as he pulled his feet off the counter and nearly fell out of his chair. "What? Manager?" Then he grinned. "We don't have no manager. It's just Beth and me runs the place."

Hunter shoved the picture in the man's face. "Have you seen this girl before? She'd be older by now."

He scratched his stubble and shook his head. "Naw. Naw, she don't look familiar to me." He turned his head over his shoulder. "Beth! Got cops out here. They need you."

A short squatty woman dressed in what was closer to a bath robe than a dress stumbled out of the back room. "George, what the hell are you yelling about?"

Barkley and Hunter repeated the routine with Beth and when they were convinced that neither George nor Beth had seen Valerie, they were out the door and in the truck leaving smoke in the air as they powered toward the Valley View Motel.

Back in its heyday, the Valley View Motel would have been referred to as a motor lodge. It was made up of two one-story, red brick buildings facing an open courtyard and parking area. Each building housed ten individual rooms, some with covered carports. Both buildings were surrounded by unkempt shrubs and trees. The lighted plastic sign that stood on a pole by the curb on Lancaster was busted out with its fluorescent tubes and wires exposed.

Once again, both men were out of the truck on the run. They entered the lobby door to find themselves in a tiny standing room facing a sliding glass window. Cigarette smoke and the years of filth oozed from the walls and God knows what else. Barkley's hand started pounding on the desk bell, the sound echoing off the walls.

"Hang on, hang on." A scratchy voice wrapped around the corner. "What the hell…" The man walked around the corner and stopped in his tracks when he saw both Barkley and Hunter standing at the window, glaring at him with their badges pressed against the glass.

He waddled over, opened the glass, scratched his exposed belly and looked at them with bloodshot eyes. "Can I help you?"

Hunter pushed the photo up so fast, the man swayed back. "Have you seen this girl? She's older now, might be with a guy."

He blinked several times, focused on Hunter's phone. He nodded. "Can't be sure, but I think she came in with her husband."

"She's sixteen, asshole. She doesn't have a husband. What room is she in?"

The man looked down at his desk. "I'm not really supposed to give out that..." When he looked back up, the barrel of Barkley's Sig Sauer P226 was two inches from his nose.

"The fucking room number! Now!"

His eyes flew wide and his hands jerked up. "Room six, across the courtyard on your left!"

Both men were in a full sprint, weapons drawn, moving across the courtyard diagonally toward room six. Hunter got there first and shouldered up beside the door. Barkley never slowed down. He brought his leg up in stride, kicked the door and barreled through.

Hunter followed on Barkley's heels, gun up, looked to the bed and stopped in his tracks.

"Oh, Jesus."

Chapter 24

Barkley stood outside the motel room, his back against the red brick, his jaw set and his eyes lost in a distant stare. The image of the girl, lying on the bed, her white shirt discolored with two crimson star bursts, her eyes open and vacant, wouldn't leave his mind. He didn't want it to leave his mind. He wanted it burned into his memory so that he'd never forget.

This was his fault. He had authorized reaching out to her via the email ruse. They were monitoring her. They saw through us. Another girl was dead. He was once again an hour too late.

If I hadn't decided to go to Austin this morning. If I'd been closer.

He could hear Hunter inside on the phone gathering the troops, getting them here. Barkley didn't want to be in there. He couldn't be, at least not yet. His chest felt like it was in a vise, it was hard to breathe. If he went inside, the pressure would crush him completely.

Reyes' car bounded into the parking lot and screeched to a stop a few feet in front of him. He heard Sanders and Reyes' voices, amped up, excited. There were questions, he answered, they went past him into the room. What did they ask? What did they say? His brain was in a fog. He couldn't think. All he could see were those two blood stains.

* * * *

"Doc, this is Hunter. Unfortunately, you were right about being needed again before this was done." He finished providing the details and hung up as Reyes and Sanders came through the door. Both instinctively looked toward the bed and cringed.

Sanders' shoulders sank as he stared at the girl. "What

happened?"

"We were too late." Hunter's voice was strained. He rubbed his forehead. "Hell, she's still warm. We couldn't have them missed by more than an hour."

Reyes shook his head. "An hour? Damn. No wonder Barkley looks like he's going to puke." He turned back to Hunter. "How did you even find her?"

"Barkley's ruse worked. She responded and they were able to track her IP address to a little store around the corner. We figured she had to be within walking distance so we started hitting the motels." He paused, shook his head. "This was our second stop."

Hunter was shook up but trying to keep it together. It wasn't working very well. He tried changing the subject. "Did you guys get everything processed at the bank?"

Sanders grinned. "Yeah. Final count was five hundred and sixty thousand dollars. All one hundred dollar bills. All neatly packed."

"Get anything from the scene?"

Sanders shook his head. "Absolutely nothing. No prints on the box or the drawer. Only the money in the box and Stacy indicated that the shear nature of used currency means that DNA or prints off the bills will be almost useless and would take an army to process."

Hunter chewed on the inside of his cheek. "So, really, all we know is that James had a big stash of money and there's nothing at either location that links it to anything."

"Yep." Reyes smiled. "One hell of a waste of cash."

Hunter nodded. "You guys stay here and wait for Stacy and Doc. I'm going to take Barkley and talk to the desk clerk."

Sanders raised an eyebrow. "Good luck with that. He seemed pretty catatonic when we pulled up."

* * * *

Another girl dead. Jesus, we've got to figure this out.

Stacy Morgan bit her lip, her eyes locked in concentration. She was in route from the bank to the Valley View Motel. She had wrapped up the processing of the safety deposit box and contents and had left Lieutenant Sprabary with two patrol units to transport the cash to the high security evidence facility where it would be held pending trial and disposition.

She thought about the girl and the hell she must have gone through since her abduction eighteen months ago. Her throat constricted as she tightened her grip on the steering wheel.

How they had manipulated her to get her to play the role of bait?

She blinked away tears and thought about the scene she would process in moments when she arrived.

She called Hunter on her cell phone. It kicked over to voicemail and she listened to his message. "Hey Cowboy, it's me. I'm on my way." She paused. "Just checking to make sure you're okay. See you in a minute." She paused again, started to say more but didn't. She punched off, dropped the phone in the console of the CSI van and accelerated.

Her tension seemed to grow with every minute of the short trip. When she pulled into the parking lot of the Valley View Motel, amid the chaos of unmarked and patrol cars, she saw the Medical Examiner's van parked in front of room six and almost lost it.

Those bastards! We'll get those bastards if I have to work twenty-four/seven to make it happen!

She stepped into the doorway to find Doc frowning as he stood by the bed.

"How dreadful." The body of Valerie Bryant was positioned as if she'd just been watching TV or reading a book. "She never saw it coming, did she?"

Sanders shook his head. "Doesn't appear so Doc. I'm guessing no one heard it either." He pointed to an empty one liter plastic bottle with the bottle blown out. "Poor man's silencer."

"I've seen more murder scenes than I care to remember and I'll never understand how someone can murder a child." Doc looked at the make shift silencer. "In this case, clearly premeditated." He shook his head and began his examination.

Stacy eyed Sanders who nodded. "Cowboy seems to think they barely missed the guy. Any idea on time of death?"

"Give me a moment or two." He reached over and gently moved her jaw. "Almost no rigidity. Rigor has barely started." Next he checked her body temperature, looked over at Billy his eyes solemn. "Unfortunately, I believe Cowboy was right. Certainly less than four hours. Probably closer to two. Anything more, we'll need to determine on the table."

"Stop tromping all over my crime scene!" Stacy moved in from the door and glared at them. "Unless you are one of my CSIs or Doc, I want you out of this room now."

Sanders smiled. "We're investigating."

She nodded toward the door. "You need to go find the answers out there. If there are any answers in this room, I'll find them. Now go." She didn't return his smile as he stepped out of the room, she merely started surveying the area from top to bottom.

Stacy saw the plastic bottle. *From the position of the plastic bottle to the body, the gunman had to be standing at the foot of the bed.* She continued to survey. *He was standing at the foot of the bed. Probably had his back to her as he attached the bottle.* Her eyes traced the movements in her mind. *He just turned and fired. She never had a chance. The bastard.*

A couple of half empty Pepsi bottles sat on the night stand. *If we're lucky, we'll get some prints.* Her mind processed not only everything she saw but those she didn't. *No clothes. No suitcases. Only one pair of girls shoes. He took the time to clean out everything.* She looked back at the bottles and frowned. *Those were hers. I won't find his prints anywhere in this room.*

The room smelled of mold mixed with the copper scent of Valerie's blood. She walked into the bathroom, looked at the toilet and smiled when she noticed the seat up and droplets of overspray on the rim. *Good boy. You may not have left any prints, but since I doubt Valerie left that, I'll get your DNA.*

* * * *

"Look asshole, I want a name!" Barkley had the desk clerk pressed against the wall, stuttering, stammering and sweating.

"I... I... I already told you. They registered as Mr. and Mrs.

Smith. This isn't exactly The Ritz. They paid in cash for a week. I didn't ask questions."

Hunter slapped his hand against the wall. The man startled. "What did he look like?"

His eyes blinking rapidly and his jaw flapping. "White guy. M... M... Maybe forty. Dark hair."

Barkley glared at him. "How tall?"

"Shorter than you."

"Everybody's shorter than me. How did he compare to you?"

The man thought for a moment. "He was about my height."

Hunter shook his head and rolled his eyes. "Great. You just described half the male population in Tarrant County." He sneered at the guy. "Including yourself, you dumbass." He looked at Barkley who hadn't stopped glaring at the clerk since they walked in. "This is useless. He doesn't know shit."

"I still want him down at the station looking at mug shots and working with an artist. Call a patrol car."

"We can just take our pick from the dozen or so that have pulled up in the last ten minutes." He looked back at the man and motioned toward the door. "Let's go. You've got some work to do."

Chapter 25

"I need to speak with you now!" The man behind the desk slammed his phone down and drummed his fingers on his desk.

Quick footsteps down the hall announced the underling. "Yes."

"What the hell is going on with the girl?" The man behind the desk waved for the door to be closed, his eyes like daggers.

The underling stepped into the office and closed the door behind him to make sure they wouldn't be overheard. "I just hea…"

"Is this what happens when you track it personally and get your best man on it?"

"There was a situation. He had to think fast." The underling was standing in front of his desk.

"Think? Is that what you call it? Leaving a dead girl in a motel room is not thinking! It's stupid!" The man stood up and directed his underling to sit.

"Well, you see…"

The man's hand shot up for silence. "I don't want to hear it. I'll ask you when I want something." He paced for a moment, stopped at the window and squinted against the sun streaming in. He gathered himself and calmed. "This is getting messy. Why did your best man feel the need to take this action?"

"I was monitoring her electronic contacts, emails, FaceBook, those kinds of things."

"And why did she have access to that in the first place?"

The underling shrugged. "In order for her to play her part, she needed them. It's the way teenagers communicate these days. It would have raised suspicion if she didn't." He paused until the man signaled for him to continue. "This morning she got an email and responded to it.

I noticed it and realized that something wasn't right. I had our tech guy trace it and it turned out to be a government IP address." He leaned forward. "It had to be law enforcement so I called our guy to take care of it. I meant for him to get her out of there."

"And he decides to kill her?" There was a sneer in the man's voice.

The underling stammered, look at his hand. "I must not have been clear."

The man was silent, continued to pace and rub his temples. "How did the cops get her email in the first place?"

"Not sure. This wasn't the email address she used while working at any of the schools. We disabled those as soon as she left. This was the address attached to her FaceBook account. My only guess is that they got a subpoena for that account."

"We clearly haven't given these cops enough credit." The man took a deep breath and sat down behind the desk. "They found our premium package and somehow tied that to our Haltom City location." He shook his head in disbelief. "They must have also tied that to our girl." He leaned back, looked toward the ceiling. "From there, they were not only able to find her email address but they were able to contact her and physically locate her so quickly that our guy was almost caught in the room with her."

The underling nodded, but didn't speak.

The man behind the desk leaned forward, his eyes boring into the underling. "Last time we spoke, I asked you to get information on the investigation. Did you find anything?"

"Yes." The underling relaxed for the first time since he'd entered the room. "Interesting stuff. It started off as a straight FWPD homicide investigation led by a detective named Jake Hunter. Once they found our Haltom City location, they brought in a Texas Ranger named Colt Barkley."

The man smiled slyly. "Barkley, huh? Interesting. His reputation precedes him. He could be a challenge."

"He's not the only one. My sources say Hunter is one of the best around. His Dad is a former Texas Ranger legend and his girlfriend is the lead CSI.

"Girlfriend? Hmm…"

The underling raised an eyebrow. "You don't want…"

The man behind the desk raised his hand and cut him off. "There's nothing to do at this point. If they get closer, we may have to become more proactive."

Chapter 26

"We need to go after Sledge hard and now!" Barkley stood and stared out the window of the conference room, the setting sun created an orange glow around his silhouette.

"All we've got on him is that his company happened to hired two scumbags out of a couple of thousand employees." Hunter sat hunched over, elbows on his knees and hands running through his hair. His eyes looked dejected.

"Goddamn it!" Barkley's voice boomed as he turned and threw a marker across the room. It hit the whiteboard with a loud crack and such force, it left a dent. Sanders and Hunter swapped glances. Barkley continued his mini tirade by kicking the back of a chair before he slumped against the wall. "Sorry. I'm just… Fuck it. I don't know what I am right now."

Hunter nodded. "For the record, I agree." His eyes were intense but empathetic when he looked at Barkley. Barkley nodded and calmed.

Reyes had taken the motel clerk in to get a better description of Valerie's killer. The other three detectives had left Stacy and her team under the watchful eyes of several patrolmen, working the motel scene. They wanted to get back to the station and regroup. Based on her mood, they didn't expect to see her for a while.

"Billy, why don't you order a couple of pizzas and let Reyes know where we are." Hunter stood and stared at the whiteboard. "We're going to be here a while."

As Sanders made the call and Hunter processed the whiteboard, Barkley slowly edged out of his funk and joined Hunter. Their eyes absorbed everything on the board.

"What are these phone numbers?" Barkley broke the silence and pointed to two sets of numbers and names on the board.

"They were numbers found on a notepad in James' apartment. The first one is a nearby Vietnamese restaurant. My guess is that's where most of Madison's meals came from when she was still alive." Hunter pointed to the second one. "This one's interesting. It's the direct line number to a Dr. Spencer Lamar, a general practitioner over off Riverside Drive."

"Have we spoken to him?"

Hunter shook his head. "Not yet."

"Maybe he's their off-the-books doctor and where they got the Propofol?"

"James didn't have any major illnesses and he didn't seem to be the type to socialize with doctors." Hunter nodded. "So yeah, that's what I'm thinking."

"What else do we know about the doctor?"

"Nothing at this point, haven't done a background yet."

Barkley nodded and folded his arms. "I'll get my guys to do that first thing in the morning." He jutted his chin toward the board. "What else did we get from his place?"

"Just the box key that led to the money."

"Money?" Barkley arched an eyebrow.

"Oh shit. I never got the chance to tell you." Hunter grinned. "That safety deposit key we found was to a box at Woodhaven National. We found over a half million in neatly packed one hundred dollar bills."

Now both eyebrows went up and he let out a low whistle. "Was there anything that indicated what it was for or why it was there?"

Hunter shook his head. "No clue. Could have been anything. Maybe he was skimming from his boss or running his own girls on the side or maybe this was a cash fund to keep the business running."

Barkley's face was intense, his mind clearly processing this information. "We need to think about how we can use this information."

"Let me know if you come up with something."

They were both lost in thought when Sanders walked in with the pizza and Reyes. The scent of garlic and pepperoni filled the room. They took a moment to get drinks and grab some slices but got back to the whiteboard and the conversation quickly.

Barkley gulped down a slice in record time. "Any more from our motel clerk?"

Reyes shook his head. "Generic white guy in a generic sedan."

A frown played across Barkley's face before he waved it away. "So, we've got the doctor, the money and the two cellmates. One of them, along with James used to work for Sledge." He stopped, shook his head. "Damn, I think that guy's dirty." He continued before they could respond. "We've also got the second cellmate and Warrick Turner."

"Who we've had no luck finding." Sanders turned his hands up.

"What else?" Barkley looked at Hunter.

Hunter shrugged. "Doc said he'd have the autopsy on Valerie done early tomorrow so maybe we'll get something there." He winced when he saw how Barkley reacted to mentioning the girl. "Sorry man."

Barkley didn't speak, just shook his head and closed his eyes.

"With the fervor that Stacy had at the hotel, there's a good chance she'll turn something up. We'll get that in the morning as well."

Barkley stood and stretched, accentuating his height. He flashed his cocky smile. "I always believe that if you don't have any coconuts, you go shake every tree you've got until some fall out." He looked at Hunter. "You up for shaking some trees?"

"Hell yeah. What do you have in mind?"

He looked at Reyes and Sanders. "Let's let these guys chase down the autopsy results, the background check on the doctor and whatever comes out of the motel. Meanwhile, you and I can pay visits to everyone on that board we can find." He pointed. "At the very least, that's the doctor, the cellmate Paul Raymond and Lance Sledge."

Hunter smiled. "You really think we can get in to see Sledge?"

"Who knows? If we don't get in to see him, we'll get high enough to rattle his cage." He shrugged. "Like you said, we don't have anything on any of these guys. All I'm trying to do is see how they react to our visit and see if we can bluff them into making a move."

Hunter raised his Diet Coke. "When all else fails, here's to a good bluff!"

Chapter 27

"You didn't get to me in time." The sound of the girl's voice made him turn to the right. When he saw her, he was drawn to her eyes. They were hazel, hypnotic, the pupils were wide and her expression grim. "You knew where I was. What took you so long?"

Hunter tried to speak but no sound came.

"At least they came for you." Another girl's voice made him turn back to the left. He recognized the penetrating blue eyes and the golden hair. "They didn't even look for me." Her eyes locked onto Hunter. "Why didn't you look for me?"

"What about me?" Another voice, this time from behind him. As he turned the voices started coming from all directions. "What about me? Why aren't you looking for me? You didn't make it in time."

His head swiveled with each new accusation. In every direction were the sad eyes of young girls… Valerie, Madison, Krysti, Hallie, girls he didn't know. Eyes of every color and shape, all sad, hopeless, pleading. "Where are you? Help me."

The voices kept coming, on top of each other, getting louder and louder, more jumbled, creating a cacophony of cries.

When it reached a crescendo, Hunter sat bolt up in his bed, the alarm buzzing through the haze. The air conditioned air hit his sweat and jolted him to his senses. His heart raced and his chest heaved as his brain registered his surroundings.

Six A.M. Wednesday.

This has got to stop.

* * * *

"Who's first on our list?" Barkley was already jacked up for the day and all business as he climbed into Hunter's SUV. He turned to Hunter and smirked as the truck started moving. "You look tired."

"I'm fine, just a rough night." Hunter steered the truck out of the parking lot. "Doctor Spencer Lamar." Hunter pointed to a manila folder on the seat. "I just got his file from Sanders, but haven't reviewed it yet."

Barkley flipped it open, started reading highlights aloud. "General Practitioner, thirty-eight years old, residency at Parkland, studied medicine at Tulane Medical, lives on Vaquero Club Drive in Westlake…"

"Whoa." Hunter interrupted Barkley. He was awake now. "Wait a minute. He lives in Vaquero?"

Barkley shrugged. "Is that a problem?"

"Drew Bledsoe lives in Vaquero. The Jonas Brothers own a home in Vaquero. Vaquero is the Beverly Hills of Texas. If a general practitioner is living there, then treating the common cold for people barely above the poverty line must pay one hell of a lot more than I thought."

Barkley smiled as they pulled into a parking lot of a small office building. "Sounds like our doctor has some explaining to do."

The receptionist's eyes widened as she craned her neck upward to see the serious looks and the two badges displayed. "Can I help you?"

Hunter set his jaw. "We need a few minutes of Doctor Lamar's time."

"I don't suppose you have an appointment?"

"This won't take long."

She disappeared around the corner. A moment later, she was back signaling them to follow her to his office at the end of the hall. The doctor was already standing behind his desk when they entered. He smiled, extended his hand. "Gentlemen, how can I help?"

Hunter surveyed the room noting multiple framed diplomas and certificates, a wall of photos from various charity golf outings and a bookshelf full of the standard medical reference books. Hmm… No family pictures or trinkets.

After quick introductions, they all sat. Sun streamed in through a large arched window and Hunter had to reposition himself as he took the lead. "Doctor, are you familiar with a man named James Le James?"

The doctor made a show of thinking. "The name doesn't sound familiar." He picked up the phone and spoke. "Judy, do we have a patient named James Le James?" He held up a finger. "Okay, thanks."

He looked back to the detectives. "I'm sorry I couldn't help gentlemen, but he doesn't appear to be a patient." He started to stand.

"Didn't expect him to be." Hunter remained seated, his words and tone stopped the doctor in mid-rise.

He sat. "I'm a bit confused…"

"James Le James murdered a young woman last week and in turn was executed with a bullet to his forehead." Barkley's voice blared, stopping the doctor in midsentence. He leaned forward and glared. "What we want to know is why James had your direct office phone number written down in his apartment?"

The doctor lurched back in his chair, his face slack-jawed. "What? There must be a mistake. I have no…"

Hunter cut him off this time. "Doctor, James was a key player in a major human trafficking ring, one that uses the services of at least one medical professional. Is that medical professional you?"

"What? No!" His face was flushed now.

Not letting him catch his breath, Hunter continued. "Are you familiar with the drug Propofol?"

"Well, as a doctor, I've heard of it. I don't use it in my practice. It's for surgical procedures."

Barkley tagged in. "I understand you live in Vaquero?"

"Yes, but…"

"Awfully nice neighborhood for a young general practitioner." Barkley raised an eyebrow.

"What are you implying?" The doctor collected himself, leaned forward. "Gentlemen, I'm sorry I couldn't help you with this James person, but I need to get back to my patients." He stood prompting Barkley and Hunter to follow suit.

Barkley flashed a cocky grin, sarcasm dripped in his voice. "Thank you for your time Doctor. We'll be in touch." He spun and took a step toward the door, stopped and looked back. "Oh, by the way, any idea why James had over a half million dollars in a safety deposit box?"

The doctor's eyes widened and his mouth opened and closed. He cleared his throat. "As I said, I don't know him. Have a nice day."

* * * *

Hunter looked over as Barkley snickered in the passenger seat. He pulled the SUV out of the parking lot and smiled. "Barkley, you are one sadistic bastard. I knew I liked you."

"I have to admit that playing bad cop is one of the great joys in life."

"You do it well. Did you see…" Hunter was interrupted by his phone. He answered it as he steered the truck towards downtown. After several short responses, he clicked off with a "Thanks" and turned to Barkley. "They got the ballistics back from the bullets taken from Valerie. They are a match to one that killed James. Not surprising, but good to know it was the same prick that did both."

Barkley's mood went dark. "The bastard was so arrogant; he didn't even get rid of the gun. I can't wait to shove it up his ass."

Before Hunter could comment, his phone rang again. He looked at the caller ID and punched decline.

Barkley smirked. "Hiding from your girlfriend?"

"Pain in the ass newspaper guy." He smiled. "If I don't talk to him, I won't have to lie to him."

They had made it downtown to one of the two nearly identical high rises on the eastern edge of town most people still refer to as the Bass Towers. As Hunter navigated the parking garage, Barkley picked up the next manila folder.

"So this is our boy Lance Sledge." As before, he read some of the highlights. "Sledge Properties, hotels, restaurants, investment properties, on the boards of several corporations, owns a two hundred acre ranch in Parker County."

"Yeah, it's not too far from my folk's place. It's just barely outside of Fort Worth near where I-20 and I-30 merge. That land is pure gold."

"Let's go see if we can mine some gold from good old Lance."

They stepped off the elevator on the thirtieth floor into a lavish reception area. There was a no-nonsense woman manning the desk. Barkley was in full strut as he stepped across the lobby and flashed his badge and a lopsided grin before Hunter caught up. "I'm Detective Colt Barkley with the Texas Rangers. I'm here to see Mr. Lance Sledge."

The woman's expression never changed. "I'm sorry. Mr. Sledge is out of the..."

She was interrupted by the ding of the elevator and the commotion of a group of men stepping off. They were led by a man in his late fifties with a full head of gray hair, an Armani suit, an unlit cigar and what looked to be handmade, leather shoes.

Barkley didn't miss a beat. He was across the lobby and in front of the group before the woman could intervene. "Mr. Sledge, I'm Detective Colt Barkley with the Texas Rangers. I need a few minutes of your time."

The bodies of his entourage recoiled at the intrusion. One man stepped forward. "Sir, if you don't have an appoi..."

"It's all right Bill." Sledge signaled for him to retreat as his eyes locked onto Barkley's, his face inscrutable. "It just so happens that I have a few minutes between meetings and we always want to help our friends in law enforcement." He waved off his troops without breaking eye contact with Barkley. "I'll see you in the boardroom in five minutes." They stumbled away with uniform looks of disbelief.

He pointed toward a set of ornate wooden double doors. "Shall we, gentlemen?"

They entered a palatial office lined with a sitting area, mahogany bookshelves with matching conference table and desk. Sledge directed them to the conference table, pointed to two chairs on one side and sat at one end. "How can I help you today, detectives?"

With no preamble, Barkley jumped in. "We'd like to discuss two of your former employees, James Le James and Mark Cooper."

His face remained stolid. "I'm afraid I've never heard those names. Sledge Properties employs over fifteen hundred people state wide. Perhaps I can get you in contact with our Human Resources department."

"I'm sure all of those workers are legal." Without waiting for his response, Barkley continued. "These two men were cellmates during their time in the state penitentiary, were both employed by you and then became part of a human trafficking ring."

Sledge rolled his cigar around in his fingers. "Detective, our business requires a large number of low skilled laborers... Low skilled *legal* laborers, so I'm sure that some of our employees have difficult pasts. I'm not sure how..."

"One of these men brutally murdered a sixteen year old girl and was rewarded for his deed by being executed by his boss." Barkley cocked his head. "Are you sure you've never heard of either of them?"

Sledge matched Barkley's cockiness with a derisive smile. "Detective, I'm a dog man. I've got several out on the ranch. One thing I've found is that when a dog sees something it doesn't understand, it tends to bark a lot." He leaned back in his chair. "Now, that's all right, it's normal, it's in the dog's nature." He looked down at his cigar and back at Barkley. "However, once you've calmed the dog and explained the situation, you expect that dog to stop barking. But some mutts..." He grinned. "Some mutts just aren't bred well enough to respond properly." His eyes burned into Barkley. "Now those mutts, those mutts just won't stop barking. Eventually, you have no choice but to put them down."

Neither man flinched or broke eye contact for a long moment. Sledge finally stood. "I trust you can see yourselves out."

Barkley and Hunter moved toward the door. As he'd done with the doctor, Barkley paused. "I don't suppose you'd have any idea why James would have a half million dollars in cash in a safety deposit box."

Sledge was placid and pointed to the door. "Have a nice day, detective."

* * * *

Hunter smirked but kept quiet on the ride down in the crowded elevator. He wasn't sure which he was most impressed with, the fact that

Barkley had actually managed to get an audience with Sledge or the vehemence with which they had been dispatched. When they finally reached the parking garage, the smirk quickly grew to a smile and then laughter. "I guess from now on we should refer to you as Detective Bark! - ley."

Barkley's simmering façade cracked. He smiled and shook his head. "That arrogant prick! It's going to be a pleasure bringing him down."

"Yeah, well. I think we're going to need something a little more tangible than his company hiring a couple of losers." Hunter hit the ignition and backed out of his space.

"We'll get there. Our objective was to shake the trees and he clearly wasn't happy to see us."

Hunter's smile didn't fade until his phone rang and he saw Sprabary on the caller ID. He shot Barkley a look, then answered. "Hunter."

"You need to get that writer back in his cage." Sprabary's voice blared through the phone loud enough to get Barkley's attention. He didn't bother with niceties. "He's calling everybody up the food chain and squawking about connecting the dots between Madison Harper, Valerie Bryant and Caitlin Gardner."

"Shit." Hunter shook his head as he guided the SUV through the downtown streets to get to the west side of town. "I was hoping we'd get this thing done before he figured it out."

"I think that boat has sailed. Do what you can to minimize it." Sprabary was off the line before Hunter had a chance to respond.

It was Barkley's turn to smirk. "Is he always that pleasant?"

"Hell, that's him on a good day. Call Sanders and Reyes and tell them to meet us at Tillman's on Crockett. We'll grab something to eat before we visit our next victim. It's on our way." He held up his phone. "I've got to get ahold of Kipton."

As they made their way west on Seventh Street, Hunter dialed Kipton but got no answer. He left a message and a few turns later, they pulled into Tillman's parking. "Grab that file and we can review while we eat."

* * * *

Tillman's Roadhouse specializes in gourmet chuck-wagon cuisine serving everything from brisket, steaks and ribs to burgers. Red meat, beans and potatoes. As they like to advertise, it's the perfect marriage of rustic and lush.

They were seated by the hostess and glanced through the menu long enough to make up their minds. "While we're waiting for the guys, what do we know about Raymond?"

Hunter spoke more to himself than Barkley as he reached over and picked up the file. It was his turn to read the highlights out loud. "Let me see… Loser, loser and loser. Dropped out of high school, busted for pot and stealing cars, finally sent to prison after a bar fight in which he cut a guy." He paused to butter up a biscuit, tear off a chunk and pop it in his mouth. "Hmm… Just like James, his cellmate, he was mostly a model prisoner. When he got out, he went to work for his cousin and appears to have been clean ever since."

Barkley nodded. "He's not our target, he's not bright enough to be the boss. It's the cousin we want to jack up. What do you have on him?"

"In comparison, quite boring. Garret Bronson has no criminal record. He grew up in Houston, went to business school at Xavier, worked for a few years in the trading group for the Bass Brothers and started Camelot Oil and Gas ten years ago." He shuffled through some pages. "Don't have the detailed financials on the company but based on the personal information, cousin Garret has done quite well for himself."

Barkley started to comment but Sanders and Reyes' arrival derailed the thought. They signaled for the waitress and placed their orders. As they waited for their food, Hunter regaled Sanders and Reyes with the story of their encounter with Lance Sledge.

Their food was served and Sanders took a man sized bite of brisket and mumbled. "So, other than having some fun ruffling feathers, what did you learn?"

Barkley raised an eyebrow. "We learned you should never play poker with Sledge. He's got ice in his veins and doesn't bluff. I'm sure he's dirty as the day is long, but he knows we've got nothing on him. He didn't flinch."

Hunter jumped in. "Our doctor on the other hand, he was completely shook up. Maybe it was just being intimidated by the badge..."

"I don't think so." Barkley was using a bite of steak on his fork as a pointer. "Did you see how he reacted to my comment about James having that money?"

Hunter nodded. "Yeah, he tried to recover but his face went pale for a split second."

"Exactly."

The four of them continued to speculate and analyze the conversations as they wolfed down their meals. Sanders and Reyes provided more details on Valerie's autopsy but nothing eye-popping.

As the conversation slid toward sports and current events, Hunter's mind drifted back to the dream that woke him that morning. The eyes played back in his mind. What kept clawing at him even more than the girls he recognized, were the eyes of the ones he didn't. So many.

"Hey, you ready to roll?" Barkley's voice brought him back.

"Yeah, we've got work to do."

Chapter 28

"So, where are these guys located?" Barkley climbed into Hunter's SUV.

"A high-end office building." He looked at his phone for the details. "It looks like they're at the corner of Bailey and West Seventh."

The drive was just a couple of blocks, barely worth getting in the truck. They turned onto West Seventh, drove a block and were looking at brand new buildings lining both sides of the street. They were all part of Museum Place, a twelve acre revitalization development full of high end office space, condominiums and restaurants just on the edge of the Fort Worth Cultural District.

"Nice digs." Barkley surveyed the area after Hunter had found a parking spot on the street.

"Yeah, nice and expensive." Hunter squinted against the sun's reflection off the mirrored glass, pointed to the building on the north side of the street. "Camelot Oil and Gas is on the second floor."

Camelot's reception area wasn't large but it was high end with scraped hard wood floors, handmade Persian Serapi rugs and antique furniture including a Georgian Period mahogany desk where a stunning brunette sat looking bored. Hunter and Barkley swapped smirks and jockeyed to see who got to badge her first. Barkley won and went through his routine introduction and asked to see both Paul Raymond and Garret Bronson.

She eyed his credentials. "I'll see if they're available, Detective Barkley." She sauntered down a short hall and through an open door while both detectives gawked.

"I should have gone into oil and gas." Barkley's eyes hadn't left the hall.

Before Hunter could comment, she reappeared, steamed up the picture frames with her look at Barkley and motioned for them to come to her. "It'll be a few minutes." She directed them to a conference room suited for about ten people. "Please make yourselves comfortable. There are waters in the fridge." Both men nodded and smiled.

Barkley shook his head after she left and then purposely stood behind the chair at the head of the table. Hunter walked around so that he would be in the middle of the table facing the door. Though they had not discussed it, Hunter realized their movements covered both power positions in the room. *I like the way Barkley thinks. When dealing with Alpha dogs, every move matters.*

He surveyed the conference room, noted the numerous framed pictures on the walls of men and their expensive toys, sports cars, boats and motorcycles. There were multiple men in the pictures but one constant face. While the furniture was more modern, it was still extremely high end. When the two men walked into the conference room, Hunter knew immediately which one was Bronson and which was Raymond. Only one Alpha dog. Bronson, the one constant in all the pictures, looked like he just stepped out of a spread in GQ advertising Masculine Elegance. Even his business casual attire looked custom tailored including the shirts with French cut sleeves and cufflinks. His hair, skin and nails were flawless.

Bronson flashed a perfect smile and extended his hand first to Hunter, then Barkley as he made his way into the room. "Gentlemen, welcome to Camelot. I'm Garret Bronson, CEO." He pointed to the other man. "This is Paul Raymond, my head of operations. How can we help you?"

There was a momentary stand off as Bronson expected Barkley to move but was met only with Barkley's cocky grin as he sat at the head of the table. When Barkley motioned for Bronson to sit, he reluctantly complied.

"We're here to discuss one of Paul's acquaintances, James Le James." Barkley switched his focus to Paul Raymond but kept Bronson in his field of vision.

Both men's faces twitched but only briefly. "That's a name I haven't heard in a while." Raymond's voice was tight.

"Have you seen him since you got out of Eastham?"

His face had gone flush. "No. I cut all ties to that life."

"It seems your buddy has been living and working just down the street from you ever since his release, and you haven't so much as bumped into him?"

"That's what he said." Bronson cut in, his voice confident. "That was part of the deal I made with my cousin when I gave him a chance to work with me and learn the business. I insisted that he cut all ties with his criminal past. He's done just that. Since he's been out, his record is spotless."

Barkley turned back to Bronson. "What exactly is your business?"

"We're energy brokers. We also own interests in a number of drilling operations around the state."

"How big is the company?"

Bronson paused, tapped his finger on the table. "Detective, we're a privately held company and that information is confidential."

Barkley caught Bronson with a momentary glare that melted into a smile. "Of course, I understand." He turned back to Raymond. "James' business has been pretty confidential as well. Last week he murdered a sixteen-year-old girl, one that he'd kidnapped and was in the process of selling as a sex slave."

Raymond's eyes grew wide. "What? That's not... I mean..."

"He was rewarded for his efforts with a bullet to the forehead." Hunter snapped at Raymond but focused his eyes on Bronson to see his reaction. There was none.

"Like I said, I haven't seen James in years and I have no idea what he's done since he was rel..."

"Detectives." Bronson cut him off and paused until everyone looked at him. His jaw was set and his eyes were calm. "I'm not sure how else we can help you since we've had no contact with this person." He stood. "Unless there's something else, we have a business to run."

Barkley stared at him from his seat for a long moment, then slowly rose until he was towering over him, never losing eye contact.

"Yes, I'm sure you do." He stepped around Bronson and to the door closer to Raymond. His eyes locked on him. "Any idea how your buddy from prison managed to accumulate a half million dollars in cash?"

Raymond's mouth dropped. "What?"

"That's right. That low rent scum you used to do in the pen, had a half million in cash in a safety deposit box. How do you think he managed that?"

"Paul!" Bronson's voice whipped Raymond's head around but Bronson was glaring at Barkley. "Have a nice day, Detective."

Barkley smiled and swaggered down the hall.

Both detectives were smiling broadly as Hunter pulled out of the parking spot and moved down West Seventh. Barkley stretched out in the passenger seat. "You sure we don't have any other trees to shake? This is just starting to get fun." He shook his head. "That was an interesting pair."

"Yeah, Paul's not a very good liar. He's seen James since his release." Hunter smiled. "And he was completely freaked when you mentioned the money."

Barkley shrugged. "You're probably right, but he could've just been surprised that a low life scum like James had that kind of money."

The ringing of Hunter's phone kept him from commenting. "Hunter."

"So you finally got around to calling me?" Kipton's voice dripped with sarcasm.

"I've been busy."

"I was able to figure that out on my own, no thanks to you. You can read about it on the front page in the morning."

Hunter shifted in his seat as he steered the truck back towards the station. "What exactly am I going to read?"

By the time they were sitting in the parking lot, Kipton had spent fifteen minutes outlining the details of his story including the connection between Madison Harper and Valerie Bryant, that Valerie Bryant and Caitlin Gardner were the same person and that both Madison and Caitlin had been apparently kidnapped by the same people. He had background on Caitlin but hadn't made the connection between the girls and James or the Haltom City holding center.

"Andre, we're in the middle of a sensitive investigation. I need you to hold the story."

"I can't do that. It's out of my hands now. If you'd have bothered to call me back, I might have been able to do something."

"Listen to me, Andre. This thing's big and there's more to it than you know but if you want to know the rest, I need you to hold the story."

"Sorry. You're too late. Next time call me back." Kipton clicked off.

Hunter dropped his phone into the console. "Damn it."

"Well." Barkley reached for the door handle. "We wanted to shake some trees." He looked back and smiled. "Get ready to pick up some coconuts."

Chapter 29

"Those bastards were in my office. They came to my place of business." The man behind the desk was stalking back and forth. "That's unacceptable."

His underling just nodded. The rant had been going on for almost an hour.

"The cocky one... Barkley, that son of a bitch." He gripped the back of his chair, his fingers dug into the leather as he looked around his office. "The way he spoke to me." He shook his head. "The other one... Hunter. He wasn't much better." He looked at his underling. "He's the local one, right?"

"Yes."

"You said it's Hunter's team that's running the investigation, right? And Barkley's the state guy?"

"Right. Hunter and his partner, Billy Sanders, another FWPD detective named Jimmy Reyes and Hunter's apparent girlfriend, Stacy Morgan is the lead CSI on the case. They've been on the case since James... uh..." The underling didn't finish his sentence.

"We need to know everything they're doing, everywhere they go and everything they see. If you need to bring in some contractors, do so." He glared at the underling. "I want professionals who can't be tied back to us. This is surveillance only at this point. If we decide to be proactive, we need to know where they are vulnerable."

"What about Barkley?"

The man sat in his chair and drummed his fingers on his desk. "I need to think about him. State guys are harder targets. I've got some friends that might be able to make him go away without action on our part. Besides, if we need to be proactive with him, I'll do it personally."

The underling looked at the man. "Do you think that's smart?"

A smile spread across the man's face. "Now that's priceless, you questioning me about being smart." The smile slid away. "I'll determine what is or isn't smart for this organization." He jabbed his finger at the air. "Nobody talks to me like that... Nobody. I don't give a damn what kind of badge he's got. I've got more pull in this state than he'll ever have."

The underling nodded. "I'll get right on it. Do we need to temporarily shut down the operations or move our merchandise?"

The man shook his head. "No. They've got nothing concrete. If they did, they wouldn't have come here to talk, they would have kicked the doors down." He waved for the underling to leave. "Get me some information so we can fight this battle the right way. We'll move when it makes sense. Meanwhile, I've got some phone calls to make."

Chapter 30

"I thought you were going to talk to that damn reporter!" Hunter's peaceful morning drive down I-35W to FWPD's Central Station was interrupted by an irate Lieutenant Sprabary blasting through the phone.

"I did talk with him." Hunter paused to change lanes. "By the time we connected, he'd already submitted the piece and my offer for additional insight wasn't worth him fighting with his boss to pull the story."

"Jesus, that guy's a pain in the ass."

Hunter grinned as he sensed that Sprabary was more bark than bite this morning. "The good news is that unless he got something more than he had yesterday, all he really knows is that there's a connection between Madison and Valerie."

"The problem is that he's connected enough dots that our traffickers may decide to pack up and move on."

"That may not be the worst thing." Hunter was now exiting into downtown. "If they start making unplanned moves, there's a chance they'll make a mistake. I'm about five minutes out. I'll read the article when I get there and we'll assess the impact."

"We'll talk." Sprabary clicked off. Hunter moved more aggressively through traffic to get back to the station and read the story himself.

* * * *

Sources close to the investigation say it's unclear whether Caitlin Gardner was a victim or possibly a co-conspirator. She enrolled at Eastern Hills

High School under the name of Valerie Bryant and became friends with Madison Harper a few months before Madison's disappearance. Friends say the two had become inseparable.

Barkley's brow furrowed as his eyes devoured the story in a matter of minutes. He had read the first part of the story, which outlined Madison Harper's disappearance and murder and then continued on as Kipton outlined how Caitlin was found in the Valley View Motel. He nodded his head as he confirmed the writer had yet to connect the disappearances with human trafficking. Kipton had chosen to go down the serial kidnapper angle.

That won't last long. Once other media outlets get ahold of this, they'll figure it out.

He finished the story, put the paper down on the conference room table and turned to the window. People jostled each other on the city sidewalk, and his mind flashed back to Valerie's body in the motel. He saw the wet brownish red stains on her white shirt, her eyes, innocent even in death.

How did I let it happen again? I set her up.

He pressed his forehead to the cool glass, closed his eyes and let his mind drift, reviewing the conversations and reactions of the four men they'd spoken to the day before. All seemed evasive, like they were hiding secrets. The real question he had to answer was if those secrets had anything to do with human trafficking.

"Are you okay?" Hunter's voice broke him from his lethargy.

"No, but Madison and Valerie are worse, so it doesn't matter."

Barkley turned to see Hunter standing in the doorway with two cups of coffee in his hands. He offered one up. "Thought you might be here early." His eyes cut to the table where the newspaper lay. "I'm guessing you weren't reading the sports?"

"According to your newspaper friend, the Police have no leads at this time."

Hunter shrugged. "If we're lucky the bad guys will believe that and we can gain ground on them."

Barkley nodded his head, ran his hands through his hair. "Let's make sure we're lucky."

* * * *

The photographs caught Stacy's eye as she walked past the HDTV monitor that hung on the wall in the break room at the forensics lab. They were pictures of Madison and Valerie with their names subtitled beneath them. She grabbed the remote and turned up the volume.

"Newspaper reports this morning linked the disappearances and subsequent murders of two Texas teens. Misty Covington is reporting from in front of Eastern Hills High School. Misty, what can you tell us?"

"Thanks Steve. Madison Harper befriended Valerie Bryant several months ago when the second girl transferred to the high school. What Madison didn't know was that Valerie's real name was Caitlin Gardner and she'd been missing from Amarillo for almost fifteen months at the time."

The report switched to a recorded story detailing the background to both Madison's and Valerie's disappearances and murders. It was nothing that Stacy didn't already know and really only scratched the surface of the case. Until an annoying song about bubbles drilled into her consciousness, she didn't realize the story had ended, the station had gone to commercial and she was still staring at the screen.

Her stomach quivered. She flashed back to the smiling faces of the two girls on the TV but as she thought about them, they transformed into the lifeless images she saw at the two scenes. Her mind flashed to the holding center, the dirty mats, the child's shirt. She blinked away the urge to cry, took a deep breath, steadied herself and headed back to her station, leaving her still warm coffee sitting in the break room.

* * * *

"This is Glen Sullivan and we're back, here on WBAP 820 am. Today we are discussing the story that broke this morning about the two murdered teen girls, one from Fort Worth and one from Amarillo. We are joined now by Sheriff Blake Haskins of Potter County. Welcome Sheriff Haskins."

The man behind the desk was now behind the wheel of his black

BWM Z4 convertible, the engine rumbled beneath him. In the previous radio segment, the host had provided the background on the case. He had chosen the convertible because of the beautiful weather but now had to turn up the volume so he could hear over the wind noise. He listened as the Sheriff told how they had originally believed Caitlin Gardner was a runaway but now it seems clear that she had been kidnapped.

There was nothing new in the information and nothing pointing to his organization or even to human trafficking in general. He continued to listen and zip through traffic on his way to his office.

"Sheriff, my screener has a call on the line she thinks we need to take. Let me punch it up. Sarah from Austin, you're on The Glen Sullivan show on WBAP, what do you say?"

"Hey Glen, big fan. Listening to you online. I wanted to let you know that last year, there was a Valerie Bryant that went to Westlake High School here in Austin. She was only here for a few months but the strange thing is that she was here when Hallie Boyer went missing."

"Holy cow! Sheriff, when did Caitlin Gardner go missing?"

"It was over eighteen months ago so that would be in the time window. That's very interesting information. First I've heard of any connection to a third missing girl."

"Wow Sarah, thanks for your call. So we may be talking about multiple kidnapping victims…"

The voice continued but the man behind the wheel was no longer listening. His face had gone flush and he'd begun to sweat all over. A horn blasted as he swerved out of his lane. He made a dismissive hand gesture, regained his composure and punched his blue tooth. "Be in the office in ten minutes! We need to talk."

Chapter 31

"How was Sprabary's temperature?" Sanders smirked when Hunter walked into the conference room shortly before lunch. He'd been in Sprabary's office since midmorning and had that rode hard look.

"One might get the impression that he doesn't appreciate the press." He smiled, looked around the room and noticed Barkley missing. "Where's our favorite Ranger?"

Sanders shrugged. "Said he had some things to run down and he'd be back this afternoon."

"You hungry?"

"Always."

Hunter pursed his lips. "Round up Reyes and meet me downstairs. We'll grab some lunch and review where we stand."

"Will do. I've got a few interesting tidbits to pass along."

They decided there wasn't a major time constraint and made their way to North Side to eat family style Tex-Mex at Joe T. Garcia's. Joe T's is a Fort Worth institution known for their classic food and strong margaritas. It started with the Garcia family serving meals in the front room of their home on North Commerce Street back in 1935. Since then, it has grown to cover most of a city block with multiple buildings, a huge courtyard and the capacity to seat close to 1,200 at one time. The original family home is still there and now serves as the reception area for the restaurant.

They were seated in the courtyard area under a grouping of big trees and beside an enormous concrete fountain. It was still early enough in May that, with a little breeze, the heat was manageable.

After they placed their order and Jimmy showed off his Spanish skills by chatting up the waitress, Hunter gave them a rundown of the meeting with Paul Raymond and Garret Bronson. They got a kick out of Barkley's gamesmanship.

"So, while I was making sure that Barkley stayed at least within sight of the boundaries, what did you guys find out?"

Sanders had brought a stack of folders with him and now opened the top one. "Let's start with our Doctor. Definitely making more money than the typical General Practitioner. I ran financials on him going all the way back to college." He flipped through a few pages. "This guy was basically broke until about five years ago. While he was making low six figures through his clinic, he had only been in practice for three years and between the startup costs and his student loans, he was over a quarter million in debt. In a very short period of time, the practice almost tripled in revenue. On top of that, over a two year period of time, he got a series of lump sums from an unknown source that allowed him to pay off his loans. Now he's debt free and supposedly pulling down five hundred plus a year." He shook his head. "For a small GP office, no way is that normal money."

"You couldn't find a source for the payments?"

"Wire transfers from an offshore bank account."

"What about his tax returns?"

Sanders leaned back, rolled and stretched his shoulder. "He's got some good accountants. I had our experts look them over. He claimed the lump sums as gifts from family and all the rest as revenue from work. He's written a big fat check to Uncle Sam each of the last five years and according to our guys, he's as clean as a whistle."

Hunter looked at Reyes. "No way to combine that with the phone number in James' apartment and get a warrant for his medical records?"

"Not a chance. We're going to have to connect him directly with either James or one of the girls."

The food was served, the aroma enveloped the table and the guys spent a few minutes stacking their plates with tacos, enchiladas, rice and refried beans. Hunter continued to ponder the information about the doctor as he took a bite. His taste buds were treated to the unique combination of chili powder, salt, garlic and pepper that infuse

Joe T's enchilada sauce.

"Five years ago, huh? Seems like that time frame keeps popping up." Hunter crunched into a taco.

Sanders nodded. "Same time that James and Turner both fell off the grid."

Hunter shook his head and took another bite. "So what else did you find?"

"Nothing else worth mentioning on the doctor." Sanders grinned. "But how about this…" He opened a second file, held up a legal document. "Sledge Properties owns the Valley View Motel."

Hunter stopped in mid bite. "No kidding." He smiled. "Oh, Barkley's gonna love that."

Sanders' grin faded. "Don't get too excited. The corporation owns it. There's no way to link it directly to Lance Sledge and without that link, it's just one more piece of circumstantial nothing."

"Yeah." Hunter nodded. "But it is one more piece."

They finished off the last morsels and leaned back, satisfaction on their faces, the sounds of dishes and silverware clinking around them. Hunter absorbed the moment and scanned the courtyard while he thought about Sledge, how smug he looked and how good it would feel to wipe that look off his face.

He shook his head at the thought of how much further they had to go. "Do we have anything else that ties this to Sledge?"

Reyes and Sanders both shrugged and shook their heads. Hunter watched the water ripple in the fountain as his mind continued to process. "What else?"

Sanders leaned forward. "I've got feelers out with everyone I know to find Warrick Turner, even checked with his former parole officer. He said he'd dig into his files and see if he can find a friend, relative or associate that might have a current address. Haven't heard back from anyone yet."

Hunter waived to the waitress for the check as the busboy cleared away the few remaining remnants.

Sanders pulled out the next folder. "The last guy you visited, Garret Bronson… Not so easy to profile. His personal finances basically don't exist. Everything's tied up in the company and since it's a privately held corporation, we couldn't get detailed financials." He smiled. "But... I spent some time yesterday going through the company press releases and public records that I could locate and I noticed two points of interest."

As he placed cash down to cover their check, Hunter arched an eyebrow. "What's that?"

"Based on property acquisitions, Camelot Oil and Gas has been steadily growing since it was founded. Not abnormal except when you consider that the oil and gas industry is boom or bust and it totally went in the shitter during the global financial crisis in 2008 and 2009. During which, Camelot went on a buying spree."

"So they had to have money coming in from somewhere." Hunter rubbed his chin and grinned. "Your mother would be so proud that those business classes you took in school are paying off."

"She might be proud but I think she'd be happier if I didn't have to carry a gun to do my business." Sanders leaned in. "Now, for the second point of interest. Camelot either has offices or owns properties in Amarillo, Austin, Houston and Fort Worth... All the cities where girls have gone missing."

Hunter scrunched his face. "Yeah, but aren't those also all major cities in the industry?"

"Sure, but..." Sanders smiled. "Hey, I'm just trying to connect dots wherever I can."

That brought laughter from both Reyes and Hunter.

"Problem is, if you connect too many dots with too many suspects, nobody stands out anymore. All you've done now is convince me that they're all guilty." Hunter nodded for them to leave.

As they stood, Sanders' phone rang. "Sanders." He held up a finger to Hunter and Reyes so they'd stop. "Yeah... Okay..." He pulled out his notepad. "What was that address again?" He scribbled on the pad. "Dude, if this is solid, I owe you one." He hung up and looked at Hunter. "We may have Turner."

Chapter 32

The three detectives jogged across East Commerce, dust kicked up behind them and drifted with the breeze as they headed for the SUV. Hunter barked orders as he reached for his keys and Sanders and Reyes arched around to the passenger side.

"Billy, where are we going?"

"The Antigua Village Apartments on East Rosedale Street, apartment 1013. It's at the corner of Rosedale and Andrew." Sanders climbed into the front passenger seat.

"Reyes, call Barkley to let him know what's going on and see if he can meet us there, then call dispatch and get a patrol unit on the way. Make sure they don't move if they get there first."

"On it." Reyes was in the back seat dialing as Hunter hit the ignition.

Hunter punched it and turned heads as he left skid marks in the parking lot. He hit his lights to clear out some traffic and burst through a red light. His mind raced as he wrestled with the steering wheel. *Finally, a lead on one of the actual perps.* When he got up to speed, he turned to Sanders. "What's the story?"

"That was Turner's former parole officer. He tracked down an ex-girlfriend who was more than happy to tell him where, as she stated it, 'that cheating prick and his no good whore' live." Sanders chuckled.

From the backseat, Reyes chimed in. "Left a message for Barkley giving him the address. We'll have patrol backup by the time we get there."

"Great." Hunter scanned the traffic as he maneuvered in between cars. His pulse had notched up with the adrenaline coursing through his system. He squinted against the sun. "Billy, can you pull up something on your phone so we can get the lay of the land?"

"Already on it, looking at Google Earth right now. The complex has ten individual two story buildings. I'm guessing based on the apartment number, he's probably in building ten on the bottom floor but I don't know which building is building ten."

Hunter nodded. "I'd guess it's in the back of the complex. They typically number them from front to back."

"Good point." Sanders scrolled for a moment on his phone. "In that case, the complex backs up to some open fields and a park to the west, a wooded area and a couple of warehouses to the south. We can position the patrol toward the front of the complex to cut off any vehicular escape. Reyes can cover the back in case he goes out the window and you and I can go pop this asshole."

"I'd prefer to avoid popping. We need this guy to talk."

Sanders nodded, pocketed his phone and focused his eyes intently on the road in front of them. They were now moving fast westbound on Rosedale.

"What's the intel on who else might be in the apartment?"

"Don't have anything. We can stop in at the office and see what they can tell us."

When they pulled into the complex off East Rosedale, the patrol unit was already waiting for them. Hunter slipped the truck into a parking spot. "Jimmy, get the patrol set. I want him positioned at the front of the complex ready to block the exit if needed, but tell him to be as inconspicuous as possible. Tell him we don't know what this guy drives but we'll be on channel two, so if he bolts this way, we'll call him."

"Will do." Reyes was out the door.

Hunter turned to Sanders. "Let's go."

Their badges were already out as they burst through the door of the office. Heads turned but Hunter didn't wait to get to the front desk. "Fort Worth Police, I need to know who lives in apartment 1013!"

His sense of urgency transferred to the woman behind the desk as she sat up in her chair, her hands slapped on the keyboard. She stared at the screen for a moment. "It's rented to a Tabitha Johnson."

"No one else?"

She shook her head. "It's a one bedroom. She's the only one on the lease."

"Thank you."

* * * *

The throw away phone he'd started using the week before rang in his pocket. It could only be one of a small group of people. The underling tensed. "Yes."

"It's me."

"What do you need?"

"I'm not sure what, but something's happening and I thought you should know. That guy… Those cops you wanted me to follow are on the move."

"What do you mean, on the move?" The underling's stomach churned and he bit the inside of his lip.

"They were eating lunch in North Side. The black one got a phone call and the next thing I know, they're out of the restaurant and gone. I couldn't follow them without being obvious but I'm tracking them on my tablet. The GPS unit I put on his truck shows they've stopped in the five thousand block of East Rosedale. They got there in a hurry so I thought it might be important."

"Yes. Good thinking." The underling paused, thought for a moment. "Get there as soon as you can and see what's going on." He stopped, raised his voice. "Observe only! Call me when you know something."

The underling clicked off, grabbed his laptop and tapped the address into MapQuest, didn't see anything special. Switched over to Google Earth and zoomed in on the area. An apartment complex? He drummed his fingers on the desk, scrolled through everyone involved in the organization. His eyes widened. Warrick Turner!

"Shit!"

He grabbed for his phone.

* * * *

Reyes was climbing into the backseat as they bolted from the office. Hunter had the truck in reverse almost before the engine cranked. He quickly weaved through the parking lot but slowed to a more casual pace as they approached building ten.

The Antigua Village Apartments were the generic box styled two story buildings that seemed to sprout like weeds back in the seventies. With multicolored pinkish toned bricks accented with dull green trim and almost no distinctive architectural features, they looked more like minimum security prison dormitories than apartment. The front of each building was just a series of flat windows with a main entrance in the center of its bland exterior and supplemental entrances on each end of the building.

Hunter pulled into an empty space toward the south end of the structure and let the truck idle for a moment while he scanned the building. "Jimmy, we'll walk down through the main entrance. You can get to the back from there and we can clear that area before moving down the hall. Hook a left behind the building, the apartment should be midway down. Be on channel two. We'll let you know if he's moving."

He turned off the truck but waited to get out. "Guys, be ready. This asshole will be armed, but we don't shoot unless we have to. Let's be careful."

No shade, Hunter could feel the late May heat and it seemed as if all air movement had stopped. The Tex-Mex lunch gurgled in his stomach as they walked through the main entrance, paused to draw their weapons. Hunter and Sanders moved quickly down the hallway, their eyes adjusting to the dim lighting and found the door for 1013 midway down on their right.

Hunter positioned Sanders on the far side of the door with a few quick, silent hand gestures and shouldered up against the near side, his right arm pressed against the frame, his Glock pointed toward the floor. He nodded to Sanders to try the doorknob.

As he reached forward, movement behind Sanders flickered in Hunter's peripheral vision. The sound of a cell phone ringing and something crashing to the floor caused him to look past Sanders down the hall. When his eyes registered the bag of groceries broken on the floor, he looked up to see a scraggly blond haired man standing at the end of the hall dropping a cell phone and raising a pistol. His instincts took over and everything seemed to move in slow motion.

"Gun!"

He grabbed Sanders by his shirt and pulled him to the floor as three gunshots exploded in the hall. Bullets ripped through the doorframe where Sanders' head had been a split second before. Splinters and plaster flew in all directions and rained down on the detectives as they scrambled for nonexistent cover.

Both men reacted as trained, rolled onto their stomachs and returned fire, but hit nothing but drywall as the man had already disappeared around the corner. Sanders was up, flying and halfway down the hall before Hunter was even on his feet.

"Shots fired! Heading out of the south entrance!" Hunter screamed into his handheld as his legs pumped, running down the hall. He jumped over the bag of groceries and cell phone as his lungs sucked in the acrid smell of burnt gun powder.

Hunter rounded the corner and his eyes were assaulted by the sun. He reached the doorway just in time to watch Sanders dive behind his SUV, hear another volley of shots fired and see the windows in his truck explode into a rain shower of falling glass. His head swiveled in the direction of the shots and saw the shooter across the parking lot turn and head toward a thick stand of oak trees.

"Are you hit?" Hunter moved toward Sanders.

"I'm fine!" Sanders was up again blasting across the open parking lot headed for the trees.

Hunter stopped in the spot where Sanders had been. "Billy!" He aimed at the trees ready to provide cover if he saw the suspect. He saw nothing and bolted across the parking lot in hot pursuit of his partner. "Billy!" He reached the trees, caught a glimpse of Sanders about twenty feet ahead as he carelessly rounded the corner of what looked to be a warehouse.

The four quick blasts followed almost instantly. Hunter's heart sank as he slammed his shoulder against the wall at the corner of the warehouse. All sound except for the ringing of the shots seemed to have stopped. He leveled his gun and rounded the corner expecting the worst and ready to fire.

He pulled his weapon up when instead of seeing his partner lying on the ground in a pool of blood, he realized he was aiming at Billy's back. Billy's shoulders rose and fell heavily as he stood over the suspect. Hunter looked past him to see a man he assumed to be Turner on the ground with a cluster of bullet holes in the center of his chest.

"Behind you Billy." Hunter knew never to surprise someone who was amped up on adrenaline and holding a gun.

Sanders nodded and holstered his weapon and Hunter walked up and stood beside him.

"Damn it." Hunter frowned.

Gunpowder hung in the still, cool air of the shaded area as Hunter and Sanders stood over the body. Both men's chests heaved as they tried to catch their breaths. The sound of footsteps from behind them turned their heads and they saw Reyes jogging toward them holstering his weapon.

As he joined them, he first looked down at the body and then made eye contact with Hunter, asking the silent question of who did the shooting. Hunter nodded toward Sanders in answer.

Reyes smiled, put his hand on Sanders' shoulder. "Don't suppose you could've just winged him?"

Incredulous, Sanders just stared at him as he continued to take deep breaths.

Reyes shrugged. "I'm just sayin'."

Chapter 33

"Hey dumbass, what do you think you are, bulletproof?" Hunter's voice had a tightness that Sanders had rarely heard and his eyes were like lasers burning a hole through steel.

"What do you mean?"

Hunter's eyes flared and his voice went up several decibels. "What I mean is your complete lack of procedure. This isn't some made-for-TV combat movie. Those were real fucking bullets!"

"He was getting away."

"I don't give a damn about him getting away. I give a damn about my partner getting shot." Hunter looked away and clenched his jaw.

"I'm sorry."

Hunter turned back, jabbed his finger in the air toward Sanders. "Being sorry is bullshit. Running around corners without looking is bullshit. Running across open parking lots without cover is bullshit. What kind of crap is that?" Hunter ran his hand through his hair. "I don't want you to be sorry. I want you to be alive." He paused, softened his tone. "I've gotten used to you."

Sanders tried to hide his smirk. "Thanks, I think."

Hunter shook his head, started to walk off but turned back. "I will say this... That was damn nice bullet placement." A smile broke out across his face as he turned and walked back toward the parking lot.

"No shit." Reyes was still standing, staring at the suspect. "Four shots all within a two inch circle. Damn nice shooting." He smiled. "Someone's been practicing."

The patrolman who had been posted at the front of the complex pulled up as Hunter cleared the trees and stepped into the parking lot.

Hunter flagged him down. "Call it in. We need the ME out here for a suspect fatality over in the woods." He pointed over toward his SUV and then to the building. "We've got three areas that are going to need perimeters set up so you're going to need a bunch of units out here. Get CSI rolling. Request Stacy Morgan, this is an ongoing case."

As he moved toward his SUV, Barkley pulled up and jumped out, leaving his truck parked sideways in the middle of the parking lot. "What the hell happened?"

"We found Warrick Turner." He gestured back toward the trees. "He's got four slugs in his chest."

"Shit."

"My thoughts exactly." Hunter pointed toward the building. "We never made it into the apartment. He supposedly lived with his girlfriend. Come with me so we can see if she's home."

Barkley turned to follow Hunter but started laughing when he saw Hunter's SUV. "You need to complain to the valet."

"Yeah I know." Hunter shook his head. "Sanders decided to use my truck as cover the second time the guy started shooting at him." He grinned, gestured toward the trees. "The third time was the charm."

They walked into the building and retraced their steps. They stopped and inspected the holes in the sheetrock from where Hunter and Sanders returned fire. Barkley smirked, Hunter shrugged. They stepped over the broken groceries and the dropped cell phone and walked down the hall. When they got back to the apartment door, Hunter looked at the damage inflicted on the wall, doorframe and door.

He pointed to the frame. "Sanders' head was right there about a millisecond before those hit."

Barkley raised an eyebrow. "He's living a charmed life." He reached toward the door. "Let's see if the little woman is home."

* * * *

"This place is crawling with cops." The voice on the phone was pitched up higher than normal.

The underling had figured out that somehow the police had

found Warrick Turner and he knew the man behind the desk wasn't pleased. "Tell me what's going on."

"It looks like a war zone. All the activity is at the back of the complex and it's pretty spread out. Something's going on inside the building, that cop's Ford Explorer got shot up pretty good and people are walking in and out of a wooded area behind the complex."

"What kind of first responder vehicles are there?"

"All cops, no fire department or ambulance. The Medical Examiner just showed up so somebody's not breathing anymore."

The underling processed that for a moment. "Does it look like they've arrested anyone?"

"If they have, they've either got them inside or they've already dragged them off."

The underling smiled. *Maybe they solved my problem for me*. "What about CSI? Are they there?"

"No, I don't... Oh, wait. Spoke too soon. The CSI truck just pulled up."

"Good. That means your partner should be arriving soon. Connect with him. Continue to observe. Let me know if anything major happens." The underling paused, thought through what he had heard. "Be ready. We may be shifting gears."

* * * *

"No need to knock the door down." A pissed off voice came through the thin walls. The groggy looking woman's eyes flew wide when she opened the door and was met with two badges, two drawn weapons and two intense looking detectives. "What the hell?"

"Tabitha Johnson?" Hunter asked the question as he pushed through the half opened door. "Is there anyone else in the apartment?" His gun moved from side to side.

"Yes, uh, what? No." She staggered back from the door, her eyes strained to focus. "I mean yes, I'm Tabitha Johnson and no, no one else is here." She watched as Hunter cleared the room then turned to see Barkley's gun pointed directly at her. Her hands shot straight up as she stumbled backwards. "I didn't do nothing. What the hell is this about?"

As Hunter moved to the bedroom, Barkley nodded to a chair. "Sit down, Miss Johnson and keep your hands visible." He glanced around the messy, cramped room. "Have you been asleep?"

"Yeah, why?"

He cocked his head. "You didn't hear all the commotion in the hall?"

She looked toward the door as if it held an answer. "I work nights so I took a sleeping pill and used some earplugs. What commotion?"

"Clear." Hunter's voice rang out from the bedroom a moment before he reentered the room. His phone buzzed in his pocket but he ignored it. Without giving her a chance to get her bearings, Hunter sat on the table directly in front of her, glared at her and started. "Does Warrick Turner live here with you?"

"Yeah, why?" She looked around as if noticing for the first time she was missing something. "Where is he?"

"Did you expect him to be here? I thought you just said no one else was supposed to be here."

Her face was blank as she seemed to consider that question. She shrugged. "Yeah, I guess. I don't remember his schedule." Concern washed across her face. "Why? Is he in some kind of trouble?"

Ignoring her question and his once again buzzing phone, Hunter continued. "Where does Warrick work?"

"I don't remember the name of the place. It's a machine shop over in Haltom City."

"Do you know where the shop is?"

"No. I ain't never been there." She scratched her head and gave a halfhearted attempt at straightening her Medusa-inspired, peroxide blonde hair.

Hunter leaned back. Jesus, this woman is dense. "Let me get this straight. You don't know where he is, you don't know if he should be here, you don't know the name of the company he works for and you don't know where the company is. What exactly do you know?" Before she could answer, he continued. "You've never seen one of his company checks?"

She looked apprehensive, started to squirm. "You guys aren't here because he gets paid under the table? I mean, look, he just does it to avoid taxes."

Barkley exhaled. "Was he supposed to be working today?"

She shrugged. "Maybe, his shifts change all the time. Look, if you need to talk to him, I can just call..."

"That won't be necessary." Hunter jumped back in. "Do you know any of his friends or work associates?"

"Not really. He talks about them sometimes, but he always uses their nicknames like Bombo, Chickenfoot and Slider." Her grogginess had passed and was quickly being replaced by annoyance. "Like I said, if you want, I can call his cell phone."

Hunter looked at Barkley who returned a shrug. He turned to the woman, locked his eyes on hers. "Miss Johnson, that won't be necessary, I'm afraid I have some bad news for you."

* * * *

"Nine millimeter." Reyes picked up Turner's gun by the edge of the trigger guard using the fingertips of his gloved hand. He stood, dropped it into an evidence bag and shook his head. "This guy was clearly an asshole but unless he used a different gun, he's not the guy who took out James or Valerie."

Sanders nodded but didn't respond. He stood with his fists on his hips and stared into the branches. The adrenaline had dissipated and the reality of the shooting had started to sink in. *Not again.* He stepped over, leaned his back against a tree and turned in the direction of the body but the scene didn't seem to register. His mind was a million miles away. He reached up and rubbed his shoulder.

"Billy, it was a good shoot. What the hell else were you going to do? You came around the corner and saw a gun pointed at you. It was either shoot or be shot." Reyes shrugged. "There's only one answer to that question."

Sanders turned his head, looked off as if trying to find the horizon hidden by all the branches. "I shouldn't have rounded the corner like that…"

"Bullshit! You were doing your job." Reyes stepped in front of Billy, looked up at him and made sure he made eye contact. "That son of a bitch shot at both you and Cowboy. He was trying to kill you and your partner." Reyes reached out, put his hand on Billy's shoulder. "He would have, too, if you hadn't reacted."

Sanders lowered his head but nodded.

Reyes shook his shoulder enough to get him to look up. "Don't ever doubt yourself. The minute you do, it'll be you in the body bag and that would really piss me off."

A slight smile broke across Sanders' face. "I hear you." He looked back toward the parking lot just as Doc walked up.

"Gentlemen, it's always great to see you in a vertical position after one of these events. Tell me, which one of you did the honors?"

Billy's hand raised just enough and Doc nodded as he walked past and observed the body in situ. "Hmm… Well, I must say lad, quite impressive marksmanship."

"So I've heard." Sanders smiled and turned toward the parking lot. "I'm going to find Hunter and see if he's found anything or anyone in the apartment."

* * * *

Where is he? Where's the team? I don't see any of them.

Stacy strained to make sense of the chaos as she pulled up to the scene in the CSI truck. She climbed out and did a quick survey of the area. Her heart rate jumped when she saw Hunter's bullet riddled SUV. His phone had gone to voicemail every time she'd called him on the way. Dispatch termed this an officer-involved shooting with a fatality but didn't give details. They had specifically requested her so she knew it had to be the Madison Harper case.

She stepped forward, flashed her badge at the patrolman, bolted under the tape and headed toward his truck continuously searching faces to find someone from the team. The bullet holes and shattered glass sent a chill up her spine. Seeing no visible signs of carnage kept her somewhat calm.

"Stacy." Sanders' voice came from behind her, and she spun around.

"Where is he?" Her voice came out far more panicked than she'd intended.

Sanders raised his hands to calm her. "Cowboy's fine. I think he's inside talking to the girlfriend."

"Who was shot?" The urgency had receded but hadn't disappeared.

Guilt flashed across his face. "Warrick Turner." He hardened his expression and nodded to the building. "He ambushed us in the hall." He then nodded back to the wooded area. "We finally got him over in the woods."

She looked at Hunter's truck. "Looks like he went out blazing."

Sanders chuckled. "Yeah, more business for Hunter's body shop."

"Hey, Stacy." Hunter emerged from the apartment building and headed toward them.

Stacy fought the initial urge to run to him. In spite of Sanders telling her Hunter was fine, her eyes did a quick inventory of his lean frame. Once she was satisfied he was fine, her urge quickly transformed into anger with the fact that he hadn't answered his phone. "Nice to see you're okay." Her angry tone was unmistakable.

"Sorry about not picking up. Barkley and I were interviewing Turner's girlfriend, Tabitha."

"Tabitha? Really?" She couldn't hide her smirk. "What were her parents thinking?"

That brought a round of laughter and broke the tension.

Hunter caught Stacy's attention and nodded toward the building. "Why don't I walk you through the scene so you can figure out how to deploy your team?"

Barkley got the hint and looked at Sanders. "You mind walking me down to Turner and giving me a run down?"

Sanders nodded and the two of them moved back toward the

trees.

Hunter started to turn back to the building but stopped when he felt Stacy's soft touch on his arm. Those beautiful green eyes locked on his. He smiled softly answering her unasked question.

Chapter 34

"What is the allure of being a criminal if all it's going to get you is living in this shit hole with a drugged out skank named Tabitha?" Sanders' voice came from the bedroom as he and Hunter made an initial search of Turner's place. The tiny apartment had the look of a well-worn fraternity house.

Stacy was getting her team mobilized to work each of the key areas, the apartment, hallway, parking lot and woods. Barkley had taken Tabitha Johnson downtown for a more detailed conversation and to get her out of the way while they searched the apartment. Reyes was busy interviewing neighbors and managing the overall scene.

"Beats digging ditches for a living." Hunter's initial anger with Sanders' recklessness had dissipated but was quickly being replaced with a building angst at what appeared to be another dead end. He had gone through every scrap of paper he could find in the kitchen area and hadn't found anything useful.

Sanders grinned, rubbed his shoulder. "I guess it's true that some people will do anything to avoid an honest day's work."

Hunter slammed a junk drawer. "Have you found anything useful in there?" His voice was all business.

"I've got some 9mm shells, a baseball bat and a military grade knife all within reach of the bed. Looks like Turner didn't sleep too well at night." He paused, exhaled heavily. "Other than that, it's just a messy bedroom with low rent clothes and miscellaneous crap. I'm hitting the closet next. Maybe we'll get lucky there."

"Yeah…" Hunter didn't finish his sentence. He just shook his head, wondered if they were ever going to catch a break, and went to work in the small living room.

* * * *

After finishing assignments to her team, Stacy's focus shifted to the woods. She wanted to work from the wooded area back to the building. The sun was already starting to sink toward the horizon and she didn't want to work outside in the dark. Based on the size of the crime scene, she figured to be here a while and this way, when it was dark, she'd be working inside the building.

Hunter had provided her a rundown of the sequence of events. Now, as she followed the path of the gun battle through the trees, butterflies flew through her stomach. *Billy, what were you thinking, running through these trees without knowing where Turner was? Do you have a death wish?*

Rounding the corner of the warehouse, she saw the bloodstain left by the body. It had coated a large patch of dried grass and leaves and soaked into the dirt. She noted where the body had landed, how close it was to the corner. She shook her head. Billy's reflexes are amazing.

She looked back to the bloodstain, pictured the man whose body was loaded in the van. Her mind drifted to Madison and her slashed throat, then to Valerie and her blood soaked white shirt. *You got what you deserved you asshole. Even if you didn't pull the trigger, you were part of it.*

Shaking the thoughts away, she continued processing. The four spent shell casings lay off to the right. She carefully retrieved them, bagged them and tagged them as evidence. She then spent the next twenty minutes carefully measuring and sketching the scene. Even though it seemed clear cut, Internal Affairs would be required to investigate and she knew they'd want a detailed scene analysis.

"Anything of interest?" Reyes' voice startled her.

She turned to him, smiled and shook her head. "Looks pretty straight forward to me, but..." Her voice trailed off.

"Yeah, I know. IAD will need it. They just pulled up." He frowned. "I'm sure they'll make it more painful than necessary on Billy since it's his second shooting since he's been in Homicide."

"He'll be fine." She smiled. 'Hunter may bust his chops but he won't let anyone else."

* * * *

"Ms. Johnson, please calm down." Barkley's patience had just about run out. Tabitha Johnson had started out in shock at the news that Warrick Turner had been shot. As they got closer to the station, the shock began to wear off and her belligerence had started to grow.

"Don't tell me to calm down. You murdered my boyfriend!"

Barkley had escorted her to an interview room without incident but the confined space and stark white walls seemed to amp up her agitation. He kept his voice as calm as possible. "Ma'am, I wasn't involved in the shooting. There will be a full investigation into the circumstances, but in the meantime, as it seems your… boyfriend… was involved in a human trafficking ring, I need you to calm down and answer my questions."

"A human what?"

"Human trafficking ma'am. Modern day slavery." Barkley's frown was so condescending, it oozed. "Warrick Turner's fingerprints were found at a human holding center and since he clearly wasn't a victim…"

"He worked at a machine shop." All of the fight had gone out of her voice. It was barely above a whisper now. She stared down at the table. "He told me he worked at a machine shop."

"Yeah, one that pays in cash and works strange random shifts." Barkley's tone was now more conciliatory. "Ms. Johnson, how long had you known Warrick Turner?"

"About a year."

"How long has he lived with you?"

"Six months."

"I know you said you didn't know his friends but I need you to really think. Did you ever meet or see any of his friends or associates?"

She sat for a moment, her eyes slightly glazed as if she was going back into shock. "I do remember this one guy who gave him a ride once when his truck broke down." She curled up her nose. "Sleazy looking guy with greasy blondish hair and kind of a crooked toothed smile."

Barkley cocked his head. "What kind of truck does he drive?"

"An old piece-of-shit Chevy Pickup. It was parked right by the entrance to the building." She went on to provide him the year, color and the portion of the license plate she could remember.

Barkley made a note to himself, then picked up a folder, rifled through it and pulled out a photo of James Le James. "Is this the guy?"

Her head nodded. "Yeah, that's him. I think Warrick referred to him as Wang Chung." She shivered. "Only met him once but he gave me the creeps."

* * * *

"Nothing… Just clothes and shoes, some extra bedding, a box full of old CD's and DVD's and a bunch of paperback romance novels." Sanders had finished his search of the closet and now stood in the doorway to the bedroom. "Anything out here?"

"Absolutely nothing." Hunter leaned his back against the tiny living room's wall, folded his arms tight across his chest and stared at the opposite wall no more than twelve feet away. His shoulders ached and his whole body felt heavy, the effect of the adrenaline rush followed by the lack of new evidence. *It's one more dead end.*

He looked at his watch, almost five o'clock. Any normal person would be getting ready to go home. Who knew how long they'd be going tonight. He pushed off the wall and took a step toward the door. "Let's go see if Stacy or Reyes have turned up anything."

Hunter stopped after another step when a man he didn't recognize appeared in the doorway and flashed a badge. "Detective Green, IAD, which one of you is Sanders?"

"He is." Hunter nodded over his shoulder. "I'm Jake Hunter, Lead Detective on this investigation. How can I help you?"

"Unless you're Billy Sanders, you can't." He looked past Hunter. "Detective Sanders, I need to speak with you regarding the shooting incident."

Hunter stepped forward placing himself between Detective

Green and Billy. "I'm the lead detec..."

"Cowboy!" Sanders' voice stopped him in mid-sentence. "It's okay. I can handle this." He looked at the man in the doorway. "Detective Green, where would you like to talk?"

"Why don't we start in the hall and then you can walk me through the sequence of events." A condescending smirk played across his face as he nodded toward Hunter, turned and stepped down the hall.

Sanders patted Hunter on the shoulder as he passed him on his way toward the door. "I'm good, Jake. I've been through it before."

* * * *

As he guided his truck onto I-30 east out of downtown, Barkley punched Hunter's number into his phone.

"Hunter."

"Hey Cowboy, it's Barkley. I'm headed back your direction. Any update?"

"It's like walking through a maze that doesn't have an exit. We keep finding pieces to the puzzle but each piece is its own dead end." Hunter's frustration was palpable. "Warrick Turner was definitely part of the operation and he was without a doubt a scumbag, but since he decided to go out in a blaze of glory, we're left once again looking at a brick wall."

"Yep. Not to add to that frustration but Tabitha Johnson fits into your description. She identified one of Turner's associates but it turned out to be the late James Le James so the loop just circles back on itself." He accelerated and changed lanes to pass a car. "I did get one other piece of information from her. Turner drove a 1999 Chevy Pickup, blue. License plate starts with an XP. She says it's parked right by the entrance to the building. We need to make sure to process it."

"Will do."

"Other than that, she was useless."

"Shit." Hunter's response was more a mumble than a word.

Both men were silent for a moment before Hunter continued. "To make matters worse, Internal Affairs just landed and are grilling

Billy about the shooting."

"The shooting was good, right?"

Hunter paused. "It was either shoot or be shot. He's fine."

"Okay." Barkley sounded relieved. "We'll regroup when I get there. See you in ten."

Chapter 35

"How's it going?"

The sun had become a glowing orange ball on the horizon toward Fort Worth and the moon had risen over Dallas. They had taped off the area surrounding Turner's truck and Stacy was set up to process it. The other outside scenes were complete but her night was still long from over. She looked up, moved a rogue strand of hair out of her face. "It's going to be a while but we're getting there."

Hunter smiled. The scene wasn't as chaotic as earlier in the afternoon. The ME team, IAD investigator and most of the patrol units were gone. "We've wrapped up inside. Is there anything we can do to help you?"

"You can get the rest of these people out of here so I don't have to stumble over them anymore." She glanced over toward the building and noticed Billy standing by himself, leaning against the wall. "Is he okay?"

"He will be… Tough day. We'll get him something to eat, maybe a cold beer. He'll be fine." He looked at her, concern in his eyes. "How about you? Don't suppose I can convince you to let this wait until the morning?"

She shook her head. "So, exactly how do you plan to take Billy anywhere with all the glass shot out of your truck?"

Hunter's shoulders slumped at the reminder. "I've got a tow truck on the way and Barkley's going to swing me by the motor pool to get a loaner."

Stacy smiled, began to giggle. "Hopefully this one will smell better than the last one."

The sound of her laughter and the comfort of her smile pulled him out of the events of the day and for a moment there was no crime scene, no murdered teenage girls, no slaves and no bad guys to hunt down. His spirits lifted in spite of the weariness that permeated his body. "Can I bring you anything?"

"I'm good." She nodded toward the CSI truck. "I've got caffeine reinforcements. I shouldn't be here too late."

Hunter took a step toward her but stopped himself. Even though their inner circle knew they were dating, going in for a goodnight kiss at a crime scene would not be appropriate. He stopped, smiled and discreetly blew her a kiss. "I'll make sure a patrolman stays with you. Don't let him leave until you're ready to go."

"I'm fine. Go take care of your partner."

She watched him walk away and then turned back toward Turner's truck and exhaled. *Where to begin?*

She decided to start inside and work out, but needed to dust the door handle before she opened it. Finding no usable prints, she opened the driver's side door and surveyed the interior. Nothing much of note, a Fritos bag on the floorboard, a QuikTrip reusable coffee mug in the cup holder, the odor from years of sweat and grime. Her eye caught on the disposable QuikTrip coffee cup. *If Turner had his own reusable mug, he wouldn't need a disposable. Someone else's DNA?*

She saved and labeled the remaining contents from each cup, then did the same for the cups themselves. From there, she bagged and tagged every piece of trash, half eaten French fry and chewed piece of gum she found. With the possibility of finding DNA other than Turner's, she felt a second wave of energy.

Next she printed the interior. It was slow going as she collected prints in all of the expected places. Although she couldn't do formal comparisons in an ever-darkening parking lot, she was able to examine enough to feel pretty sure all the prints were from the same person, presumably Turner.

When she applied the powder to the curved surface of the driver's side door, where the window recedes into the door, her breath caught. She was looking at a perfect, complete set of prints. Four from the left hand and four from the right. Someone had stood outside the truck while the window was down and had gripped the door with both hands with their fingers on the inside of the window and their thumbs on the outside.

Her excitement started to grow. *Turner would have no reason to be in that position in his own truck. These had to be someone else's prints.* She carefully lifted the prints and cataloged them so she could do a quick comparison. Using a small tripod light and a magnifying glass, she looked at the ridges, curves and swirls of the patterns from the door and then looked at the patterns from the dashboard area. Her lips curled slowly into a smile. *I've got you now.*

She moved to the outside of the driver's door and captured the thumbprints exactly where she'd expected them to be. Whoever these belonged to had left her a present tied in a bow. She found herself humming and tapping her toes as she spent the next thirty minutes moving around the rest of the truck. The possibility of identifying another bad guy had her buzzing.

"Officer?" She signaled the lone patrolman over from where he'd been leaning against his patrol unit. "Can you call in a tow truck? We need this pickup taken to the lab."

"Yes ma'am."

It was well past eight and the sun had completely disappeared. She nodded toward the building. "I'll be working in the apartment for a bit. I should be finished by the time they get it taken away. Just let me know when they're gone."

He gave her a thumbs up as he spoke into his radio. She stored all the evidence taken from the pickup in the CSI truck before she went into the building.

She set down her collection kits and ran her hand along the shattered doorframe and ripped up door to the apartment. She'd just passed the bullet holes in the wall. Thoughts of Hunter and Billy diving for the ground as the bullets flew past their heads ran through her mind. *Oh Cowboy. You've got to be more careful.*

Over the next forty-five minutes, she focused on prints but knew that if was pointless since most would be Tabitha Johnson's or Turner's. Anything else found would likely belong to any number of police personnel who had trampled in and out that day.

When she finished and walked out to the parking lot, night had taken over. She looked at her watch and saw that it was close to nine-thirty. Her stomach growled as if to punctuate her realization of the time.

She heard the sounds of the tow truck as it pulled away with the pickup riding piggy back. The officer stepped over and offered to help carry a box of items she'd collected. "How's it looking in there? Any idea how much longer?"

"I'm done. You can take off any time you'd like. All I have to do is grab my kit from inside and I'm gone myself."

The officer loaded the box into the CSI truck and Stacy walked back toward the building. "Have a good evening ma'am."

She waved over her shoulder. "You too. Thanks for staying."

Stacy reentered the building and once again retraced the steps of the gun battle. As she moved, she thought about the prints and DNA evidence from the pickup. She reached the apartment, packed up her kit, secured the door, headed back down the hall and out of the building. What earlier was a multipoint crime scene with teams of law enforcement crawling all over it was now just a dark, quiet parking lot.

She was pleased with the outcome of the day. They had finally caught a break on the case. Her mind drifted to Madison and Valerie. Maybe now we can get you justice. As she reached the CSI truck and opened the back, she thought about what she had seen at the Haltom City holding center, about the people who had been held there. Maybe now we can find you.

She loaded her kit, secured the evidence boxes and closed the back hatch. Her heart lurched when she turned to see the barrel of a gun pointed directly at her forehead. She opened her mouth but no sound came out as a hand covered a rag over her face. Her next breath sucked in the acrid odor of chloroform and her eyes widened only long enough to see a blur before everything went black.

Chapter 36

"Here's to damn fine bullet placement!" Hunter smiled and lifted his frosted mug.

Sanders rolled his eyes but raised his glass to join Hunter's and Barkley's in a toast.

Reyes joined in. "Here's to being alive."

After the four detectives had been summarily dismissed from the scene by Stacy, they decided to head back to downtown for some relaxation at The Flying Saucer.

"I'm just bummed I was late for the fireworks." Barkley looked at Sanders. "So give me the details. How'd it go down?"

Sanders shifted in his seat and stared for a moment at his beer before Hunter came to his rescue. "You don't need to hear his version. I had a better view of the events anyway."

Reyes laughed. "From what I understand Cowboy, the only view you had was of Sanders' ass and even that was from quite a distance."

That brought a round of laughter from the group. After calming them with his hands, Hunter responded. "What do you expect? He was a division one running back. Once he took off, there wasn't a chance in hell of me catching him."

Barkley pulled them back. "Seriously, what happened?"

"Billy and I took the front and had Reyes out back in case someone decided to bolt out the back." Hunter had put down his beer and was using his hands as he spoke. "We were all set to knock on the door when we hear a crash at the end of the hall. I looked past Sanders and there was Turner already drawing down on us."

"Holy crap! That'll certainly ruin your plans." Barkley took a drink but kept his eyes intently on Hunter.

"So I grabbed Billy by the shirt and pulled him towards me." Hunter paused for dramatic effect. "Saving his life I might add since the bullets tore through the door frame right where his head had been."

"Saving my life? I thought you were just pulling me over there to use me as a shield."

Hunter chuckled but continued. "We both rolled over and returned fire but Turner had already bolted." He cocked his eye toward Sanders. "Next thing I know this son of a bitch is halfway down the hall and moving like someone shot him out of a cannon. All I could do is scramble, chase after him and watch as the rest of the events unfolded.

"I made it out of the building just in time to see my truck get riddled with bullets and watch all the glass fly everywhere." He looked over at Sanders. "You had to use my truck for cover?" Sanders just shrugged as Hunter waved him off and went on with the story. "I tried to get him to slow down but Rambo here was up and gone again before I even made it to my truck.

"He flew across the parking lot and disappeared into the woods and I didn't catch up again until I saw him tear around the corner of that building and instantly heard four shots." Hunter stopped, his face went dark. "Based on the timing, I didn't think there was anyway those shots came from Billy." He looked down and cleared his throat. "Thank God, Quickdraw McGraw here proved me wrong."

Sanders smiled and they raised their glasses to salute the last comment.

"What I want to know is why didn't you just wing the son of bitch?" Barkley grinned. "I mean, I'm impressed with your shooting and all, but…" He shrugged.

Sanders nodded. "That seems to be the question of the day." He shook his head with a look of wonder. "Man, he was standing there with his gun up and all I did was react. To be honest, it scared the shit out of me. I thought I was dead."

Hunter pointed at him with a stern look. "Next time you don't listen to your partner, you might be… But I'm damn glad you're not."

The moment was interrupted as the waitress confirmed that

another round was in order. After she was on her way, Hunter cocked his head at Barkley. "Speaking of being late, where were you all day?"

"Oh yes, my day. While you boys were taking bullets from Turner, I was taking bullets from my boss." That got everyone's attention. "For almost two hours, I got to listen to him tell me in explicit detail about how his boss had chewed his ass because his boss' boss had gotten a call from the Governor complaining about how one of his detectives was harassing a prominent constituent."

"You're kidding me." Sanders' eyes went wide.

"I wish I was. It was no fun. Trust me, I'd much rather have been with you guys."

Hunter smiled. "Well, you said you wanted to shake some trees. I guess you did." He shook his head. "Damn. The Governor? You don't fool around when you piss people off."

"One of my many talents." Barkley smiled, turned to Sanders. "I understand I'm not the only one whose ass was in a bind today. How did your conversation go with IAD?"

Sanders shrugged, exhaled. "Who knows? I just walked him through what happened." He smirked toward Hunter. "I might have left out those parts when you were yelling at me to slow down."

"I'll keep that in mind if they want my version of events."

Sanders tipped his glass to Hunter. "Other than that, he just asked a bunch of detail questions and I answered them. Routine."

"There's nothing routine when it comes to IAD." Reyes shook his head and frowned.

"Well…" Barkley raised his glass. "Any day that ends with a bad guy going down and all the good guys still standing is a good day as far as I'm concerned."

"Amen!" Reyes smiled.

"I just wish we'd have gotten something… Anything that got us a step closer to these scumbags." Hunter frowned into his beer and looked at his watch. Seeing how late it was prompted him to check his phone for messages.

Barkley watched Hunter. "Something will pop. Every one of these pawns we take out puts a little more pressure on the big dog. He'll make a mistake eventually."

"How many more people have to die before eventually gets here?"

Chapter 37

"It's awfully late for you to be calling." The man behind the desk seemed annoyed. He was at home and he rarely took calls at home but this was a special situation.

"Sorry about that but I thought you might want an update." The underling was calling from his car.

"I hope it's better news than earlier."

The underling hesitated. Earlier in the day, the man behind the desk had gone on a tirade when he heard the news about Warrick Turner. He was intensely concerned about there being any connection to the organization. "Our guys watched closely all afternoon. They said it didn't look like the cops were overly excited. In fact, they seemed to be dejected."

"So we've got body language experts now, do we?" The man frowned.

"Not exactly." The underling spoke quickly, stammering slightly. "They've just been around a lot and have seen how cops react when they think they've found something."

"If you say so." The man paused. "Did we get a chance to take any action?"

"Yes." The underling relaxed a little. "The package was acquired." He smiled as he spoke. "It was just as you predicted. She stayed later than everyone else. It was easy. No one saw a thing."

"They damn well better not have. Did you leave the truck where it was?"

"Yes, just like you said." The underling squirmed in his seat as he made his way through the empty streets of downtown. "I don't understand why you wanted it left like that."

The man chuckled low. "I want them to know that we hit them in their own backyard, at their own secured crime scene, out in public. They've pissed me off and they might as well have kicked a cobra."

The underling returned the chuckle although his seemed much more nervous. "Well, I think they'll get the message."

"Damn right they will." The man paused. "Where did you take her?"

"We've got her at the central location with the latest batch from Mexico. We're moving them through over the next couple of days. We can keep her there as long as we need. What's your game plan for her?"

"You let me worry about the game plan. You just keep her safe and sound for now. I want you to handle it personally."

"That's where I'm headed right now."

"Good. I'll let you know what to do tomorrow."

Chapter 38

"Hello, you've reached the voicemail of Stacy Morgan. I'm not available at the moment but please leave a message and I'll return your call as soon as I can."

It was ten o'clock and that was the fourth time Hunter had called with no response. He'd already left two previous messages. This time he just hit end and sat in his loaner unit in the parking lot of The Flying Saucer. *She's just working late. She's a professional. She didn't need you babysitting her before so she doesn't need it now.*

He had left the guys to finish their last round so that he could ease his mind by getting in touch with her. That, and with Turner's death, he figured the next day was going to be long and filled with numerous painful conversations with Sprabary and IAD.

His finger tapped on the steering wheel and he chewed on the inside of his cheek as he let the phone fall into the drink holder in the console. *I'll try her again on my way home.*

The ignition cranked and he slipped the car into gear but he paused again as his stomach twisted. He shook his head to chase away any bad thoughts, let his foot off the brake and headed down the street.

Downtown Fort Worth at ten o'clock on a Thursday night was lively but not crazy. He made his way through the Sunset Square area, weaving past small groups of people, catching the ever changing aromas from the restaurants and the patchwork of music from the various clubs.

It only took a few moments to circle back on Fifth Street and get to the I-35 North entrance ramp. As he pushed his loaner toward home his mind was reliving the day, finding Turner, the shooting, processing the scene, watching Stacy push the hair out of her face and seeing her smile. *She's beautiful even when she's exhausted.*

His hand reached for his phone, punched send. "Hello, you've reached the voicemail of Stacy Mor..." He punched end and let it drop again. *She was exhausted. Why would she stay so late when she was this tired and there was so little left to process?*

His gut wrenched and his throat tightened. Without thinking, he accelerated, flipped on his lights and steered the car off the Northside Drive exit. He busted through the light at the bottom of the ramp, circled under the overpass and was back on I-35 moving south in a matter of seconds.

If she had found something worth staying for, she'd be back at the lab by now. That's a straight shot down I-35. He was exiting in less than five minutes. Another two minutes and he pulled into the parking lot of the Forensic Science Labs.

The lot was empty except for three cars. Two were the night shift attendees for the morgue and the third was Stacy's Ford Escape. Hunter stared at the parking lot, its emptiness seemed to squeeze his chest like a vise. The CSI van wasn't there.

He jumped from the car and raced up the walk to the night entrance. His finger jammed on the buzzer, almost pushing it through the wall. An attendee ambled down the hall and Hunter rapped his badge on the window to speed him up.

"How can I hel..."

"Have you seen CSI Morgan?" Hunter was in the door and moving down the hall looking over his shoulder for an answer.

"No. As far as I know, it's just Darren and me and a bunch of stiffs."

Hunter never saw the attendee's confused look. His last words were spoken to an empty hall as Hunter had already disappeared around the corner. Her work station was empty, dark and quiet when Hunter bolted into the room. His eyes searched the area, looked around the floor. She hasn't been here. Shit.

He ran back down the hall, pulverizing the send button on his phone as if the force of his finger could make her answer. "Hello, you've reached the voicem..."

Damnit! Where the hell are you Stacy?

The sound of his tires ripping across the concrete parking lot echoed off the hospital buildings. He retraced his path and in seconds was back on the access road to I-35, heading north to the next major intersection. This time he not only had his lights flashing but his sirens were shattering the night's calm.

Even with busting every traffic light along Rosedale, the four miles from the freeway to the crime scene seemed to take a lifetime. His mind kept replaying her smile and his finger kept pounding the redial button.

He took several deep breaths. *She's fine. I'm overreacting. This is just crazy paranoia.*

He killed the siren when he finally got to the entrance of The Antiqua Village Apartments but he didn't slow down as he turned into the parking lot. The suspension of the loaner unit did little to absorb the speed bumps as Hunter gunned it to the back of the complex.

The car screeched to a halt and Hunter's mind froze as the CSI truck sat in the glare of the headlights. Hunter killed the engine, rolled down the window and held his breath. There was no movement, no sign of life by the truck or anywhere in the parking lot. The only sounds drifted in from the wooded area where Turner had been shot.

Hunter opened the door and drew his Glock. He slipped a small flashlight into his pocket and moved slowly toward the truck, his head swiveled from side to side, his finger rested on the trigger guard ready to slip to the trigger at any moment. "Stace?" He spoke in a calm, normal volume then stopped and listened for a response. "Stace, it's Jake. Are you there?"

He dropped his left hand to his pocket, found his phone and without looking, hit the redial button. His hand left the phone in his pocket and returned to support his weapon. A few seconds passed and the silence was shattered by the echoing synthesized chimes of a ringtone. The sound was coming from the other side of the CSI truck.

"Stace! Are you there?"

He hesitated. His feet felt like they were glued to the parking lot. He was suddenly aware of the sweat dripping off his forehead. A deep breath and three quick steps and he was to the truck. Instinct and training took over. He cleared around the back of the truck, reached over and checked the door latch. Locked.

The echoing chimes had grown louder but now stopped. He could now hear Stacy's voice coming from his pocket. "You have reached the…" He slid his hand to his pocket, felt around and hit the end button.

Another quick breath and he rounded the side of the truck. It took a moment for his brain to register the glowing light coming from the ground through the cracked display of Stacy's phone. Stacy wasn't there, just her broken phone and her keys.

Hunter felt his knees start to buckle and leaned his shoulder against the truck for support. *"Oh God! Where is she?"*

"Stacy!" His scream shocked him with its volume. "Stacy!" No response.

He moved quickly around the front of the truck so that he had cleared all sides. No Stacy. His eyes scanned the rest of the parking lot as he walked back to where her phone and keys lay. His chest squeezed tight. He grabbed the flashlight from his pocket and began a quick search of the area around the truck. Nothing but her phone and keys.

He holstered his Glock and pulled out his phone to dial Sanders. His brain seemed to lock for a moment as he realized his hands were shaking. He swallowed hard, clenched his jaw and controlled his hands long enough to hit Billy's speed dial.

"Damn Cowboy, you missed me so bad, you couldn't wait till in the morning?"

"Stacy's missing!"

The laughter in Billy's voice disappeared. "What do you mean, she's missing?"

"I couldn't get her on the phone so I came back to the scene. The CSI truck is here, the keys and her broken phone are lying in the parking lot beside the truck. They've got her."

"Who's got… What? Dude, this is a mistake. She must have…"

"Billy, listen to me. It's no mistake. Call Reyes and whoever's working CSI tonight and get down here. We need every resource we can find. I'll call Barkley and Sprabary." Hunter stopped to catch his breath.

"I'm on it. I'll be there in twenty minutes." Sanders clicked off.

The silence of the parking lot seemed to close in on him. His mind raced but went in too many directions at once to make sense. *Who took her? Why? Are these people truly that crazy? Kidnap a cop?*

Chapter 39

"This can't be good." Barkley sounded as if it was the middle of the afternoon, not almost eleven o'clock at night. His intensity and focus didn't seem to have an off switch.

"It's not. Stacy's missing. I think the traffickers have her." Hunter had calmed slightly and was now operating as if on a mission.

There was silence on the line for a few seconds. "Where are you?"

"At the scene. I've already contacted Billy and he's reaching out to Reyes."

"I'll be there in fifteen."

The line went dead. Hunter had called dispatch after he'd spoken with Sanders and the first unit pulled up before he could dial again. He moved toward the patrol car with his badge displayed and was barking orders before either officer was out of the car. "I want this entire parking lot taped off. We've got an abducted officer. We need a Sergeant down here now. When he gets here, direct him to me."

The officers nodded and moved to set up the perimeter as more units began to arrive. Hunter walked back toward the CSI truck poking at his phone as he walked.

"Sprabary."

"Lieutenant, this is Hunter. We have a situation that needs your attention…" Hunter spent the next ten minutes providing the details not only on Stacy's possible abduction but on the follow up to the shooting and the minimal evidence they found at the scene.

As he signed off with the lieutenant, Sanders ducked under the perimeter tape strode toward him, his shirttail was out as he clipped his holster to his belt. "Anything new?"

Hunter shook his head. "I'm just getting things set up. Barkley's on his way and the lieutenant is up to speed." Hunter's eyes surveyed the activity that had started and avoided looking at Sanders.

"Are you okay?" Billy's voice was concerned, his eyes staring at Hunter.

Hunter had his hands on his hips and looked down for a moment. "There was supposed to be a patrolman here with her until she left. I need to find out what the hell happened." Before Sanders could respond, Hunter was already on the phone.

"Fort Worth Police Department, Harrison speaking."

"Harrison, this is Jake Hunter."

"How's my favorite Cowboy? Aren't I the one who's supposed to call you in the middle of the night?" He belly-laughed as if that was the funniest joke ever told.

"Harry, we've got a CSI who's possibly been abducted. She was working a scene in the five thousand block of East Rosedale. There was supposed to be a patrolman with her until she left. I need to know that patrolman's name and phone number."

"Shit Cowboy. Give me second. I'll have it for you." Hold music came on. With every phone call and every minute that passed, Hunter could feel his anxiety growing. He'd started off shocked and surprised, passed through scared to calm and now he was getting pissed. This was a fuck up of biblical proportions and he intended to fry some ass along the way to finding her.

"Here you go Cowboy. It was a rookie named Travis Daniels. Don't know him. Here's his number." He read it off. "What else do you need?"

"Enough self-control not to kill this idiot." Hunter clicked off and banged in the number.

"Yeah." The voice on the other end of the line had clearly been sound asleep.

"Officer Daniels?"

"Yes." Hunter's tone put Daniels on alert.

"This is Detective Jake Hunter. Why the hell did you leave my CSI alone at a crime scene?"

"Huh? What? I... uh..."

"You were supposed to be here until she left. You weren't and now she's been abducted." Hunter's decibel level had crept up with each sentence and was now just one notch below a scream.

"What? No... I mean... She was all packed up to go. She said she was done and I could leave. What the he..."

"She wasn't done and when you left, someone kidnapped her. I'd suggest that if you have any concern for your future that you get your ass back down to this scene and help with the search. I'd also suggest that when you get here, if you value your life, you will report to the Sergeant in charge and avoid me at all costs!" Hunter jabbed the end button so hard he had to shake his finger to ease the sting.

The level of activity had skyrocketed in the few minutes that Hunter had been on the phone. The perimeter was set up, close to a dozen patrol cars were on the scene and a Sergeant had a command post set up and was getting briefed by Sanders. Hunter headed their direction. When he stepped up, the Sergeant nodded. "Your partner got me caught up. We've got the site secured, CSI is on its way and as soon as some reinforcements arrive, I'll have them start a grid search of the expanded area." He pointed toward the park. "We'll start with the open area and then move to the woods. We'll keep expanding the grid until it doesn't make sense." He gave Hunter a reassuring look. "If she's anywhere close by, we'll find her."

Hunter listened, nodded and tried to keep his composure, but the meaning of the words chipped away at his armor. He'd only been thinking in terms of Stacy being abducted, not the possibility that she'd been injured or murdered and dumped somewhere nearby. The thought threatened to overwhelm him. "Keep me posted."

His own voice sounded alien to him. He walked away with no particular destination in mind. He just needed to breathe. His heart was pounding and the sound of the blood rushing through his ears seemed to drown out all of the chaos surrounding him.

"Hunter? Hunter? Are you okay?"

Sanders' voice broke through but only momentarily. "I just need a minute Billy." He stepped under the perimeter tape and walked to his loaner unit. He leaned over, placed both elbows on the roof of the car and put his head in his hands, staring down at the glossy black finish. *What the hell is going on? Nobody kidnaps a cop. Who are we dealing with?*

"We'll find her." Barkley's voice boomed across the hood of the car as if answering Hunter's thoughts. "I contacted my boss on the drive over here. Since this is an officer-involved abduction, we can provide support. We're mobilizing a task force. The entire strength of the Texas Rangers is going to come crashing down on their ass before the sun comes up. How are you doing?"

Hunter looked across the car. "I don't know. We've got nothing to go on."

"I don't know about that. I got a phone call from Anne Robinson as I was leaving the Saucer. Didn't think it was a major deal when I spoke to her. I figured I'd just catch you up in the morning."

Hunter raised an eyebrow.

"She told me that one of her volunteers had made a rescue of a day laborer. Based on the location, sounds like it might be the guys we're looking for. She said they found the guy in Haltom City. That holding center you raided was in Haltom City, right?"

Hunter nodded. "Yeah, but we've already shut it down and they've moved on to somewhere else."

"Might be worth calling her back to get more details." Barkley looked at his watch. "I know it's late but she's a bit of a night owl and she's a crusader. She won't mind."

Hunter scanned the scene. The Sergeant had the CSI team already engaged. With one of their own missing, they appeared to be analyzing every speck of dust within a fifty foot radius of the abandoned truck. He also had lines of officers and recruits walking shoulder to shoulder across the open field with flashlights. Reyes had arrived and was working with Sanders knocking on every door in the complex to find someone who saw or heard anything. A wave of hopelessness and helplessness washed over Hunter. He looked over at Barkley and shrugged. "Can't hurt."

The two men sat in Hunter's car while Barkley put his phone on speaker and dialed Anne's number. "Hey Sweetie. Isn't it past your bedtime?"

"Anne, I've got you on speaker. I'm here with Jake Hunter. Sorry about calling so late but we needed to get more information about the rescue you told me about earlier tonight. Can you run down the details for Jake?"

"Sure. Hey Jake. As I told Colt earlier, one of my volunteers rescued a young man who said he'd been held in a building over in Haltom City. The way he described it, it sounded very similar to what you had found over in that area."

"Could the guy give you a description of his captors?" Hunter seemed to be going through the motions.

"Only vaguely. Seems that all sleazy white scumbags look alike when you're being held against your will. I just found it interesting since I remember you mentioning something about Haltom City."

Hunter nodded at the phone. "Well I appreciate your thinking of us but we already shut that location down over a week ago."

"Oh?" She sounded confused. "That's odd since my volunteer only found this man earlier today and he indicated he had escaped last night when they were moving him out of a location in Haltom City."

"Last night? In Haltom City? Are you sure?" Hunter crinkled up his face, looked at Barkley and shook his head.

"Positive. He was very sure about the location. In fact, hang on just a second." The sound of papers shuffling came through the speaker. "Here it is. He said the building was located on Higgins Street and it was definitely last night."

Hunter's eyes went wide and he slammed his fist on the steering wheel. "Holy shit! It's the second location!" He looked at Barkley. Barkley looked confused. "I know where she is." He turned to the phone. "Anne, thank you so much. This has been incredibly helpful but we have to go!" He hung up Barkley's phone.

Before Barkley could ask, Hunter was on his phone. "Billy, get Reyes and meet me at my car. I know where Stacy is at and we're going to go get her."

Chapter 40

"Damn it! I can't believe we missed that. There was a second location all along." Hunter paced beside his car looking slightly manic talking to himself and waving his hands. He looked up to see that Reyes and Sanders had arrived. They had joined Barkley and were eyeing him warily as if they thought he'd lost him mind.

Hunter looked at Sanders and Reyes. "Here's what we've got guys. Remember when we narrowed our search for where Madison had been held, we identified two different buildings in Haltom City? Both fit the profile but we made the call to hit the Earl Street location first because it was the best fit."

Reyes and Sanders both nodded while Barkley watched the conversation unfold.

Hunter was emphatic now. "We never hit the second location!"

"Why would we? We didn't need to. We found what we were looking for in the first location." Reyes shrugged. "Hell, finding that one was like finding a needle in a haystack."

He nodded. "Exactly, who finds two needles at the same time? But we screwed up. That second location is another holding center and if we'd hit it that day, this whole thing might have been over right then." He put his fist to his mouth and bit down on his lip. "Damn it, I can't believe we missed it."

"Cowboy, what are you talking about?" Sanders seemed confused.

"They've got Stacy at that second location."

Sanders and Reyes now looked even more confused than before. Barkley stepped in to bridge the gap. "I got a call from Anne Robinson tonight. One of her volunteers rescued a victim early this morning. The victim claimed to have been held in a building *last night* on Higgins Street in Haltom City."

"Meaning he escaped from the second location..." Hunter picked up the sentence from Barkley. "The one we decided we didn't need to hit because we'd already found where they'd held Madison."

Understanding washed across Sanders' face. "Which means that's where they're holding Stacy now!"

"Exactly!" Hunter went into command mode. "Reyes, turn over the crime scene to the Sergeant. Tell him we're running down a lead. Billy, get a tactical unit in place and ready to roll. Have them meet us in the parking lot of the El Rancho Supermarket at Belknap and Beach in one hour. I'm going to go wake up a judge to make sure our original search warrant is still valid." He turned to Barkley. "You with me?"

Barkley grinned. "Are you kidding? This is why I woke up this morning!"

They broke like a football team leaving the huddle, all moving in different directions but in synch as if choreographed. Hunter's adrenaline was pumping. All the weariness from earlier in the day was gone. He finally felt like they were on top of it. He looked at his watch. It was almost midnight. Her smile played across his mind. His chest tightened and he felt his face flush. *If they hurt her...*

"Are you okay?"

Hunter turned to see Barkley looking down at him, an odd excitement in his eyes. "I'm better than okay. I'm pissed!"

Barkley flashed his lopsided smile and raised an eyebrow. "Let's roll then." He held up his keys. "I'll meet you at the station since I doubt we're coming back here tonight. We'll ride together to the rendezvous. I'll get the Rangers tactical guys on alert as backup."

Hunter nodded and watched as Barkley stepped up into his truck. His mind was already mapping the assault plan. He would be the first one through the door and God help anyone who got in his way.

On the drive to the station, alone with his thoughts, his mind seemed schizophrenic. One minute he was pumped on adrenaline, the next it felt like the weight of the world was on his shoulders and the only thing he wanted to do was puke. It wasn't fear, at least not for himself.

Kicking down doors was part of the job and he'd done it so many times, it was like walking in the park. But this was the first time someone close to him was going to be on the other side, in danger and depending on him to save them. *Why did I leave her alone? I'm off drinking beer with the boys and she's the one they get.*

Everything seemed to take too long for Hunter. Even though, the normal fifteen minutes from the scene to the station were cut to ten with lights and sirens, it still felt like hours. The few minutes it took to find the original search warrant in the filing cabinet seemed to drag. His mind seemed to be teetering on the edge of a meltdown. He struggled to punch in Judge Spicer's phone number. *Come on. Answer.*

"Hello." The voice was tired but sounded as if midnight calls weren't out of the ordinary.

"Judge Spicer, Detective Jake Hunter with Homicide, I'm sorry for waking you but we have an emergency…" Hunter spent the next ten minutes going over the details with the judge and explaining the urgency of moving before daylight.

"Are you sure she's there?"

"Sir, nothing's guaranteed but we have a high level of confidence. Worst case scenario is that we bust in on an empty warehouse. We'll replace the front door and apologize to the owner."

The judge gave a short laugh. "I wish it was that simple Detective, but your point is valid. Consider the warrant back in force. Have the documents faxed over to my office and I'll sign them retroactively in the morning." He paused for a moment. "Good luck Detective. Bring her home safe."

"I will sir. Thank you."

Hunter hung up, looked over his desk at Barkley. "We're green. Let's go." He looked at his watch. "We've got twenty minutes to be in place."

The FWPD SWAT team's truck looked more like a tank and stood out like a sore thumb in the grocery store parking lot at one o'clock in the morning. Anyone passing by knew that something nasty was about to go down. Fortunately for the team, the traffic in the area was light.

When Hunter came to a stop, he could see that Reyes and Sanders were already huddled with the SWAT Team Leader looking at a tablet, fingers pointed and heads nodded. He popped the trunk and as he got out talked over the car to Barkley. "I've got an extra vest you can use. I'm going in first and I want you and Sanders on my shoulders."

Barkley nodded as he checked the magazine in his Sig. Both men suited up quickly and quietly, and Barkley followed Hunter over to the planning group.

The SWAT Team Leader saw Hunter, smiled and extended his hand. "Cowboy, good to see you."

"Zeke, how the hell are you? It's been a while."

The man looked more like an accountant than a SWAT Team Leader. His slender frame seemed swallowed up by his uniform, vest and all the paraphernalia that came with his role. His small eyes looked as if they should have wire rimmed glasses balanced delicately on his nose. "I'm good." His smile disappeared. "I understand the bad guys have Stacy."

"Not for much longer." Hunter gestured toward Barkley. "Zeke Dickson, meet Colt Barkley, Texas Ranger."

Zeke extended his hand, looked up at Barkley and smiled. "Are all Rangers this tall?"

"I barely made the height requirement."

Hunter shook his head and refocused the conversation. "Zeke, I assume that Reyes and Sanders brought you up to speed on the basics." Dickson nodded. "I want your guys taking the back door, following my team in the front and providing support and perimeter security. I'm going in first with Barkley and Sanders on my shoulders. Reyes will manage the scene and coordinate evac of any victims or casualties."

Reyes nodded. "I've got paramedics on alert and a wagon in the neighborhood."

"I don't need to remind anyone that if this is our location, we will likely have multiple potential hostages in the building including one of our own. Don't fire unless you have to and if you do, make damn sure you're on target."

Everyone nodded and Hunter continued. "We're going in fast

and hard. We go straight from the vehicles to breach. No announcement until we're in the door. We're taking two vehicles. Barkley and Sanders with me in the lead car. Jimmy, I want you riding with SWAT." He paused and looked around the circle of men. Each had his own look but there was no mistaking that they were ready.

"Let's go."

As planned, Hunter headed northeast on Belknap with the SWAT truck on his tail. Sanders was in the back seat and Barkley was riding shotgun and snickering as he tightened his vest.

Hunter furrowed his brow and glanced at Barkley. "What's so funny?"

"Just got a kick out of your CPA looking SWAT leader."

Hunter smiled as he accelerated. "Don't underestimate Zeke. I've seen him take down an NFL linebacker and make the man cry like a baby. Never forget the old saying about the size of the fight in the dog."

Barkley nodded. "I'll keep that in mind."

When Hunter turned left on Higgins, he killed his lights and the SWAT driver followed suit. The next four blocks were covered in seconds and Hunter slammed his car into the parking area in front of a small, non-descript warehouse at the corner of Higgins and Goldie.

By the time he had the car stopped and turned off, the SWAT team had moved into place. As he jumped from the car, he absorbed the building. *It's too quiet.* The three detectives drew their weapons and in a few strides were at the front door.

There was no hesitation. The SWAT battering ram manned by two huge officers was pulled back and shoved forward. They may as well have used dynamite with the force provided. The door blew open with pieces flying in all directions. The two officers were out of the way before the door had hit the backstop.

Hunter, Barkley and Sanders were in, guns up and shouting. "Police! Police!" The powerful flashlights from the SWAT team followed them in and illuminated the room. It seemed to only highlight the empty echoes that met them.

The three detectives stood within a few feet of the door, staring at an almost identical setup as they had found a few blocks down the road. As with the first case, this one was just as empty. Hunter moved his gun from side to side as his eyes searched the shadows for any sign of movement. "Main room clear. Let's move on the small rooms."

As with the previous location, there were two smaller rooms used for special guests. He led Barkley and Sanders to them following perfect protocol but knowing they'd find nothing. With each step, his heart seemed to tear a little further out of his chest.

They cleared each room. The sounds of the raid continued as SWAT members followed suit and cleared every closet and corner, their voices crawling over each other. Hunter holstered his Glock, his chest heaving, lungs searching for oxygen.

Someone had found the light switch. Hunter looked around. Cages with mats and blankets strewn about, the smell of old sweat and human waste, the signs of bondage and pain were everywhere. But the victims were missing.

"Hunter." Zekes voice turned his head. "We've got fast food wrappers and left overs in the trash that can't be more than a day old. Someone was here very recently."

Hunter nodded but couldn't seem to make his voice work. His shoulders slumped as he turned and walked out of the building. The fresh, clean night air filled his lungs but the taint from inside the building didn't go away. *We missed them… again.*

"Damnit!" He slammed his fist down on the trunk of his car. The sound echoed down the empty street.

"Hunter?" Sanders' voice came from behind him but he didn't turn around.

"How did we miss them? Where the hell are they, Billy?"

Sanders didn't answer. The rest of the team was in full action, setting up a perimeter, calling in CSI, beginning to work the scene. Hunter didn't move. He just stared blankly off into the distance. The night seemed darker than before. That blackness matched the feeling in his soul.

Chapter 41

His lips gently touched hers, the taste of the full bodied Cabernet lingered on his breath. A very good year. She playfully bit his bottom lip and walked her fingers up the lapel of his jacket. When they reached his chin, she pushed back just far enough to smile and look into his eyes. She could swim in those eyes. Deep, blue, warm. When he smiled, the left side of his mouth always went up slightly more than the right side and the creases at the edge of his eyes were just visible.

What was the line from that Jimmy Buffet song? 'Wrinkles only go where the smiles have been'. I guess he's smiled just the right amount.

His face slacked. He began to pull back. The picture started to blur, then fade. Darkness took over. She was floating now, up. There were muffled sounds. A dull light hung above her. She wanted to go back to him, to his lips, to the wine. She tried to swim down but the light kept getting closer, brighter.

Please don't go. Jake, where are you?

A dull thump brought her eyes open. She blinked rapidly, trying to focus. The light sent jolts of pain through her head. She squinted and tried to turn away. Her head moved but her body seemed stuck.

What's wrong with my arm? Why won't it move?

Stacy lifted her head and looked down. The room spun and her pulse raced She squeezed her eyes shut until the room stopped. She kept them shut as she got control of her breathing and slowed her pulse.

Again, she opened her eyes. This time the pain abated and the images were clear.

I have to be dreaming. This can't be real.

She closed her eyes. As if to test herself, she tried to move her left arm. It was stuck, held in place. She opened her eyes and looked down to see the leather restraints. Now her heart pounded. Her head whipped around as she took in the small room, the dull white cabinets, the metal table, the straps on her arms and legs. Her mind raced back to processing the crime scene in Haltom City. She knew what kind of place she was in.

Oh God. How did I get here?

Her mind raced, trying to remember something, anything. It was just a blur. She pictured a parking lot, Hunter smiling at her, his SUV shredded by bullets.

Is Jake all right?

She couldn't remember but she felt sure he wasn't hurt. She shook the thought away. Figuring out how she got here was a waste of time.

Concentrate. How do I get out of here?

Her eyes surveyed the room. It was almost identical to the room in the building she'd processed a week ago.

Plain cabinets, white countertops, wooden door. I'm sure it's locked.

She looked down at her clothes which seemed clean and then closely at both of her arms.

No needle marks. I can't have been here too long.

Other than her, the table she was strapped to and the dull cabinets, the room appeared completely empty.

She strained to listen through the door. There was movement, voices, people. She pictured the cages in the other building, the thin mats, the worn blankets and the child's shirt. Her stomach turned but she fought back the bile.

Screaming didn't seem like a good plan. Whoever was out there either couldn't help, or worse. She laid her head back, tried to control her heart rate. The blood rushed through her ears, her face felt flush. It seemed as if someone had turned the thermostat to high. Sweat dripped down the side of her face. She began to take slow, deep breaths.

Stay calm. If they were going to hurt you, it would've already happened. If they wanted you dead, well… Oh God!

Fear raced through her as she heard footsteps approaching. She squeezed her eyes shut to make the sound and fear go away.

Chapter 42

"What are you finding in there?" Hunter directed his question to Tom Lovett, Stacy's right hand on the CSI team. But every question, every thought seemed to require a force of will. He struggled to focus. He'd been so sure they'd find her here. The disappointment threatened to overwhelm him.

"Nothing and everything." They stood in the parking area just outside the front entrance. Tom pointed south. "It's just like the location down the street. I've got so many prints and so much DNA that it's going to take weeks to get through and when we do, it's likely going to just be more victims as opposed to perpetrators." Lovett shook his head, his face drooped and his eyes looked hopeless.

Hunter exploded. "I want every CSI in this department dedicated to this case. This is one of our own they've got. I don't give a damn about anything el..." Hunter stopped when he felt Sanders' hand on his shoulder and he realized how irrational he sounded. "Sorry Tom. I'm just..." He shook his head.

Sanders stepped in and looked at Tom. "How soon do you think you can get this working?"

"The problem we've got right now is that we haven't even started processing the stuff from this afternoon's scene."

"This takes priority." Hunter's look was intense. "There was nothing at the scene this afternoon that was going to lead us anywhere. We need to focus here and on the pieces that might lead us to the bad guys. Prints off the fast food wrappers, prints off the light switches and cabinet doors, things the victims wouldn't likely have touched."

Hunter looked at his watch. It was almost four in the morning. He surveyed the area until he saw Reyes coming out of the building and headed toward him. "Jimmy, can you manage the scene until Tom and his crew get done? By that time, you'll need to get some breakfast and some sleep. I'm going to drag Sanders and Barkley back to the station to see where we go from here."

"No problem Cowboy. We got it covered."

The silence on the drive back to the station amplified the dead end they were facing. These guys were pros. Even with two of the bad guys dead, there was no connection to the organization. There were at least four high profile teenage girls abducted but they'd only found traces of two and they were dead. This was now the second time the organization was one step ahead of them leaving nothing but a pile of useless evidence to process.

As he parked in back of the station, Hunter replayed the night in his mind, hearing her phone in the empty parking lot, finding her keys in the glow of the broken display, breaking through the door expecting to find her only to be left grasping at straws.

He killed the engine, got out and moved toward the door. "I'll get some coffee brewing and meet you guys in the conference room."

Sanders nodded and followed. Barkley pulled out his phone. "I'll check with my team and be there in a minute."

The smell of coffee, even break room coffee, helped fight off the fatigue of what was quickly becoming a twenty-four hour shift. The three detectives reconvened in the conference room where Sanders clicked away on his laptop while Hunter paced like a caged animal and Barkley jotted notes on his pad.

"One thing this tells us is that these guys are heavily focused on the DFW area and specifically, northeast Tarrant County." Barkley spoke as he continued to write.

Hunter stopped pacing, curiosity covered his face as he looked at Barkley. "How do you figure?"

"We know they have a least three locations. The two we've already found were within a few blocks of each other. Since they were clearly moving assets between locations, I think we can safely assume that another location is also close by." He looked up at Hunter. "Stop thinking like a cop and start thinking about supply chain and logistics.

They're not going to shuffle resources over major distances. It's too expensive, too risky and their customers have delivery expectations. This is a business first and foremost."

Hunter nodded and began pacing again. "Okay, let's say you're right. How does that help us?"

"It means we know where the haystack is and we just need to find that next needle."

"Son of a bitch!" Sanders stop clicking. "I may not have found the next needle but you're not going to believe this..."

Hunter and Barkley both turned to Sanders. "Well?"

"The building we raided tonight. Guess who owns it?" Sanders shook his head in disbelief as the other two stared at him. "Jackson Bell."

Barkley shrugged as if the name meant nothing and Hunter expression registered confusion at first and then slowly transformed into revelation. "Jackson Bell as in the same Jackson Bell that owned the first building we raided?"

Sanders nodded. "The very same one."

Hunter's face turned red and his pacing turned to stalking. "That son of a bitch deserves an Oscar for his performance. Unbelievable!" He looked at Barkley. "Reyes and I both interviewed this guy. He came off as innocent as a lamb." He turned back to Sanders. "Get his address. We're going to give Mr. Bell a wakeup call."

"Already got it." Sanders ripped a paper out of his notebook and held it out for Hunter.

In minutes they were in Hunter's car and speeding northeast out of town. Hunter spent most of the time during the drive pounding his fist on the dashboard and muttering about making mistakes, not searching the second building, not seeing through Bell's lies, not staying with Stacy at the scene.

"Cowboy! Take a breath." Barkley eyed him from the passenger seat. "Beating up the car isn't going to get her back any sooner." He stretched and yawned. "We need you thinking straight and you need to be calm to do that." He beamed one of his cocky grins and nodded. "Relax. We're going to get these guys."

Hunter's first urge was to lash out but reason took control. He knew Barkley was right and by the time they had taken the Haltom Road exit, he was back under control.

The sun hadn't risen yet but the sky was starting to lighten as they turned into a neighborhood just east of Haltom Road. Bell's house was a single story, red brick colonial on the right.

Since they were officially out of their jurisdiction, they didn't have a search warrant and this was a residence which likely included a family. Instead of kicking the door in, they just started pounding on it and screaming at the top of their lungs. "Fort Worth Police, open the door!"

Their approach netted immediate results as the lights flashed on and panicked voices could be heard from inside. A man's voice came through the door. "I'm coming. Hold on."

When the door cracked open, Hunter shoved it the rest of the way and in seconds had Bell up against the wall. "Jackson Bell, you are under arrest for human trafficking. You have the right to remain…"

A shriek came from his wife. "What's happening?"

"It's okay honey. It'll be okay." Bell tried to calm his wife.

Hunter grabbed him by the arm. "I wouldn't count on that Mr. Bell." The sound of crying came from the hall as two little boys stumbled out of their rooms, one dragging a stuffed rabbit. Now the wife seemed torn between rescuing her husband and comforting her boys. The scene continued to melt into chaos as Hunter finished the Miranda reading. He jammed the cuffs on Bell's wrists, shoved him against the wall and leaned into his ear. "You son of a bitch. You lied to me. You knew all along. Now you're going to jail and if the cop they kidnapped dies, I'll personally see to it that you get the needle!"

"What? Kidnapped? "Oh God."

Hunter dragged him stumbling out the front door and across the yard wearing a pair of faded sweat pants and wife beater T-shirt. They tossed him in the back seat like he was a sack of potatoes. As he fired up the engine, Barkley extracted himself from the panicked grip of Bell's wife and trotted across the yard.

His door was just closing as Hunter hit the gas leaving Bell's wife hysterical, clutching her sons in the front yard.

Barkley shook his head and grinned. "Damn glad you calmed down. I would've hated to have seen you pissed off."

Hunter gripped the wheel. "I'm just getting warmed up."

He glared into the rearview mirror at Bell who was slumped in the back seat shaking his head and mumbling. "You don't understand." The blubbering declarations of them not understanding continued throughout the ride back to the station. By the time Hunter cuffed him to the table in the interrogation room, he was crying and slobbering and begging to talk to his wife. Hunter left him without a word.

Standing in the hall, Hunter leaned against the wall and took a deep breath. He needed to get his mind straight and be under control before walking back in that room. Stacy's life depended on it. He looked at his watch: seven o'clock. Based on the information from Patrolman Daniels, she'd been gone for close to ten hours.

Where is she? What have they done to her? Concentrate!

As if reading his mind, Sanders appeared with a cup of coffee in each hand. He handed one to Hunter. "You look like you could use some java." Hunter nodded and they both sipped for a moment. Sanders pointed toward the room. "Do you need any help in there?"

Hunter shook his head. "What I need is for you to keep doing what you've been doing. It seems that while I've been running around halfcocked, you keep coming up with real leads." He smiled. "Nice work on finding Bell."

Folding his hands around his coffee in front of him, Sanders bowed his head and put on a Chinese accent that was every bit as bad as Hunters. "You have taught me well, Master."

Hunter laughed. "Master my ass." He pushed off the wall, stepped toward the door and toasted Sanders with his coffee. "Thanks."

"Mr. Bell, let me be clear about your situ…"

"Is my family okay? I need to talk to my wife!" His eyes were wide and sweat poured off his forehead as he tried to stand but was stopped by the cuffs connected to the chair.

"What you need to do Mr. Bell is sit…"

"You don't understand. You don't know who you're dealing with." He sat back down, shaking his head, hunching his shoulders, crying.

"Then tell me who I'm dealing with." Hunter leaned on the table towering over the man.

His head almost shook off his neck, the moaning and crying in his voice made his answer almost unintelligible. "I can't... I won't... My family..."

"Mr. Bell, if you're worried about your family, we can protect them."

"No you can't. These people... They're crazy." His voice trailed off as his eyes went almost catatonic.

"Mr. Bell..."

"I want my lawyer! I want my lawyer now!" He dropped his head into his hands and his shoulders shook with sobs.

Hunter stood up, exhaled and ran his hand through his hair. He felt his face go flush and realized both of his hands were clenched into fists, one was crushing the file he held. He took a deep breath, turned and exited the room without another word.

The look on Hunter's face when he charged into the conference room told the story. Sanders looked up momentarily from his laptop but didn't say anything. Barkley raised an eyebrow. "Lawyered up, huh?"

Hunter's normal pacing was more like stomping as he moved back and forth across the room with his arms folded across his chest. "He's scared to death. They've threatened his family."

"We can protect them."

"He doesn't believe us and won't say a word." Hunter stopped at the window and looked out at the city coming to life.

"So where does that leave us?"

"Nowhere! Absolutely nowhere." Hunter pulled out a chair and slumped into it.

"Maybe not." Sanders' voice stopped the conversation. "I think I may have something."

Both Hunter and Barkley turned to Sanders with anticipation.

"So I was thinking that if they used Bell for two of their locations, why not more?" Hunter sat up straight, signaled for him to keep going. "I've spent the last thirty minutes searching property records to see if he owned other buildings." He smiled. "As it turns out, he does. Exactly one more and with a similar profile to the others, five thousand square foot light commercial warehouse in Northeast Tarrant County."

"Holy crap! Nice work Billy." He jumped up and joined Sanders at his laptop. Billy spent the next several minutes walking him through the details.

"This is great." Hunter looked as if he'd just been injected with straight caffeine. "I'll contact Judge Spicer to get the paper going. Billy, can you reach out to Zeke to let him know we'll need his team again?"

He looked at Barkley who just smiled and opened his hands. "I love it when a plan comes together."

Chapter 43

"Detective Hunter, it's not often that people call me after the search warrant is executed. Why do I get the impression that you're not just calling to tell me how it went?"

"Good morning Judge Spicer." Hunter cleared his throat. "No sir, I'm not. The good news is that the raid went as planned and no one was injured. Unfortunately, we did not find CSI Morgan."

Hunter could almost feel the judge stiffen through the phone line. "Did you have the wrong place?"

"No sir. It was most definitely a human trafficking holding center and we're hopeful that the evidence collected there will help us find and prosecute the people responsible. We apparently missed them by mere hours. No one was at the location."

"That's unfortunate Detective. How is it that I can help you?"

"Well, sir. We need another search warrant." Hunter went on to explain the connection between the first and second locations, and how Jackson Bell had owned a third property in the area that fit the profile of a holding center.

After a number of questions around the details, the judge spent several minutes reviewing the paperwork before he finally consented. "Good luck Detective. I hope this one proves to be where they're holding Ms. Morgan."

"Yes sir, you and I both. Thanks for your time." Hunter gave Sanders a thumbs up as he hung up the phone. "We've got the paper."

Sanders nodded. "Zeke's on his way up so we can plan things before we leave. I've got a map of the area on the board." He pointed to the board as Zeke walked into the conference room.

"Hey guys, I hear we have another location." Zeke saw the map and walked over to it as Hunter, Barkley and Sanders got up as well.

Hunter stepped up to the map, ran his finger north and south on Edith Lane just east of Beach Street. "Right there." He tapped the map. "Address is 2917."

"Yeah, I'm familiar with this area. All those buildings back up to a run down, ratty old cemetery." Zeke pointed at the map to the area just behind a row of small warehouses.

"It's called the Peoples Burial Park." Sanders' voice was more stern and louder than usual. Everyone turned to see his face without its normal smile, his jawline rigid. "I've got relatives who are resting there."

"Sorry Billy, I didn't mea…"

"It was founded in the early 1930's and was built adjacent to two older cemeteries where I'm sure I have older ancestors." He cocked his head, continued. "You know when my Daddy was growing up, folks who looked like you wouldn't allow black folks to be buried anywhere near them, and since we also couldn't hold the same kind of jobs or make the same kind of money, a run down, ratty piece of land on the outskirts of town was where we were relegated. It might not be much but it still has meaning."

Zeke held up his hands and nodded. "I stand corrected. My apologies."

Sanders waved it off. "No problem." He nodded back to the board. "Let's get this thing planned."

"All right." Hunter got everyone's attention. "The warehouse we're hitting is white and has a big eight ball painted on the front of the building. Used to house a company that manufactured pool tables." Hunter smiled. "You can't miss it."

He moved to the whiteboard and drew an outline of the building. "Very similar to the location at Higgins and Earl, there are three rollup garage doors on the front of the building toward the south end and a pedestrian entrance toward the north end. As far as we know, there's nothing unique about the layout." He turned to the team. "Based on the last two locations, my guess is that the inside will be very similar."

"Same basic plan as before?" Barkley looked at Hunter. "You

lead Sanders and me in the front, SWAT takes the back and perimeter?"

Hunter nodded. "Exactly." He turned to the rest of the team. "We'll have to move quickly. We're doing this in broad daylight. Zeke, your team will have to access through the cemetery. I'll take one of your guys with me to provide support on the front."

"Sounds good."

"There's a Dollar General around the corner on Beach. Let's meet up on the southwest corner of their parking lot in thirty minutes." Hunter looked at his watch. "That'll give us a few minutes for final logistics and then we'll hit the building right at nine."

Zeke turned to head to the door. "We'll see you there."

Thirty minutes later, the sun was already high in the sky and the parking lot was busy. The team got some curious stares as they gathered, strapped on their vests, checked their weapons, confirmed the plan one last time and mounted up like the cavalry riding into battle.

They pulled out of the parking lot onto 28th to drive past the Peoples Burial Park. As they slowed to let Zeke's team pull into the cemetery and get positioned, Hunter looked out at the small headstones. His mind drifted to Gina as it often did when he was confronted with death. It'd been over five years since that night and while the pain had lessened, the memory was just as vivid.

Even having lost his wife at a young age, he didn't spend much time thinking about what happens when it's your time. The little thought he'd put into it and all the death he'd seen in his job had convinced him long ago that it really didn't matter much where they decided to bury you or by whom. For that matter, he didn't see much point in the whole cemetery concept. He had no desire to be buried. If it hadn't been for Gina's parents, he would have cremated her remains and spread them in the mountains of New Mexico, her favorite place.

Sanders worked the hand held radio staying in touch with Zeke. "Turning left onto Edith, thirty seconds from target."

"Roger that. We're in position."

Twenty seconds later they came to a stop in front of the building, poured out of the car and set up at the door. "Breaching door now." Sanders slid the hand held into his pocket as the SWAT officer slammed the door with the battering ram. The metal frame screeched as the door blew open. Like before, Hunter led with Barkley on his left shoulder and Sanders on his right.

Time seemed to slow as his eyes adjusted to the dark room. Hunter moved in screaming. "Fort Worth Police, don't move!" He took a step forward, his mind registered flashes, people in a cage on his left, doors to rooms straight ahead.

There was movement on his left, someone standing. He saw the man's arm, raising a gun in his direction. He swung his Glock that way but heard the shots before he could get turned, a quick double tap. The man staggered back, two overlapping circles of red grew on his chest before he seemed to understand what had happened. He was dead before he hit the ground.

Movement to Hunter's right made him swing back that direction. A second man stood, his gun raised also. Again, he turned. Another double tap before he could pull the trigger. An identical set of perfect red circles on his chest. He too fell in place.

Time warped back to real speed, people in the cage were on the ground yelling, crying. Barkley moved in their direction followed by SWAT. He stopped to check the first downed gunman, shook his head. Sanders knelt beside the second gunman shoved his gun away, needlessly checked for a pulse. Hunter saw the two closed doors on the back wall, his heart jumped out of his chest as he bolted forward.

Please be there.

He slammed into the first door with his shoulder. The frame exploded inward and Hunter went with it, crashed head first into the metal table and fell to the ground. He was up in and instant, surveying the small room.

Empty.

Warm liquid flowed down the side of his temple. "Clear!" He swiped quickly at his face, slinging blood off to the side, ran back out of the room and moved to the next door. Without the momentum of running across the room, he stopped, kicked the door just above the handle and watched it swing violently away.

This time under control, he saw someone on the table, strapped down. Auburn hair, that beautiful little scar. "Stacy?" He moved into the room, blood streamed down his face. He flicked it away. "Stacy!" She was there, her face pale, eyes closed, leather restraints held her down. He reached over, checked her pulse. It was faint but there. "Sanders, call an ambulance now!"

"On its way."

Barkley was at the door, took one look at Hunter and shouted back over his shoulder. "Make that two, Billy."

"You got it."

Barkley holstered his Sig, moved to the cabinets and started rummaging. Hunter's hand alternated between checking Stacy for injuries and wiping the blood from his face. He heard a box rip open. A moment later, Barkley's hand held a large gauze pad. "Here, put this on your head."

With the blood flow stopped, Hunter focused on Stacy. He saw the needle marks on her arm. He gently touched her face. "Stace, wake up baby. We've got you. You're all right." She moaned and her head moved. He kept talking to her, gently coaxing her to wake up and holding her hand. Barkley unstrapped the restraints.

"She's coming around. We got her Cowboy." Barkley nodded, smiled. "Nice work."

The sound of the paramedic's gurney turned Hunter toward the door. The first guy in the door looked at Hunter, reached for the bloody gauze. Hunter swatted at his hand. "Not me." He thumbed over his shoulder. "Her."

"You're bleeding." Hunter barely heard her weak voice. He spun to see her groggy, green eyes looking up at him.

"It's nothing, baby. Are you okay?" Hunter smiled and caressed her cheek.

Her eyes seemed to dance around the room as if she was watching butterflies, her voice sounded high and distant. "I'm tired... Where are we?"

"Detective, we need you in there." The paramedic pushed past him to get to Stacy, started checking her vital signs and calling them out to his partner.

Hunter started to object but Barkley stepped in front of him. "She's in good hands Cowboy. Let's step out and get you cleaned up." He relented, kept the gauze pressed to his head and turned for the door.

As they moved back through the open area, the full SWAT team had moved in. There were about twenty people still in the cage, huddled together, their eyes wide. Fear seemed to radiate from them. They were almost uniformly tan with brown eyes and dark hair. The little conversation that could be heard seemed to be a mixture of Spanish and Vietnamese.

The two gunmen were in heaps where they'd fallen, their chests soaked in blood, their eyes vacant and glazed. Hunter pointed. "Were they the only bad guys?"

"As far as we know." Barkley shook his head. "Neither exactly looks like the big boss." He nodded toward the cage. "I've called in for a bus to transport the victims. We'll process them through John Peter Smith first to make sure they're okay. By the time they get through that, I'll have a processing center set up with translators." He frowned. "Hopefully, they can tell us more than the two dead guys."

They stepped through the door to the parking area, shielded their eyes against the sun and saw Sanders directing the scene. A second ambulance pulled in the lot where a half dozen patrol cars were parked at random angles.

Sanders noticed them, walked over and smirked. "Cowboy, uh… That was an interesting method for breaching a door. Can you show me how to do that?" He barely got the statement out before he and Barkley broke into laughter.

"Funny." Hunter frowned, started to reply but caught the sight of Stacy being wheeled to the ambulance. He spun and caught up with Stacy. "Hey." He smiled down at her as he walked along beside her.

She smiled, still fighting to wake up. She tried to reach up to his face but her hand just kind of waved around as the gurney jostled. "Are you okay?"

"Detective, we need to get her to the hospital." The paramedic started to push the gurney into the back of the ambulance.

Hunter stopped them just long enough to lean down and softly kiss her cheek. "I'll see you there." He stood at the back of the ambulance and waved as they closed the door and pulled away.

"Your turn." Hunter turned to see the paramedics from the second ambulance. "We need to get you cleaned up and transported, Detective."

He followed them to the back of their ambulance, sat down, signaled for Barkley and Sanders to come over. As they cleaned him up, he looked up at his team. "So, which one of you bad boys took those shots?"

Sanders nodded toward Barkley, raised his eyebrows. "Wasn't me. Hell, I didn't even have time to get them sighted."

Hunter looked at Barkley. "Damn fancy shooting in there my friend. Where the hell did you learn to shoot like that?"

Barkley just shrugged. "Spent some time working for Uncle Sam overseas before I joined the Rangers."

Chapter 44

"How's our special guest?" The man behind the desk answered the underling's call with a smug tone.

"Gone!"

"What? What are you talking about?" The smug tone had disappeared, his voice had shot up nearly a full octave.

"The cops… I was there… I mean…" The underling's words stumbled out of his mouth in a traffic jam of thoughts.

"Slow down and tell me what's going on!" The man behind the desk had recovered his composure and was trying to get the underling to do the same. "Step by step, what happened?"

"Okay. We had her at the Edith Lane site. I was there all night. The doctor came by and put her to sleep. Everything was under control." He paused to let his mind catch up with him. "The boys were hungry so I decided to grab some breakfast. Shit! I couldn't believe it…"

"Calm." The man behind the desk stretched the word out with a soothing tone to try to keep the man from babbling.

"Sorry. When I got back to the corner, I saw them… The cops… They came flying around the corner headed toward the warehouse. I tried to call the guys but by the time the call went through, the cops were in the parking lot and headed for the front door."

"Shit! What happened after that? What did you do?"

"I circled back around to see if I could tell. I'm not sure. All I know is that in a matter of minutes the place was swamped with cops." He paused and audibly gulped for air. "I had to get out of there."

"Okay, let me think." The man behind the desk was already up and standing at the window. His eyes looked outside toward the city but his mind didn't register the view. It was spinning, processing. "Worst case is that they retrieved the woman and they got our guys. Who was there?"

"Randy and Dirk."

"Will they talk?"

"No. No way. It'd be suicide and they know it. They know we can reach them wherever they are."

"I don't want to take any chances. You need to put our sources on alert and find out if they're alive." The man behind the desk paused. "If they are, you need to fix that immediately." He turned back to his desk, nervously rearranged a framed photo. "What about the woman? Does she know anything?"

"No. We were very careful." The underling had calmed somewhat. He was no longer stammering. "She was out like a light from the time they snatched her. The only person that she saw while there was the doctor and he was disguised. She won't know anything."

"How the hell did they find her?"

"I don't know." The underling hesitated, his voice strained again. "But they found the other Higgins location as well."

"What?"

"When I bolted from the Edith location, I happened to go by Higgins. Just habit, I guess. Cops were swarmed on that location as well."

"Son of a bitch!" The man behind the desk slammed his fist down. "Get back here now. We've got to plan our next move."

Chapter 45

"That should hold you for a while, but this needs stitches. Unless you want to leave a nasty scar on your forehead, you'll get it done soon and by somebody good." The paramedic put the final touches on a couple of butterfly bandages on Hunter's head.

"Thanks." Hunter pulled away with an annoyed look. The pungent smell of the rubbing alcohol burned his nose. "I'll take care of it. I've got to go to JPS later anyway."

Hunter escaped from the back of the ambulance and found Barkley and Sanders. When he saw Hunter patched up, Barkley cocked an eyebrow at him. "That's a good look. The chicks will dig it."

"That was the plan all along." Hunter turned to Sanders. "Where the hell is the CSI team?"

Sanders' mouth curled into a slow smile. "Seems that between our shoot out at the apartment, Stacy being out of commission and two raids on trafficking centers, we've put a bit of a strain on our resource pool."

Before Hunter could respond, Barkley cut in. "Don't worry about it. Since this scene is an active trafficking center and that's more on my side of the fence than yours, I took the liberty of calling my guys. They're on their way. Should be here in the next fifteen minutes or so."

Hunter frowned, folded his arms and started to say something but Barkley held up his hand. "I'll make sure the whole team is copied on everything they find. Just because you rammed your head though a door, don't start getting territorial on me."

Hunter pursed his lips. "Just to be clear, I hit the door with my shoulder. It was the metal examination table that damaged my head."

"I stand corrected." Barkley smiled and nodded.

Sanders nodded toward the building. "Doc got here a few minutes ago. He's already inside so hopefully we can get the stiffs out of the way soon."

The local media had caught wind of the situation early on when the calls went out for patrol backup and ambulance dispatch. They had begun to gather at the perimeter tape taking every opportunity to wave and yell questions to anyone who might pay attention. The detectives ignored them.

The first of the satellite trucks had arrived a few moments earlier and by the time the Rangers CSI team had arrived, the trail of media vehicles stretched down the street and looked like a covered wagon train crossing the prairie. Hunter directed Barkley's attention that direction when he saw the CNN truck. "Looks like we're going national."

Barkley looked down the road, saw that close to a dozen reporters and cameramen were getting set up and starting to give their onsite reports. He rubbed his forehead and sighed. "Lucky us."

"Before we get inundated, let's get your guys in the building and working." Hunter waived to the patrolman manning the perimeter tape to let the CSI team into the area.

The CSI team leader managed to see Barkley's hat towering over the crowd of first responders and walked over. Barkley met him as he moved toward the building. "Thanks for getting here so quickly. Preston Evans, Jake Hunter." He pointed to the two men as a way of introduction and they shook hands. "Let me catch you up."

Barkley walked Evans through the scene and gave him the background on the case. "We're going to need ballistics on the perp's weapons immediately. FWPD has two open homicides where the same forty-five was used. One of our bad guys was carrying a forty-five and we need to know if it's a match."

Evans took a quick look at the bodies, noted the wounds, grinned and looked at Barkley. "You need to get to the range, you left two visible entry wounds. You're getting sloppy."

"What can I say? I haven't been to bed in over twenty-four hours. Give me a break."

Hunter watched the exchange with amusement trying to

determine just how much of it was bullshit. Sanders stepped over with two wallets enclosed in evidence bags but with the drivers licenses visible. "So, our bad guys are Randall Townsend and Dirk Simpson. Townsend was the one with the forty-five. I'm guessing by the fact that they have nothing in their wallets except their licenses and cash, they're probably as off the grid as Turner and James."

"I'm sure you're right, but..." He shrugged.

Sanders nodded. "I'll get backgrounds working ASAP."

"Is there a Detective Barkley in here?" A voice boomed over the chaos. When everyone went silent and every head in the room turned to the Patrolman standing at the front door, his face went pink and he tried to shrink.

"That's me." Barkley raised his hand.

"There's a bus out front. The driver's asking for you." The Patrolman ducked back outside as Barkley nodded.

Barkley looked at Hunter and then to the door. "Let's see just how close we can get the bus to the door. I want to get these people loaded up with as little exposure to the hounds as possible."

Hunter followed Barkley to the bus. He passed a number of reporters doing live scene shots. "This is Misty Covington reporting live from Haltom City..." It looked like every station in town was there. "We've learned that a combined task force made up of Fort Worth Homicide Detectives and the Texas Rangers have raided..." The sound bites all sounded the same. "It's believed to be in connection with the murders of Madison Harper and Caitlin Gardner, A.K.A. Valerie Bryant..." The names and descriptions bounced from one reporter to the next like pinballs off bumpers.

They have no idea what's really going on here.

Barkley directed a number of Patrolmen and the bus driver to move vehicles and pull the bus in front of the warehouse door so that the bus blocked the view from onlookers. As they began the process, Barkley pulled Hunter aside. "The hounds are getting restless. Any issue with us doing a short press conference?"

Hunter looked at the crowd of media. "Doesn't look like we have much choice." He grinned at Barkley. "I assume you're well versed in saying a lot while actually saying nothing."

Barkley just gave Hunter an 'are-you-kidding' look, signaled a Patrolman over and started working out the details.

Hunter stepped back inside and saw Doc wrapping up his review of the two bodies. His team had one body zipped and loaded on a gurney and were about to load the second. "Doc, we're trying to keep you busy."

"So it seems. Was this more of Detective Sanders' handiwork?"

Hunter shook his head. "These two were courtesy of the tall Ranger."

Doc raised an eyebrow. "Cowboy, you must feel quite safe with those two gentlemen by your side. I'm not sure I've ever seen this kind of marksmanship outside a movie theater. Very impressive."

Hunter nodded. "The only issue is that they keep shooting our leads." He paused. "Not that I'm complaining. The alternative in this case would have sucked." He pointed to the door. "Try to avoid the press on your way out. Let me know if the autopsy reveals anything."

"As always." Doc waved, directed his team and the two gurneys were pushed toward the door.

Preston Evans caught Hunter's eye and signaled him over. "Hell of a scene you've got here. It's going to keep us going for a while."

"Have you found anything of interest?"

"We collected the two weapons and sent those to the lab already. I'd expect that we'll have an initial ballistics match before the day's over." Evans pointed to the cage area. "We've got so much DNA and print evidence that we'll need to think about how we process it to get you the important stuff first."

Hunter nodded. "My suggestion is that we process anything collected outside the cage first. I don't think our bad guys spent much time inside."

"Makes sense." He nodded to the two smaller rooms. "Those are a different story. We covered those with a fine toothed comb. In fact, we've already found a pair of latex gloves. If we're careful, we should be able to get prints from inside."

"How soon will you know?" Hunter's interest was piqued.

"That could be big."

"I'll rush it through, possibly today or early tomorrow." He looked at his notebook. "Other than that, just a lot of stuff to process."

"Thanks. I'll get out of your way."

Hunter stepped away but paused to look around. It was the third one of these hell holes they had found. The thought that these places existed made him shudder. His throat constricted and he had to blink rapidly when he thought of the twelve hours Stacy had spent here. *She must have been terrified.*

The Vietnamese and Spanish translators had arrived and Barkley walked them into the building and began providing information to the victims in the cage. Relief washed over the faces as they began to understand they were safe and were going to be provided medical attention, food, clothing and accommodations.

There were hugs and tears as the team spent the next twenty minutes carefully escorting them out of the building and onto the bus. Their next destination was John Peter Smith Hospital and eventually some version of freedom either here or in their home countries.

As the bus pulled away, a patrolman got Barkley and Hunter's attention. "We're all set up."

Barkley sighed. "It's show time."

Hunter shook his head and followed him toward the perimeter tape where a cluster of microphones had been hurriedly cobbled together.

Without hesitation, Barkley stepped up, adjusted his hat and found the closest camera. "Ladies and gentlemen, I'm Detective Colt Barkley of the Texas Rangers." He placed his hand on Hunter's shoulder. "This is Detective Jake Hunter of the Fort Worth Police Department. Over the last two weeks our teams have collaborated on the investigation of two homicides we believe to be related to a human trafficking organization. That investigation has culminated in raids on three facilities in Northeast Tarrant County that we believe were holding locations for human trafficking victims… slaves." He paused for effect. "This investigation is ongoing so we can only share limited information at this point but are happy to answer what questions we can."

A roar rose from the group as fifty reporters simultaneously screamed questions. Barkley and Hunter both involuntarily leaned back. Barkley raised both hands to calm the masses. "Hang on." He pointed to Misty Covington who happened to be on the front row and not surprisingly, the most attractive of the group. "How about we start with you?"

"Is this related to the Madison Harper and Valerie Bryant murders?"

"Yes."

She quickly followed up. "Have those murders been solved?"

Barkley motioned to Hunter. "Since Detective Hunter has led the homicide aspect of this case, I'll let him address that."

Hunter straightened his jacket, cleared his throat and frowned at Barkley before turning his attention to the reporter. "We had already determined that James Le James was responsible for the death of Madison Harper. We are still processing ballistics evidence but are hopeful that today's raid will lead to determining who killed Valerie."

Another roar erupted. Barkley pointed to the next reporter.

"Were there other victims found at this location and if so, how many?"

"There were, but we can't discuss numbers at this point."

A reporter jumped in. "Have you found any trace of Kristi Quinn or Hallie Boyer?"

"Can't comment on those cases." Barkley quickly pointed to the next reporter

"There are reports that a Fort Worth Officer was taken hostage yesterday. Is that related to today's raid?"

"No comment."

The press conference rapidly fell into a cadence of questions that were answered with a variety of answers that all meant 'no comment'. Hunter took note of the fact that all of the national outlets were there: CNN, Fox, MSNBC. It had become a media spectacle.

After twenty minutes of being berated, Barkley's patience had worn thin. "Thank you everyone. All further requests for information should be directed to the Media Relations Departments with the Texas

Rangers and the Fort Worth Police Department."

Without waiting for consent, he spun on his heels as another roar of questions erupted and headed for the front door of the building. Hunter nodded and followed suit, grabbed Sanders on his way and closed the door behind them.

Once inside, all three looked drained. Sanders rolled his shoulder and Barkley stretched his arms out to both sides demonstrating all six foot five of his wingspan. Hunter rubbed his neck. "What a beating."

Barkley grinned. "That? Oh, that was nothing. Just wait till they really get going. If this thing is as big as I think it is, we'll be doing that twice a day."

Hunter grimaced and shook his head. "I'll pass."

When Barkley walked over to talk with Evans, Sanders and Hunter leaned against a wall and let the exhaustion wash over them. Sanders gave Hunter a smug look. "So, remember that conversation you and I had when we first got this case?"

Hunter looked puzzled.

"The one about how blonde victims are treated."

Hunter's face scrunched in bewilderment. "Yeah?"

Sanders nodded toward the door. "How many questions were asked out there about Madison and Valerie?"

Hunter shrugged. "I don't know, a couple of dozen."

"How many were asked about all the other victims?"

Hunter didn't answer. He didn't have to. He just stared across the room at the cage and felt his chest tighten.

Chapter 46

"Detective Hunter? Detective…"

The voice seemed to come from a well, echoed and muffled. Something pushed on his shoulder.

"Detective, time to wake up."

His eyes cracked open slightly then squinted shut. The bright light left psychedelic spots playing across the back of his eyelids. He raised his hand to his face and tried again. This time he kept his eyes opened and perused his surroundings.

"You fell asleep while I was stitching you up." The doctor flashed a smile that must have cost his parents a small fortune. "We've got you taken care of." He offered his hand and helped Hunter sit up on the examination table. "As long as you take care of the wound, the scarring should be very minor."

The grogginess had lifted but the complete exhaustion had set in and weighed on Hunter's shoulders like a bag of concrete. He yawned. "Thanks for your help." After only halfway listening to the doctor's instructions, Hunter found himself alone in the curtained off space. He felt every muscle in his body creak as he examined his bloody shirt and jacket, realized he didn't have an alternative and put them back on.

Now, how do I find Stacy?

John Peter Smith Hospital is really a catch all name for the Tarrant County Hospital District or JPS Healthcare Network. It's a Level One Trauma Center which consists of eight separate buildings and two parking garages. The two main buildings are connected by a sky bridge and have over five hundred rooms. Even a veteran who has spent years roaming the halls can get lost trying to find a patient.

Since Stacy's phone had been collected as evidence, Hunter

decided to expedite his search by calling Stacy's supervisor at the Forensics Lab. He found out she had been examined, seemed to be okay but was being held for observation and was in a room on the third floor of the main building. It wasn't too far so he set off through a maze of sterile looking corridors.

The never ending pale green walls, humming florescent lights and lack of windows made it seem like it was in the middle of the night but when Hunter looked at his watch he found that it was a little after four in the afternoon. The catnap he'd taken while getting stitched up had done little to fend off the fatigue that leaked through every cell in his body.

He exited the elevator on the third floor and turned a corner when his phone rang. He glanced at the caller ID and his stomach sank when he saw Reyes' name. The realization hit that he hadn't thought about Jimmy since leaving the apartment scene when he'd told him to knock off and get some sleep. *He's going to be pissed.*

Hunter stopped walking, cleared his throat and punched his phone. "Hunter."

"Sure, just send me off to bed and then go find the bad guys." The sarcasm dripped through the phone. "That's okay. I didn't want to be part of it anyway."

"Jimmy, shit man, I'm sorry. It just kind of unfolded really quickly."

Reyes snickered. "No worries. I'm just yanking your chain." He yawned overly big. "In fact, I feel great. I'm guessing I've gotten a little more sleep than you have." Hunter nodded but didn't respond. Reyes' tone went serious. "Please tell me you found Stacy and she's okay."

"We did. She seemed to be fine physically but we sent her to JPS to get checked out. I'm looking for her room." As he spoke, Hunter absent mindedly looked down the hall and noticed a Patrolman guarding a room. "In fact, I think I just found it. I'll buzz you later and catch you up."

Hunter clicked off the call and strode down the hall. As he approached, the Patrolman noticed him, bowed up initially but relaxed once Hunter smiled and badged him. "I'm assuming this is Stacy

Morgan's room?"

The officer gestured toward the door. "The doctor just left so I'm pretty sure she's awake."

"Thanks." Hunter took a deep breath, gently cracked the door and rapped his knuckles on the wood. As his eyes adjusted from the harsh hall lighting to the soft glow of the room, he was treated to the sight of Stacy's smile beaming up at him.

His whole body relaxed at that moment as he pushed on through the door and let it shut behind him. "You are a sight for sore eyes." He went straight to her, leaned down, cupped her chin in his hand and kissed her. "You look great. How are you?"

Her deep green eyes still seemed shaky but glowed up at him. "I'm good." Her voice sounded weak but steady. For a moment, they remained nose to nose and just absorbed each other.

"I'm good too. Not that you give a shit." The harsh sound of Lieutenant Sprabary's voice shot Hunter up straight and spun him around. Sprabary could barely contain his smile but continued his gruff tone. "From the looks of it, you're the one that needs to be in the hospital bed. What the hell happened to your head?"

"Oh, uh… Hey Lieutenant…" Hunter cleared his throat. "Didn't see you there."

Sprabary cocked an eyebrow. "Clearly." He frowned. "Why don't you catch both of us up on where things stand at the warehouse and then the two of you can get back to… Mm…" He swirled his hand toward them. "Whatever it is you need to get back to." He finally couldn't resist smiling. "Why don't you start with what happened to you?"

Hunter relaxed when he saw the smile. He nodded and gave Sprabary a quick recap of the events. He ended by pointing to his forehead. "When I shouldered the first door open, I uh…" He pointed to his head. "I kind of went head first into the metal table."

The mention of the table made Stacy grip her blanket and pull it up under her chin. Hunter turned, touched her hand. "Stace, you okay?"

She nodded but her eyes were wide and staring down at the foot of the bed. He eased down onto the side of the bed, squeezed her hand

and waited until she looked up at him. She nodded again but this time looked up at him with a weak smile. "It's okay, keep going."

"You sure?"

She smiled stronger and squeezed his hand back.

His eyes absorbed her face and tried to calm her. Once he felt her relax, he continued. "There were twenty-three people in the caged area. We secured the scene and got Stacy evac'd. Doc took care of the two stiffs and we brought Barkley's team in to process the scene."

Stacy sat up straighter. "What? Why didn't you use my team?" Her jaw flexed and her eyes narrowed. "We've processed everything related to this case."

Hunter motioned for her to sit back. "Relax. Your team was already stretched thin." He realized she didn't know about the second location. "They were processing the holding center we raided about six hours earlier when we thought we'd found you the first time. Don't worry. Barkley promised he'd share everything they find. He's already sent in the guns for ballistics and some gloves for prints. We should have something back by in the morning."

He looked back to Sprabary. "Barkley's helping to expedite the evidence." He looked at his watch. "Sanders should be wrapping up the scene by now. I told them since it's Friday night, we'd regroup for lunch tomorrow to see what we've got."

The Lieutenant nodded, stood, smiled at Stacy. "Get feeling better, Morgan. If he harasses you too much, you've got my number." He turned to Hunter. "You might think about changing clothes. You look like hell." He turned toward the door and waved over his shoulder. "My office, Monday morning. Keep me posted between now and then."

It was silent until the door shut completely. Hunter turned to Stacy. "What the hell?"

She shrugged, put her hands up. "No clue." She shook her head. "He was here when I woke. He just said he was worried about me and wanted to make sure I was okay. Thank God you showed up. I have no idea what we'd have talked about."

They both broke out laughing. When it fell quiet Hunter was staring at her, his eyes had gone moist. He fought through the lump in his throat. "You scared the hell out of me." His voice was a scratchy whisper. "I thought I'd lost you."

Her face scrunched and tears squeezed from her eyes. "Thank you for not letting that happen." She pulled up as he leaned in to kiss her. They spent the next few minutes exploring each other's eyes and getting reacquainted with each other's lips.

Hunter sat on the edge of the bed but kept hold of her hand. "Are you up to telling me what happened?" He held up his hand. "If you're not or don't want to, it can wait. I'm going to have Jimmy do your official debrief tomorrow, I just wanted to understand... You know..." He stopped. "I just want to make sure you're okay."

Although her face seemed to pale slightly, she nodded. "It's fine." She closed her eyes and rubbed her temple. "There's not too much to tell. It's all really fuzzy." She looked up, squinted her eyes and shook her head. "I remember waking up and not being able to move." The memory washed over her face and she stiffened. She spoke slowly, seemingly unsure of what she was saying. "I have no idea how I got there. The lights were on but I couldn't tell what time it was or how long I'd been there."

She concentrated. He squeezed her hand for encouragement. "When I saw the room..." She shuddered and her breath got shallow. Her voice strained. "I knew... I knew where I was." Her shoulders began to shake. Her grip on Hunter's hand tightened. "I was so scared, but I was so tired and everything was so wavy." She shook her head. "I must have passed out again. I don't remember anything else until something stuck me in the arm." She strained, searching for the memory. "Someone was there but I couldn't see his face." She looked up at him. "The next thing I remembered was you standing there... You were bleeding. I thought they hurt you."

She pulled him toward her, their mouths crashed together and they kissed hard. She pulled back. "Don't ever scare me like that again."

Hunter shook his head, cocked an eyebrow. "Back at ya."

Chapter 47

"And now we go to a suburb of Fort Worth Texas where law enforcement has raided a location related to the recent murders of two teenage girls." The CNN anchor looked solemnly into the camera. *"Sofia Cox is on location. Sofia, what can you tell us?"*

"We're in Haltom City, Texas where Fort Worth Homicide detectives along with the Texas Rangers have raided a warehouse that sources say was used as a holding center for a human trafficking ring. This is the third such location that has been uncovered in this area." She had positioned herself where the camera angle would show the front of the building with the huge eight ball on the front. *"Police found the three locations during the investigation of the abductions and murders of Madison Harper and Caitlin Gardner, who also went by the name of Valerie Bryant. The girls…"*

As the onsite reporter went into a lengthy background of the two girls and provided details around their disappearances and deaths, the man behind the desk hit the mute button, dropped the remote and chewed on the inside of his mouth. The underling sat across from him watching him, fidgeting.

The man's head began to shake back and forth, slowly at first then more quickly. Like a snake striking, he grabbed the remote and threw it across the room. It exploded into fragments against the far wall. "Fuck!"

The underling jumped, reflexively put his hands up. "I know it looks bad, but…"

"Looks bad?" The man's voice seemed to vibrate the walls. "Are you kidding? We've lost three of our primary locations, over twenty of our assets and four of our guys are dead!" He glared across the desk. "Bad? Yeah, I think it looks bad."

"Even with all that..." The underling nodded without making eye contact. "They've got nothing that connects to us. As for our four guys, well... dead men can't talk."

"They might not be able to but what about the CSI?"

"She never saw anything or anyone. I made sure of that. She was out almost the whole time we had her."

The man frowned, glared across the desk. "I don't share your confidence. We need to go dark for a while."

"What about our customers?"

"Tell them it's temporary." He snorted an exasperated laugh. "Hell, give them a 'going dark' discount on the assets in our other locations. Call it a 'temporarily going out of business' sale. I want every location empty by Monday."

"What about the guys?"

The man leaned forward, more relaxed, his business side emerging. "Send them on a paid vacation to Mexico. I want all of them gone as soon as the assets are moved."

The underling nodded. "What about us?"

A smile broke across the man's face. "Us?" He shrugged. "We've got a business to run."

* * * *

Barkley settled back on the king sized bed in the Residence Inn's room that had become his temporary home for the last few weeks. The thought of dragging himself out to some chain restaurant for a nondescript dinner was too much. He reached over and opened the cardboard pizza box, the smell of garlic and oregano assaulted his nose. He tore off a slice of chicken pineapple, folded it New York style and chomped into it.

He was running on close to thirty-six hours without sleep. His mind hazily drifted through the events of that long day and a half, the scene at the apartment and the two raids. He replayed the two shots in his mind. Pulling the trigger when required was part of the job, but it was never something he enjoyed.

Big day... Productive day... But are we any closer to the big dogs?

Working through the main suspects in his head, he thought

about Lance Sledge, Spencer Lamar and Garret Bronson but struggled to see connections to any of them. His team had been combing through the financial records of Jackson Bell, the owner of the three buildings but hadn't been able to find any links to their big three. With Bell lawyered up, that looked like a dead end.

Had any of the bad guys, Warrick Turner, Randall Townsend or Dirk Simpson survived, they might have been able to get them to talk. He shook his head as he picked up his Arizona Iced Tea, tipped it back.

We had to take those shots. Otherwise, it would have been us in the morgue tonight.

Preston Evans and his team had scoured the holding center from today's raid. With the exception of the latex gloves and the ballistics on the guns, there was very little found that seemed to hold any promise. *We can hope the ballistics comes back right. At least Cowboy could officially close his case.* He smiled to himself. *Doubt my boss will care too much about that.*

He reached in and grabbed his second slice, leaned back against the headboard and took a bite. The TV had been on ever since he'd gotten to his room but he'd had it muted so he could think. A newsbreak came on and caught his attention when he saw himself and Hunter standing in front of the jumble of microphones. He smiled, reached over and turned on the sound.

As he watched and listened to the press conference, he couldn't help but critique himself, his answers, his presence. He snickered when he realized just how bloody Hunter had been. *Damn, that little cut made one hell of a mess. Cowboy's going to be pissed when he sees this.* He smiled and took another big gulp of tea.

When the newsbreak ended, he turned the television off and looked over at the clock on the nightstand. *Eight fifteen.* He picked up his phone, punched in a number and listened to it ring twice before it was answered by a little voice. "Hi Daddy."

"Hey Baby."

She giggled and he grinned in spite of the lump in his throat.

* * * *

Since Stacy wasn't in a monitored room, it was easy for Hunter to sneak in a contraband meal. He provided dinner for the patrolman guarding the door and then he and Stacy sat back to enjoy a quiet meal. After having not eaten during the time she was held and then being subjected to hospital food since her rescue, Stacy went after her tacos like she was possessed.

As he took a bite, Hunter realized that all he'd managed to grab since early that morning were some vending machine crackers. The spicy Tex-Mex was just what he needed. The room smelled like a restaurant and Stacy's smile seemed to brighten with every tortilla chip she scooped into her queso.

It wasn't long before they both relaxed and fell into idle conversation. They talked a little more about the case but tried to keep things light. She teased him about running through doors and he told her he only did that for special people. She liked that thought.

With their stomachs full and their small talk reservoir drained, they did what most couples do, they turned on the television. It was ten o'clock and the evening news was just starting.

"Welcome to the Channel Five Evening news, this is Steve Crawford and tonight we begin with a story that broke early this morning with a Police raid on a warehouse in Haltom City. Misty Covington has been on the scene all day and has continued to learn more as the day has unfolded. Misty, what's the latest?"

The scene shifted to Misty standing in a lighted spot with the big eight ball in the shadows behind her. Hunter thought that seemed a little creepy. *"Steve, we have continued to learn more about this case. We reported this morning that this raid was related to the Madison Harper and Caitlin Gardner murders. We have now learned that a Fort Worth Crime Scene Investigator who was kidnapped at a crime scene late yesterday was actually rescued from this location as part of the raid. We have confirmed through two different sources that Stacy Morgan, a ten year veteran of the Fort Worth Police Departm…"*

"How did they find out?" Stacy looked stricken as she saw her picture flash onto the screen.

Hunter turned to her and took her hand. "Stace, almost every officer in two different forces knew that you were there." His voice was calm and soothing. "There wasn't any way it was going to stay quiet." He grinned and nodded toward the television. "At least it's a nice picture of you."

She frowned, rolled her eyes and threw a wadded up napkin at him. "My life is going to be ruined and you're making jokes. You butthead."

He smiled and threw the napkin back. "It'll all blow over in a few days. You'll just have to stay off the social circuit a bit until then." He turned back to the news.

"We've also learned that this is apparently tied to a human trafficking ring with numerous other victims. Two of those other victims appear to be Kristi Quinn of Sugarland and Hallie Boyer from Austin." Their pictures popped up on the screen while Covington gave their backgrounds.

It wasn't lost on Hunter that every picture of every victim discussed on the newscast had similar features, blonde, white, suburban. Although Stacy wasn't a blonde, her auburn hair was on the lighter side of the shade and with her piercing green eyes, she certainly met the other two criteria. Hunter shook his head.

There have been hundreds of victims of this group and the only ones they want to talk about are the teenage suburban hotties.

Stacy's voice got his attention. "You look pissed. What're you thinking?"

Hunter waved it away. "Nothing really, just a conversation Billy and I had earlier."

She looked at him like a kindergarten teacher looking at one of her students. "Sharing is caring." Her voice sing-songed.

He laughed but then stopped, looked down at the floor. "We were talking about the hypocrisy of the media. Well, really, of everyone." She cocked her head and waited for him to continue. He stood and paced in the confined space while he spoke. "It's just that from the very beginning, this case has been all about the beautiful blonde teenage girls, even though we've known these scumbags were buying and selling immigrants like discount merchandise. Few, if any of those immigrants are white. It just seems like no one gives a shit about any of them. They only care about the middle class blonde girls."

She smiled at him. "Our job was to solve three murders, two of those were blonde teenage beauties and the third was one of the scumbags. It just so happened that those murders were tied to this human trafficking ring and so we've been helping Barkley with that investigation." She paused, held out her hand, which he took. "We have done and will do everything in our power to bust these guys. Think about it, you and Billy got shot at and I managed to get kidnapped. You can't ask for much more, can you?"

Hunter smiled and nodded.

She continued. "Besides, it doesn't matter what anyone thinks because it wasn't just me you rescued from that warehouse today."

Chapter 48

"Oh my gosh!" Bernard, in all his effeminate Gothness, bolted around the Starbucks' counter and headed toward Stacy. "Are you okay? I was so worried." He spoke rapidly, not letting her answer. "I saw you on the news last night and I was just sick." He started to hug her but stopped with a look on his face as if he didn't think it was appropriate. Instead, he guided her to a chair as if she were an invalid. "Here, sit down. I know your order. I'll get it going."

After watching the news the night before, Hunter had fallen asleep on the visitors chair in Stacy's room. It made for an uncomfortable night but was convenient when Stacy had been released early that morning. He had been able to get both of them home and cleaned up for their Saturday lunch meeting with the team.

Hunter laughed as Bernard flitted away. He looked at Stacy. "See, being a celebrity isn't all bad."

She frowned. "Don't confuse pity with celebrity. Being that poor woman who got kidnapped is not my idea of fame."

"Let's just hope your fame only lasts for the required fifteen minutes."

Bernard reappeared with their coffees. "Here you go Stacy. This is on the house. The least we can do. Is there anything else I can get you?"

She smiled and shook her head. "No thank you, Bernard. You're sweet."

As if noticing Hunter for the first time, Bernard raised an eyebrow. "You look like you got run over by a bus." Overnight, the bruising on his face expanded with a large yellowish purple splotch painted across his forehead. Bernard smiled. "How gallant of you

Cowboy. Taking a beating while coming to your lady's rescue."

Stacy laughed a little too hard and Hunter gave her a 'what's-so-funny' look, and then nodded to Bernard. "Yeah, that sounds like a good enough story for me. I'll go with that."

Hunter provided a few more details about how he really got his wounds, which seemed to satisfy Bernard's curiosity enough for him to get back to his duties. This allowed Hunter and Stacy to get a few minutes of quiet time before walking down the block to the station.

When Hunter and Stacy walked in, Sanders was busy clicking away at his laptop. He saw Stacy and broke into a big grin. "There she is." He stood and wrapped her into a bear hug. "It's good to see you up and about."

She smiled. "Thanks, Billy." She turned to Hunter. "I could get used to that part of this celebrity thing."

Hunter waved his finger between Stacy and Billy and deadpanned. "Yeah, he gets a onetime pass on that stuff." That brought a round of laughter between the three of them.

"What's so funny?" Reyes stepped through the conference room door.

"That you slept through the raid." Sanders smiled.

"Hey, I was just following orders." He shrugged, walked over and gave Stacy a hug as Billy had and chatted with her about how she was doing.

As they settled in, Barkley made his entrance. Even on a Saturday, he looked the part. In place of his usual suit, he wore jeans but the white Stetson, black boots and lone star badge were still on display. "Hope everyone got some rest." He looked to Hunter and Stacy. "Glad to see the two of you look better than the last time I saw you." They both nodded as he scanned the room. "Let's get this party started, shall we?"

He walked to the whiteboard, started making notes as he spoke. "First, congratulations team, you can close two more homicides. We got ballistics back and we have a winner... Mr. Randall Townsend is our guy. His gun was confirmed as the murder weapon for both James Le James and Caitlin Gardner."

"Best part is that we don't have to waste money on a trial."

Sanders grinned.

"Precisely." Barkley continued. "Next piece of good news is that we were able to lift prints off the inside of the latex gloves. The bad news is that we haven't gotten a hit on any of our databases."

"So, they weren't worn by either Townsend or Simpson?" Hunter cocked his head.

"Nope, both of those guys were in the system." Barkley smiled. "They don't strike me as the type who'd waste time with gloves anyway."

"Good point." Hunter pointed at him. "Only someone used to doing it out of habit would, someone like a doctor or nurse, someone in the profession."

"Exactly what I was thinking. We'd speculated before that we thought they might have a healthcare professional on their staff." Barkley tapped his finger on the whiteboard. "This might confirm it."

Hunter nodded, tapped some notes into his laptop. "Let me chew on that a bit. Anything else?"

Barkley shook his head. "Much like the other two locations, tons of prints and DNA but most are going to end up being victims, not bad guys. It's going to take a while to sort through." He turned to Stacy. "If you'd like, I'll have my guy Evans reach out to you on Monday so you guys can start comparing notes."

"That'd be great."

Hunter made a few more notes then turned to Sanders. "Billy, were you able to run backgrounds on Tomlinson and Simpson?"

"I've got the basics." Sanders scrolled through a few screens. "Won't surprise you that for roughly the last four years, both of these guys were completely off the grid."

"That's interesting." Hunter perked up. "Turner and James must have been early recruits with Tomlinson and Simpson coming into the organization as the next wave."

"Exactly." Sanders continued. "Also similar to the other two guys, both Tomlinson and Simpson had a long history of low level offenses. Tomlinson did time for manslaughter and had busts for B&E and possession with intent."

"So I guess he graduated from manslaughter to murder."

Sanders nodded and flipped screens again. "Simpson did time for assault and had a long list of arrests that didn't go to trial."

"Let me guess, they did their time at Eastham." Hunter cocked his head.

"Nope. It does look like they knew each other in prison but they both served their time at the Clemens Unit. I haven't found any obvious connections to James or Turner. I also have no connection with either of James' former cellmates, Cooper or Raymond." He shrugged. "I've really just scratched the surface so far. I'll keep digging."

"So, where does that leave us?" Hunter surveyed the room.

Barkley leaned forward. "The better question might be 'where does that leave me'." He paused and looked around the room at the questioning faces. "Officially, all the homicides are solved. From the FWPD standpoint, I'm guessing you guys are done."

"Absolutely not!" Barkley was surprised to hear Stacy's voice so intense. "I understand the jurisdictional side, but that's bullshit."

"Whoa there." Barkley held out his hands. "I'm not saying that from my perspective. I'd love to have this team for the whole ride. I'm saying that's probably what you're going to hear from your brass."

"I have no intention of rolling off this case until it's done. I haven't worked around the clock for the last two weeks, watched Billy and Cowboy get shot at…" She pointed to Hunter's head. "See him bleed like a stuck pig and spend twelve hours kidnapped just to walk away from the case because of jurisdiction. I'm going to see this to the end and I'll be happy to tell Sprabary or anyone else who tries to stop me!"

The room went silent, the four men swapped cheeky looks. Finally, Hunter smiled. "Yeah, um…" He pointed to Stacy. "What she said."

Chapter 49

"You're not on his calendar."

Hunter smiled at Paige McClaren's normal sour disposition. "His last words to me on Friday were 'my office, Monday morning.' So we're here as directed."

Her glare melted into a smile that looked more like she smelled something bad. "I'll see if he has time for you." She made a show of organizing her desk before walking into Sprabary's office.

"She's so pleasant." Hunter sighed at Stacy.

The two of them had done little more that eat and sleep since their meeting with the team on Saturday. Hunter felt as if he was waking from a coma. The bruising on his forehead had started to fade and the muscle soreness had transformed into stiffness. Even so, his whole being screamed from a bad case of the Mondays.

Paige returned and looked pained as she directed them toward the lieutenant's office door. Hunter made sure to catch her eye when he smiled. "Thank you Paige."

As they entered, Sprabary looked up and the scowl on his face softened as he looked at Stacy. "Well, this is a surprise." He stood and actually smiled as he directed them to sit. "I didn't expect to see you back at the grind today. How are you feeling?"

"I'm good Lieutenant. Thank you." Her smile was polite but all business. "The ordeal was more mental than anything else and I got a lot of rest this weekend. So I'm ready to get moving again." She set her jaw. "There's a lot to do to catch these guys."

Hunter hid his grin as Sprabary turned to him. "Were there any developments over the weekend?"

"We had a couple of things pop." Hunter leaned forward. "The ballistics came back from the weapons recovered from the Friday morning raid. Randall Townsend's gun was a match for the Caitlin Gardner and James Le James murders."

"Excellent Detective, your team managed to clear three murders and help the Rangers bust a human trafficking ring in a little over two weeks. Not bad."

"Well, not exactly sir."

Sprabary opened his hands and cocked his head and let his look ask the question.

"We raided three locations of the ring and rescued several victims and I'm sure we've disrupted their operation somewhat by taking out four of their thugs." Hunter shook his head. "But we haven't broken up the ring or arrested anyone involved with really running it."

"The good news is that we may have a strong lead." Stacy broke in. "The team was able to get prints from some latex gloves found at the scene."

"Did you get a hit?" Both Hunter and Stacy just shook their heads. "That sounds more like evidence, not a lead." Sprabary leaned back in his chair. "Besides, the trafficking case belongs to the Rangers. We've closed our cases."

"We want to stay on the case." The statement blurted out from Stacy as if she couldn't stop it.

Sprabary's stare toggled between the two of them. He exhaled loudly. "Hmm… The Rangers have plenty of resources. Your specialty is homicide. Doesn't seem to make much sense to me."

"Sir, we think we're very close and we've developed a strong working relationship with Detective Barkley." Hunter pleaded his case outlining everything they'd accomplished together over the last two weeks and how this team had managed to get further on this human trafficking ring than Barkley had been able to do alone.

The debate continued for ten minutes. Sprabary put up a number of objections but without his normal passion. He finally steepled his hands and pursed his lips. "Has Barkley requested your assistance?"

"He said he'd love to have this team for the whole ride." Hunter avoided eye contact since he knew no formal request had been made.

Sprabary smiled, looked at Stacy. "Miss Morgan, you don't report to me so you'll need to take up your assignment with your supervisor." She nodded. He turned to Hunter. "I can't spare all of you guys. Have Reyes get back on the homicide desk." He pointed to Hunter. "Get me a formal request from Barkley and I'll let you and Sanders have one week."

He turned back to Stacy. "If you're not feeling well, you might consider taking some time off this week."

She started to object until she saw his knowing smile. "Yes sir."

Chapter 50

"You've got the team for another week if you want it."

Barkley was alone in the conference room staring at the whiteboard. He turned to see Hunter standing in the door. His grin spread. "Damn glad to hear it. Let's get to work."

Hunter nodded. "Here's the deal. We lose Reyes, and Stacy's working off the books. I'll go grab Billy and some coffee and we'll get going."

"Good because I've been staring at this board for the last hour…" Barkley shook his head. "And as far as I'm concerned, it might as well be blank."

Hunter smiled. "No problem. I've got an idea. I'll be right back."

Ten minutes later the team was re-caffeinated and gathered back in the conference room. Barkley looked at Hunter, tossed him the dry erase marker. "All right Cowboy, you said you had an idea?"

"You made a comment on Saturday that kept gnawing at me. You said that the gloves might confirm that they have a healthcare pro on their staff."

Barkley nodded.

Hunter continued. "What if that healthcare pro is Dr. Spencer Lamar?" He stood, started pacing. "We already had him on our short list because of his connection to James Le James, right?"

"So all we need are his prints." Barkley raised his eyebrows. "I'm guessing you have a plan?"

Hunter smiled. "Yes I do."

Shortly before two that afternoon, Hunter and Barkley pulled into the parking lot of Dr. Spencer Lamar's medical practice. Hunter had a carefully prepared folder sitting on the back seat. He reached around, grabbed it and looked at Barkley. "Show time."

Barkley stretched to his full six-foot-five as the two detectives were purposefully noticeable as they strode through the door and across the waiting room. Hunter was louder than he needed to be as he badged to receptionist. "I'm Detective Hunter with the Fort Worth Police. We need to see Dr. Lamar immediately."

The receptionist, realizing that everyone in the waiting room was staring, jumped to her feet. "I'll get him." She was down the hall before Hunter could even smile.

"This way please." She was back and shuffling them out of the waiting room in less than a minute. Barkley couldn't resist tipping his hat to the startled patients.

"This borders on police harassment." Lamar was standing behind his desk, his face red and his finger stabbing at the air. "How dare you continue to barge into my place of work and disturb my patients. I should be on the phone to my law..."

"Sit down, Dr. Lamar." Hunter's bellow stopped him in midsentence. "If you cooperate with us and tell us what we need to know, we'll be out of here in five minutes."

Clearly flustered, Lamar stood for another moment then dropped into his chair. "Fine, what do you need?"

Hunter opened up the folder to show that it contained three eight by ten photos, one each of Warrick Turner, Randall Townsend and Dirk Simpson. "I need you to look at these photos and tell me if you know any of these men." Instead of handing him the photos one by one, Hunter handed him the whole folder. He deliberately left the folder closed so that Lamar would have to take each photo out to look at it.

Lamar quickly glanced at each photo, shook his head. "Just like before with the other guy, I've never seen these people." He tried to hand the folder back.

Without reaching for it, Hunter glared. "Look closely doctor. This is critical."

Lamar shuffled back through the photos and made a show of holding up each photo and staring at it for several seconds. He stacked them back up, put them in the folder and held it out to Hunter. Hunter nodded and took the folder. "That wasn't so hard, was it?"

The red tint to Lamar's face seemed to glow even brighter. "Is there anything else?"

"I think we got what we needed." Hunter stood. "As always, thanks for your cooperation."

Both detectives were laughing when they plopped into the car. Hunter took the time to slip the folder into an evidence bag, label it with the collection information and set the bag on the back seat. He hit the ignition, maneuvered out of the parking lot and looked over at Barkley. "We either just pushed the case forward or managed to get ourselves sued."

"One or the other." Barkley smiled. "We'll see."

By the time they had swung by the station, picked up Sanders and driven south to the forensics lab, it was pushing four o'clock. Although Stacy had officially put in for a few days of vacation, knowing Hunter's plan, she told her supervisor she'd be around some that afternoon to clean up paperwork.

She was set up and ready for them when they arrived. Hunter handed her the evidence bag and she took it to her workstation. She put on her latex gloves. "You're absolutely sure the photos were clean and no one other than the suspect touched them?"

"What am I, a rookie?"

"Had to ask." She carefully set the first photo into the ALS machine. This would allow her to use a laser to wash the object with an alternate spectrum of light and then use a number of filters to accentuate the print's ridges and valleys formed by body oils and sweat. Once the contrast is clear, she would be able to take a high definition photo of the print to be used for comparison.

As she started working, Hunter, Barkley and Sanders hovered. She stopped. "This is not a five minute operation. I've got to process all three photos through the ALS, take pics of them and then dust them. It's going to be a while." When they didn't immediately disappear, she glared at them. "I work faster when I'm not being watched. I'll call you when I'm ready to make the comparison." She shooed them away and pointed them in the direction of the break room.

Two hours later, she had them reconvened in her office. "Okay gentlemen." She turned on her projector and directed it to the screen. "On the left, I've got high definition photos of the prints taken from the latex glove at the scene." She hit several keys. "Now on the right are the photos of the prints from your collection today." She reached for her laptop. "Our tools automatically analyze using a minutiae-matching algorithm." She tapped a button. "Push the magic button, and…"

There was a pregnant pause as circles and lines popped on the screen. Hunter felt his spine tighten. When the flurry of movement stopped, Hunter smiled. "Son of a bitch!"

Chapter 51

"Let's go get this bastard." Sanders stood.

"Whoa there. Let's pull back on those reins." Barkley chuckled. "I appreciate your enthusiasm but we need to be careful here." He turned to Stacy. "This is great work. Can you coordinate with Preston Evans to formalize these findings and add as much depth as possible?"

"Happy to."

Barkley leaned back in his chair and surveyed the team. "Look guys, getting this print match is great. It's definitely enough to bring him in but it's not enough to hold him for very long and without a lot more corroborating evidence, a good defense lawyer will have us kicked to the curb before pretrial hearings."

Barkley watched as the excitement fizzled from the room. "We need to be very deliberate with how we approach this guy. What do we really know?" He looked at Sanders. "The print places him at the scene and I'm sure we can get one or more of the victims to identify him as having been there, but what does that really mean?"

Sanders frowned but didn't respond.

"All it means is he was there." Barkley shrugged. "A creative lawyer will come up with a dozen reasons why he was there. Look at our building owner. They threatened his family. Lamar's a doctor, right? Maybe they threatened him and forced him to come in to take care of someone?"

Hunter crossed his arms, Stacy's shoulders sank and Sanders' frown remained but they all nodded, following his logic.

"My point is that when we move on this guy, I want to nail him as a key player, not just a worker bee. That means we have to eliminate his ability to claim he was 'just there'."

"Okay, how do we do that?" Hunter pulled out his notepad.

"We use the fingerprint evidence to get us whatever warrants we need to build a bullet proof case. We need to do a deep background of his financials, every account, every transaction. I want to know where every penny is and where it came from. We need to get a history on every form of communication." He ticked off his fingers. "His cell phone, home phone and office phone. His email, text and instant messaging. Who he's spoken to, when did they talk and where possible, what did they say?"

Sanders nodded. "We can check his social networking like FaceBook, Instagram and Twitter."

"Exactly."

"What about his prescription history?" Hunter shrugged. "Maybe there's something there."

Barkley grinned. "We've got some work to do. We know this guy's involved but we're only going to get one shot at him. If he gets out on bail, he'll either run or the organization will take him out."

Hunter looked at his watch. "Let's head back over to the station. It'll be easier to work there. We can give Judge Spicer a heads up on our way. I'll order the pizza so it'll be there when we arrive." He looked at the group and smiled. "It's going to be another late night."

Chapter 52

"Anybody up for arresting a doctor?" Hunter closed his laptop and stood.

Tired smiles and head nods came from Barkley, Sanders and Stacy. The team had worked late into the evening on Monday getting the search warrants and building the case. It was now late Tuesday morning and they had done enough to get a judge to sign an arrest warrant for Dr. Spencer Lamar.

Stacy started to pack up and Hunter arched an eyebrow. "Where do you think you're going?"

"I'm going with you." She said it casually but her shoulders tensed.

Hunter shook his head. "Even if you weren't officially on vacation, you know CSI's don't go on arrests. On top of that, this guy was directly involved with your kidnapping. Legally, the department would get hammered if you were there and something went haywire."

"That's exactly why I want to be there." Her eyes were pleading. "I want to see you slap the cuffs on this scum."

An empathetic smile crossed Hunter's face. "Stace, I know how important this is for you but we have to do this by the book. You can be here when we get back and for all I care, you can spit in the bastard's face, but you can't be there for the arrest."

She frowned, crossed her arms and glared for a moment. Finally, she exhaled, sat and put her bag on the table. Her jaw was tight when she looked back up at Hunter. "Make it painful."

Barkley chuckled. "Oh, I think we can guarantee that. We're going to drag his ass out in cuffs right through the middle of his waiting room."

Stacy smiled. "Happy hunting."

* * * *

Thirty minutes later, Hunter, Barkley and Sanders pulled the loaner squad car into Dr. Lamar's parking lot. The noontime heat greeted them as they stepped across the sidewalk to the front door. As planned, they had their badges out and held high as they moved into the waiting area. Like before, Hunter took the lead as they stepped to the front desk. "We're back." He smiled at the woman behind the desk. "Where's Doctor Lamar?"

She started to pick up the phone but Barkley reached his long arm over the desk, stopped her hand. "Uh uh, don't think so. What room is he in… NOW!"

Her voice was barely audible. "Examination C."

Hunter started toward the hall. Barkley looked at Sanders. "Make sure no one alerts the doctor."

Sanders nodded, looked at the receptionist until she took her hand off the phone. He surveyed the shocked faces scattered around the room and gave them an uncomfortable shrug. "If you're waiting to see Dr. Lamar, I'm sorry but he's going to be otherwise engaged for the rest of the day."

Hunter and Barkley brushed past two stunned nurses as they moved through the small maze of halls, found the door marked Examination C and without warning, shoved it open. The woman sitting on the examination table in a hospital gown startled and the doctor spun around to see both detectives, hands resting on their weapons, glaring at him.

"Dr. Spencer Lamar, you are under arrest for human trafficking…" Hunter started talking as Barkley grabbed the doctor by the lapel of his white lab coat and planted him face first against the wall.

"Oh my God. What the…" The woman's voice was shrill as she gasped, stuttered and struggled to comprehend what was happening.

"You have the right to remain…" Hunter continued, unaffected by her blabber.

"What's this all about? You can't do this. This is harassment." Lamar was defiant as his face pushed into the powder blue wallpaper.

"Anything you say can and..."

Barkley laughed. "Doc, you have no concept of harassment. Just wait till we get you downtown." Lamar's face went pale except for the red splotches on his cheeks.

"Be used against you in a court of law." Hunter smiled at Barkley as the Ranger clicked the cuffs into place. "God I love that sound."

"Let's go Doc." Barkley sneered as he shoved him toward the door. "You can say goodbye to your patients as we march you out."

They had him down the hall and into the waiting room before he could object further. As they passed the receptionist, he looked over to her, his eyes were wide with fear. "Karen, call my lawyer. Tell him what's happened. Tell him I need him..." His voice trailed off as Barkley and Hunter dragged him out the door.

Sanders smiled and nodded to the room full of slack jawed faces. "Have a nice day."

* * * *

"So this is him." Stacy's arms were folded across her chest and her stare was so intense, it threatened to shatter the one-way glass between the observation area and the interrogation room.

The doctor sat in the harsh light, surrounded by the stark white walls and fidgeted with the cuffs chaining him to the metal table. Beads of sweat dripped down the side of his face and his eyes blinked rapidly.

"Yep." Hunter nodded. "Don't suppose you remember him?"

Her head was shaking before the question was out and her voice was quiet. "No, not at all." She plopped dejectedly into a chair. "Truth is, I can't identify any of them."

Hunter reached over and gently touched her shoulder. "It's okay, Stace. We've got this guy and we're going to get the rest of them."

She continued to stare through the glass but reached her hand up and squeezed his. "Thanks Cowboy."

* * * *

Barkley burst into the interrogation room looking like a bloodhound who had just treed a fox. His eyes smiled with a slightly crazed intensity as he folded his long frame into the chair across from Lamar and slapped a file folder onto the table. "Dr. Lamar..." He grinned. "Or can I just call you Spence?"

"I want my lawyer." Lamar stared at his hands.

Barkley leaned back and spread out like he was watching a football game on his couch. "Now, now Spence, we'll get there. But first we're going to chat."

"I want my lawyer."

The grin left Barkley's face and he sat up and leaned his elbows on the table. "Okay Spence, but understand this..." He opened the folder. "We've got your balls on a cutting block with the cleaver raised. We've got fingerprints at the scene of a human trafficking holding center. The very one where we rescued a kidnapped police officer."

Barkley looked up from the folder. "Do you know the sentence for kidnapping a law enforcement officer?" Lamar wouldn't make eye contact. "You might want to ask that lawyer when he gets here." He looked back at the folder. "We've found your offshore accounts and we can track the cash deposits going back almost five years. It's only a short time before we identifying who made the deposits, so your time is running out."

Lamar seemed to collapse further into himself with every sentence while Barkley seemed to be just getting warmed up.

"Now, I've got to hand it to you. You were clever when you used multiple different pharmacies to process your Propofol prescriptions." Barkley opened his palms. "But we do live in an electronic world these days and we were able to find an inordinate number of prescriptions filled at a number of different pharmacies for a drug that you, as a general practitioner, would have no reason to prescribe... Especially to what appears to be a fictitious patient."

The sweat flowing down the side of Lamar's face had gone from a trickle to a stream. His pupils were huge and his breathing was rapid and shallow.

Barkley stopped, put a look of concern on his face. "You don't look so good, Spence." When he got no response, he smiled. "Why don't I wrap up so that we can get you that lawyer? Did I mention that we scoured your phone records and found an inordinately high number of calls made to and from burner phones? Now, in and of itself, that's no big deal. But..." He held up a long finger. "When some of those calls happen to be to the burner phone we found in the pocket of Randall Townsend as he lay dead on the floor of the human trafficking holding center... Now that's a problem."

Barkley resumed his relaxed football watching position and glared at Lamar for almost a full minute. The man looked near collapse. His hands shook and his eyes were glazed over. His expression seemed detached as he continued to look at his hands.

"Now that I have your attention, I'm going to ask you one more time." Barkley leaned forward, picked up the folder and straightened the documents in it. "Do you want to talk to me or do you want to spend the rest of your life as some biker's bitch in the Texas State Penal system?"

His voice shook and was barely more than a whisper. "I want my lawyer."

Chapter 53

"This is getting out of control. First, the holding centers, now, Lamar. What are we going to do?" The underling shifted from one foot to the other as he stood in front of the man's desk.

"What we're going to do first is take a deep breath." The man behind the desk pointed to a chair. "Have a seat. Calm down."

The underling sat but didn't relax. He continued to move and squirm nervously. His eyes darted around and he chewed on the inside of his mouth. "What if the doctor talks?"

"He won't."

The underling looked up confused. "How can we be sure?"

"He won't talk!" This time, the man's voice boomed and the underling cowered. The man calmed and his voice returned to normal. "Trust me."

"Okay." The underling nodded.

"You've gotten the other locations cleared out of inventory and shut down, correct?"

"Yes."

"And you've gotten all the guys out of town for a while, right?" The man opened his palms.

The underling nodded.

"All right then." The man stood and walked to the window, squinted into the late afternoon sun. "I've moved some money around just in case we need it and I've cleaned up paperwork and electronic trails that lead back to the company."

"Okay."

"At this point, the worst thing we can do is panic. If the cops have any suspicions, they'll be watching. We don't want to play into their hands." He turned back to face his desk. "Other than the one fishing expedition when they were tracking down connections with James, they haven't sniffed around since. We've been very careful to make sure our guys have no connections to us so unless someone has messed up, they've got nothing on us."

"Hasn't that already happened?"

The man cocked his head. "What do you mean?"

"The doctor got arrested."

The man nodded his head. "Yes. Our friend has messed up and we do need to address that." He rubbed his chin and looked around the room. "Do we have connections into county lockup?"

The underling thought for a moment. "We've got a few contacts… Why?"

"I think we need to enlist their services."

"Exactly how?" The underling's voice was tight. He cleared his throat with a cough.

The man's eyes went dark. "We need to eliminate any possible threat to the organization." He paused. "You understand?"

"Yes."

Chapter 54

"Here's to a job well done and a doctor who's going to spend the rest of his life getting proctologic examinations from his cellmates." Sanders smiled and raised his Diet Coke. The rest of the team joined him and 'clinked' their assortment of soda cans and paper coffee cups.

After finishing up the paperwork on the arrest of Dr. Lamar, they had haphazardly reconvened in the conference room, all looking satisfied but restless. It was late afternoon and although it seemed they were at a stopping point, there was an underlying realization they hadn't quite hit the finish line.

Barkley finally addressed the elephant in the room. "Guys, I'm awfully happy about nailing our boy Spencer, but you know he's not the big dog. Whoever's really calling the shots is still out there."

Everyone nodded and Sanders smirked. "Thanks for bringing us down man."

Barkley shrugged. "Don't get me wrong. We've made a hell of a dent in this organization." He ticked off his fingers. "Three locations, four of their thugs, their landlord and their doctor." He nodded. "That's great work." He looked from Sanders to Stacy to Hunter. "But these things are like fire ant colonies. You can kill a whole bunch of mounds but the heart and soul of the colony is ten feet underground and still very much alive."

"You're right." Stacy's voice sounded determined. "I'm still on vacation and you've got these two for the rest of the week." She pointed to Sanders and Hunter. "So how do we best use that time to see if we can kill the colony?"

Before Barkley had a chance to answer, Hunter stood up, walked to the whiteboard and flipped it over so that he was looking at a blank slate. "The answers are there. We just haven't seen them yet." He turned and nodded at Barkley. "Colt just said it. We've killed some mounds and although we can't see it yet, all of those mounds are somehow connected to the colony. We have to find those connections."

He turned and started drawing what looked like a random collection of shapes on the whiteboard, squares, rectangles, circles and a couple of stars. "We're going to play connect the dots because it's impossible to work side by side with someone in an organization and not leave some kind of trail. These guys are good but they aren't perfect and all we need to do is follow the connections. Think of it as playing six degrees of separation."

Barkley stood and picked up the conversation as if he and Hunter had rehearsed. "Each one of these shapes is a person…"

"Or a crime scene." Hunter interjected.

Barkley nodded. "A person that we've already nailed, suspected as involved, or is at a crime scene. We're going to walk through all the connections between these entities that we currently know and then we're going to start digging to see what other connections we can reveal."

"Exactly." Hunter pointed to the board. "The rectangles across the bottom are the six crime scenes: the three holding centers, James' apartment, Warrick's apartment and the Valley View Motel. The two stars in the middle are our murder victims, Madison Harper and Caitlin Gardner, A.K.A. Valerie Bryant. The squares are the various players in the mix, James Le James, Warrick Turner, Randall Townsend, Dirk Simpson, Jackson Bell, Paul Raymond and Mark Cooper. Finally, the three rectangles across the top are our three original big dog suspects, Garret Bronson, Lance Sledge and Spencer Lamar.'

He turned back to the team. "Now, we're going to find all the connections we can between each one of these."

"I'll start with an example." Barkley picked up the marker and started drawing lines. "Take Madison Harper. She's directly connected to James Le James because he killed her, she's directly connected to the first holding center because that's where she was held and she's directly connected to Caitlin Gardner because they were school friends."

Hunter pointed at the lines Barkley had drawn. "Right now, let's focus first on direct connections. Once we've done that, then we can start inferring other connections. For instance, since Madison is directly connected to James and he's directly connected to Paul Raymond, Jackson Bell and Mark Cooper, then she's indirectly connected to them."

"Got it." Stacy smiled. "So Caitlin Gardner is directly connected to Randall Townsend because he killed her, she's directly connected to the Valley View Motel because that's where she was killed and she's directly connected to Madison Harper because they were school friends."

"Bingo." Barkley drew the connections and made the notations.

"Alright, so why don't we do 'scumbag zero'?" They all turned to Billy with looks that said, 'huh'. He smiled. "You know how epidemics have 'patient zero', James Le James is our 'scumbag zero'. He's at the center of it all."

There were nods around the room as Billy continued. "James is directly connected to Madison Harper because he killed her. He's directly connected to the first holding center because that's where he killed her. He's directly connected to Paul Raymond and Mark Cooper because they were cellmates. He's directly connected to Randall Townsend and his own apartment because Townsend killed him in his own apartment." He stopped and took a breath. "This could go on for a while... He's directly connected to Dr. Lamar by the phone number found in his apartment and to Lance Sledge because he used to work for him. Finally, he's directly connected to Jackson Bell and to all three holding centers because he was the guy who paid Bell the rent for all three." Sanders exhaled and wiped his brow. The group shared amazed looks.

They spent the next hour looking through their case notes, drawing lines, noting comments and trying to make as many connections as they could. They had gone through every person on the board except Warrick Turner. Hunter stepped up to the board and drew a couple of lines. "Warrick is connected to his apartment because that's where we, uh... encountered him and he's tied to the first holding center because we found his prints there."

As he paused, Stacy stared at the board. "Wait a minute. Who all is connected to Turner's apartment?"

Hunter looked and traced the single line back to Turner. "Just Turner."

"That can't be. What about the prints on the truck and the DNA from the coffee cup?"

All three of the detectives turned to her with blank looks. Hunter shrugged. "What prints and DNA?"

"That perfect set of full hand prints I took from the door of Turner's pickup and the coffee cup from the floorboard. I had packed them up with all the other evidence from the apartment scene right before they grabbed me." As she spoke, the wheels turning in her head could be seen on her face. She sat up straighter. "Didn't someone process that evidence?"

Hunter went pale. "Uh… Well… Since you were gone and the priority was to find you, we put that stuff on the back burner and then when we ended up raiding two more holding centers, we put the apartment scene as a low priority."

She picked up on his statement. "And since I haven't been officially back to work since, no one would have known to process those prints or that cup." She scrunched her face and put her hand to her forehead. "We've got to get those processed. I'll bet my paycheck that's going to give us another connection."

"I'll bet you're right." Barkley looked at his watch. "Guys, it's getting late and it's been a long day. Let's put that as our first priority for in the morning. Stacy, that's yours. Billy, now that you know what we're looking for, rerun the backgrounds in the morning on our four dead guys and look for any kind of connections to anyone or any place on this board. Go all the way back to high school."

"I'll take Bronson, Raymond and Lamar and do the same." Hunter stood and took a picture of the board with his phone.

"Perfect, Cowboy and I'll take my personal favorite, Lance Sledge." Barkley nodded at the board.

"Try to stay out of the Governor's crosshairs." Sanders smiled and the team laughed as they all packed up.

Chapter 55

"You did go home last night, didn't you?"

Barkley turned away from the white board to see Sanders standing in the doorway of the conference room. "What?"

"I think you were standing in that exact spot when we called it a night."

Barkley waved off the thought. "No, I got out of here last night. Unfortunately, I've made little progress since." He shook his head and pointed to the board. "I spent two hours after dinner last night…" He looked at his watch. "And another three hours this morning searching every aspect of Lance Sledge's life and I've come up with absolutely nothing that connects him to anyone or any place on this board other than the two ex-con's that worked for his company."

"No surprise there." Sanders sat down at a table and booted up his laptop. "He's at the top of a multi-million dollar empire. He's as close to untouchable as they get." He laughed. "Just ask the Governor."

"Maybe I'll hold on that suggestion." Barkley laughed. "I know our two lovebirds should be here anytime but I need some positive news so if you've got anything…" He tossed him the marker and sat down. "Don't keep me in suspense."

Sanders snatched it out of the air. "Not sure it's earth shattering but I've got a few interesting things." He walked to the board and drew a line from Randall Townsend to Warrick Turner and then one from Townsend to Dirk Simpson. "I checked and cross referenced the phone records on the burner phone that were found with Randall Townsend, Warrick Turner and Dirk Simpson. All three showed multiple calls going back and forth between the three of them." He shrugged. "Not surprising but it's one more link that ties them all together." He raised the marker and wiggled his eyebrows to make a point. "But wait, there's more. All three had a ton of calls to and from another burner phone, one we hadn't found and weren't aware of yet, that all stopped at the exact same time."

Barkley sat up straight and cocked his head.

"All the calls from this fourth phone stopped the day James Le James was killed." He smiled.

"Interesting." Barkley leaned forward. "So I'd suggest that we…"

"Already done." Sanders smiled. "I got the records for that burner phone and it produced two other burner phone numbers that I pulled into the mix. Those phones also had calls to and from Turner, Townsend and Simpson, but… The big nugget I found…"

"Are you panning for gold now?" Hunter smiled as he walked into the room. Sanders stopped as he and Barkley nodded to Hunter. "Don't stop on my account. You were talking about a big nugget?"

Sanders grimaced. "Well, it may not be that big. There's good news and bad news. The burner phone number connected to all of these guys, the one we think belonged to James Le James, made a phone call to the switchboard of Camelot Oil and Gas."

Both Hunter and Barkley bolted straight. Barkley's eyes went wide. "Holy shit! Are you serious?"

Sanders immediately held out his palms to tamp down the excitement. "The problem is that there was only one call and it only lasted a few seconds. For all we know, it could have been a wrong number and keep in mind, we don't have this phone and we can't tie it physically to any one on this board."

Barkley nodded his head, lost in thought as he spoke. "It's a connection and one of the first that takes us outside our little cadre of dead guys."

"Exactly." Hunter walked over to the board and drew a dotted line from Lamar to Bronson. "But it helps substantiate a very weak connection I found between Spencer Lamar and Garret Bronson. This may be a stretch but… Spencer Lamar went to med school at Tulane Medical School from 1996 to 2000. During that same timeframe, Garret

Bronson was getting his business degree from Xavier University." He put the marker in the tray and turned to Sanders and Barkley.

Both men looked confused. Sanders squinted at the board. "Okay, so what's the connection?"

"Both universities are in New Orleans."

Sanders shook his head. "No they aren't. Xavier's in Cincinnati."

Hunter smiled. "Not that Xavier, Xavier of New Orleans. It's just a few miles from Tulane. These guys were not only both in New Orleans at the same time, they spent four years within just a few miles of each other. Hell, they were probably drinking in the same bars."

Barkley smirked. "Well, it's something to add to the pot."

"It also reinforces the other connection I found." Hunter drew a line from Warrick Turner to Paul Raymond. "Almost fifteen years ago, Raymond was arrested but released on a breaking and entering charge. His companion at the time was Warrick Turner."

"Now we're getting somewhere." Barkley's eyes were wide.

Sanders nodded. "I've got one more that might help." He looked at Barkley. "I took your advice and went all the way back to high school and found that Dirk Simpson went to high school in Amarillo. That rang a bell so I checked my notes. Paul Raymond also grew up in Amarillo. He was a few years older than Simpson but at the time, Amarillo wasn't exactly New York City. There's a good chance they knew each other."

"The picture is becoming clearer." Barkley stepped to the board and retraced. "Paul Raymond was a cellmate to James Le James. We can triangulate the burner cellphone calls and connect Camelot Oil and Gas to Townsend, Turner and Simpson. We've got Spencer Lamar and Garret Bronson in the same New Orleans neighborhood for four years of college. Simpson and Raymond both grew up in Amarillo and Raymond and Turner were burglary buddies. Not exactly bullet proof but it's getting close."

"Maybe I can help." Stacy's voice wafted in from the door. All three detectives turned to see her holding up a file folder, her smile glowing. "Guess who's a perfect match for that set of prints found on the driver's side door of Turner's truck and the DNA from the cup in the floorboard?" She paused until Hunter motioned for her to continue.

"Paul Raymond."

"And that ladies and gentlemen, is a chicken dinner winner." Barkley crossed his arms, leaned back and smiled.

Chapter 56

"I can't believe you didn't want to eat at Blue Sushi." Sanders jabbed playfully at Hunter's shoulder as they walked to the car after eating at Boomerjack's Grill on West Seventh.

"I told you, it's bad form to eat lunch across the street from where you're going to arrest someone." He smiled. "Besides, I've seen you eat sushi. You'd eat so much that you wouldn't be able to move.'

Sanders thumbed over his shoulder at the restaurant as he got in the back seat. "That wasn't exactly light eating."

Barkley closed the passenger door and rubbed his stomach. "He's got a point."

Hunter shook his head, started the car and pulled out onto West Seventh. "Okay you jackoffs, let's get focused. It's early afternoon on a work day and Camelot Oil and Gas is in the middle of a heavily populated business area. The last thing we want is to end up in a shootout."

In the rearview mirror and to his right, he saw Sanders and Barkley nod. Before he could continue, his phone rang. "Hunter. What?" He shot a glance toward Barkley. "Shit. What's his status?" He frowned and shook his head as he listened. "All right, thanks."

He slammed his phone onto his thigh. "Damn it. That was Stacy. Spencer Lamar got shanked in county lockup this morning."

Barkley sighed and shook his head. "Is he alive?"

"For now, but it doesn't look good." He pounded his fist on the steering wheel.

"It is what it is." Barkley's voice was more of a growl. He was glaring forward. "Like you said, let's stay focused. Go back through the plan."

Hunter nodded. "The plan is simple. Barkley and I will go in just like we did last time... All we want to do is talk." He maneuvered the car into the middle lane as they came up on the University intersection. "Billy, we've got a patrol unit meeting us there. I want you to coordinate downstairs and cover both exits just in case something happens and either of them gets past us."

When the light turned green, they crossed and moved between the two newest buildings in the Museum One complex. He pulled into one of the angled street parking spots in front of Blue Sushi just as the patrol unit pulled in beside him.

The three detectives and the two patrolmen spent two minutes standing by the patrol unit doing a quick plan check and then walked across the street toward the six-story office building housing Camelot.

Hunter looked at Sanders and held up his hand held radio. "Stay on channel two. If something happens, I'll let you know."

"You got it, Cowboy. We'll have both exits covered." He pointed to each of the patrolmen in turn. "I want you on the north exit and you on the south exit. I'll be in the lobby where I can watch both the elevator and the stairs."

The team walked into the lobby. Barkley and Hunter waited for the elevator door to open as the patrolmen deployed and Sanders found the optimal position in the lobby.

"You ready to go orca hunting?" Barkley's eyes gleamed.

Hunter nodded. "Damn straight. I'm kind of tired of wasting time on sharks."

The elevator doors opened and the two detectives stepped on.

* * * *

Garret Bronson sat behind his desk scouring a printed out spreadsheet. Paul Raymond sat across from him with a notepad. "Have you talked with the boys over at Chesapeake about negotiating the rights to that acreage north of the speedway?"

"I've left several messages. I'm still waiting on a return call. You know how those guys are." Raymond jotted a note. "I'll try again."

Bronson nodded, circled some numbers on the printout. "Stay after them. That could be a gold mine for us." He laughed. "As good as it gets without breaking the law."

Raymond smirked. "We wouldn't want to do that, would we?"

"No we wouldn't." Bronson stood up. "How are the production rates looking for our leases out in Keller?"

"Ever since drill site 529 came online, the numbers have skyrocketed." Raymond flipped through some notes as Bronson moved to the window. "We've gone from 5,000 cubic feet in March to 7,500 in April. I expect that to be even higher in May."

Raymond continued to talk but the sound became background noise as Bronson's eyes locked onto the activity in the street below.

Shit... Okay, stay calm.

Bronson took a deep breath, turned from the window and smiled at Raymond. "It sounds like expediting that site was a good move." He casually walked back to his desk and picked up the spreadsheet again, pretended to look at it and dropped it back onto the desk. "Can you get me some updated numbers on the Roanoke leases? I'm going to hit the head."

"I'll have it for you when you get back." Raymond looked down at his laptop and began clicking away.

Bronson nodded. "Thanks." He stepped out of his office, looked over his shoulder and paused at the door until he was sure Raymond was preoccupied with his task. Instead of walking through the lobby out to the restrooms, he turned right down the hall and headed for a back exit that led directly to the parking garage.

He heard the ding from the elevator as he stepped through the door.

* * * *

Hunter and Barkley stepped off the elevator directly into the lobby of Camelot Oil and Gas. They walked toward the receptionist they had seen last time. She smiled. "Welcome to Camelot, how can I help you?"

They both had their badges out. Hunter held his up. "I'm Detective Jake Hun..."

The glass partition separating the lobby and the offices exploded into a shower of glass rain as gunshots rang out. Both men instinctively dropped to the floor as bullets ripped through the receptionist's desk. Splinters mixed with the glass flying through the air.

The receptionist shrieked and fell out of her chair.

Barkley was up on one knee behind a chair in an instant. His Sig fired three quick shots in the direction of the office. Hunter moved behind the desk, his Glock out and ready. With his free hand, he reached for the receptionist. "Are you okay?"

Her head was nodding frantically but only whimpers came out.

"Get behind me." Hunter positioned himself behind the desk between her and the line of fire. He yelled over to Barkley. "What do you see?"

"Don't have a sight line. You?"

Three more shots ripped into the desk just above Hunter's head. He flinched and the receptionist squeaked. *Thank God this desk is solid.* He peaked over the desk, raised his Glock and popped off two quick rounds but missed.

"Shit! Nothing." Hunter grabbed his hand held. "Billy, we're taking fire. Call for reinforcements."

"On it." Sanders voice crackled.

Hunter grabbed the receptionist. "Who's in there? Is it both Raymond and Bronson?"

Her head shook back and forth. "No, no..." She stammered. "Garret l-l-left... Out the back... A minute ago."

"The back? Shit! Barkley! Bronson's gone. It's just Raymond in there." He grabbed the hand held. "Billy, there's a back exit." He stopped, looked at the receptionist. "Where does it go?"

"G-g-garage."

"It goes straight to the garage. Get there now!"

"Moving!" Static screeched from the radio.

* * * *

"Let's go. Let's go." Sanders signaled to the two patrolman to follow him and he headed toward the entrance they'd come in.

He had his gun out as he burst through the door into the midday sun. Two women standing at the door screamed at the sight of his big frame crashing through the door. He was yelling into his radio for backup as he turned to his right and broke into a sprint down the sidewalk. The two patrolman lost pace within seconds.

As he came up on the corner of West Seventh and Barden Street, he heard the roar of a high performance engine and the squeal of tires. He shouldered against the wall just long enough to get settled before he swung around the corner with his gun raised.

A high-pitched whine and a flash of red moved past him coming out of the parking garage. The bright red Ferrari took a hard right and moved away from him. He stepped into the street, took aim on the license plate that read Camelot and fired twice to no effect.

All he could do was watch the car disappear over the rise in the road. He grabbed the radio. "He's gone!"

* * * *

Hunter heard Sander's garbled voice over the radio but ignored it. He slid to the back of the desk making sure to keep the receptionist safe. "Don't move." He caught Barkley's eye and gave him a hand signal.

Barkley nodded, turned his gun toward the office area and began firing. As his rounds steadily pummeled the office door and desk, Hunter scrambled around the receptionist's desk and dove for the hall. He landed in a pile of glass, slid behind a wall and turned to get a line of sight into the office.

Swapping roles, Hunter now fired into the office, his bullets steadily ripping into the desk as Barkley moved from behind the chair in the lobby. Hunter could see Raymond's leg jerk behind the desk as Barkley slid to a position on the other side of the door.

Both detectives ejected their empty magazines and reloaded in seconds. Hunter peeked around the corner, saw Raymond move his leg.

"Raymond, this is the police. There's no way out. Throw out your weapon."

A cross between a laugh and a whimper came from behind the desk followed by a flash of movement and another rain of bullets. Both Barkley and Hunter jerked back from the doorway as another whirlwind of glass and splinters peppered their faces.

Hunter heard a dry click of the trigger and reacted instantly. He jumped to his feet, flew through the door and slid past the desk with his Glock up and ready.

Raymond's eyes jerked wide, a new magazine halfway inserted into his gun.

"Drop it or die! Your call." Raymond's forehead was lined up in Hunter's sights.

Raymond's hand opened and the gun hit the floor as Barkley's Sig appeared over the top of the desk and stopped an inch from his temple. "Good decision."

Chapter 57

"When I gave you the go ahead to support Barkley for another week, I didn't expect you to shoot up half the west side." Sprabary's jaw was tight as he motioned for Hunter to sit.

It was shortly after four P.M. Hunter and Barkley had escorted Paul Raymond back to the station and had him stewing in one of the interrogation rooms while Sanders managed the crime scene with the support of Preston Evans and the Rangers CSI team.

Sprabary frowned but his voice was flat as he continued. "I've got every media outlet in the country either camped out or calling every five seconds. I've also got some attorney wanting to see me about his client who's apparently having some kind of mental breakdown."

"Yeah, that would be Camelot's receptionist. Sorry about that." Hunter winced. "Their reaction was a bit unexpected. We hadn't even identified ourselves to the poor woman before Raymond unloaded on us."

Sprabary rubbed his forehead. "Fucking criminals. They never do what you expect, do they?" He shrugged. "So where are we?"

"We've got an APB out for Bronson with people watching all airports, train and bus stations and the Rangers have units posted on all major outbound interstates. We've got Raymond sweating in a room. Barkley is waiting to start questioning him."

"Has he said anything yet?"

"Other than disparaging my mother and insisting that I procreate with myself, nothing of note." Hunter grinned. "The usual claptrap."

Sprabary nodded and thumbed toward the door. "Let me know what he says and when we locate Bronson."

Hunter took his cue, bolted Sprabary's office and found Barkley standing in the observation room glaring through the mirror at Raymond. "Is this a new interrogation technique? Just stare at him until he cracks?"

Barkley's smile was tired. "Just thinking. I thought we had both of them today." He shrugged. "I was ready to put this one in the books. We can't do that until we get Bronson and for all we know, he's halfway to Mexico by now."

"We'll get him." Hunter joined Barkley in staring through the window. "He's not an underground kind of guy. You saw all those pictures in his office. He likes his toys and the highlife too much and while he may have some contacts outside the country, I don't see him making a living in Saudi Arabia or Mexico." He paused. "All we've got to do is find him."

Barkley picked up a folder sitting on the table and held it up. "And Paul Raymond is going to tell us exactly how to do that."

Hunter looked at him with a question, but Barkley just smiled and headed toward the door. "Showtime."

When Barkley entered the stark white room, Paul Raymond immediately started ranting. "Where's my lawyer? I told you in the car I wanted my lawyer. You can't just keep me here, locked in this room..."

"Would you shut the fuck up?" Barkley plopped down in the chair across from Raymond. "For Christ's sake, you sound like my mother-in-law. You're going to get your lawyer soon enough but here's the deal, Paul. Before you do, you're going to tell me everything there is to know about Garret Bronson and his organization and you're going to help me find him today."

"Bullshit." Raymond shook his head. "I want immunity before I say anything."

Barkley spread his hands, scrunched his face and looked at Paul Raymond like he was crazy. "Paul, Paul, Paul. Are you kidding me?" He over exaggerated exasperation. "Let's see." He looked at his notebook. "I've got you on well over twenty-five counts of human trafficking, which by the time we get through with our investigation will likely be in the hundreds. I've got you on conspiracy to commit three counts of murder and four counts of kidnapping. I've got you as an accessory to murder and an accessory after the fact. Oh, and let's not forget, two counts of attempted murder of law enforcement officers." He laughed. "I'm not offering you immunity. Hell, you're going to be lucky to avoid the needle."

Raymond blustered. "What? Let me guess. You're going to offer me protection? You can't protect me inside so don't even go there." He leaned back and folded his arms across his chest.

"Really? Protection?" Barkley smirked and shook his head. "Oh no Paul, you're going to prison for the rest of what will likely be a very short life and let me give you a glimpse into your very near future." He leaned back, grinned at Raymond and talked with his hands held wide. "Sometime within the first six months of your stint in the Texas Penal System, two or three of Bronson's boys are going to catch you alone in the showers. They're going to beat you half to death and gang rape you until they get bored. When they lose interest, they're going to shiv you so many times that even your mother won't recognize you when you meet her in hell." He leaned forward, cocked his head and one side of his mouth ticked up. "I'm not offering you protection."

"Then we have nothing to talk about. I won't tell you a thing."

"That's where you're wrong Paul." Barkley ran his index finger over a folder he had laid on the table. "You see, I'm offering you something much more important than your protection." He flipped open the folder and turned the single eight-by-ten photo around. "I'm offering protection for her."

Raymond's breath caught and his eyes flew wide. He started to hyperventilate. "How the... What... You son of a bitch! No one knows about her. How did you find her?"

Barkley looked incredulous. "Really Paul? It took me all of twenty-four hours."

"Bronson doesn't know she even exists." He said it but the look of terror on his face showed he didn't believe it.

Barkley's laugh echoed off the hard white walls of the interrogation room. He stopped and shook his head. "Please don't be that dense. Come on. You've watched the man. Do you really think he doesn't know?"

Raymond's face had gone pale, a sheen of sweat covered his face. His voice was weak, almost a whisper. "He doesn't know..." He shook his head slowly and stared at the picture of the little girl.

Barkley leaned over the table and positioned his mouth a few inches from Raymond's ear. His voice sounded like Satan hissing. "He may not... Yet..." He left the thought hanging in the air as Raymond's hands began to tremble so violently the sound of the chains filled the room. "Chew on that while I go get some coffee. Then I'm going to come back in here and you're going to tell me everything you know about Garret Bronson."

A slow smile slid across Hunter's face as he watched Barkley stand and leave. When he walked into the observation room, Hunter shook his head. "Colt Barkley, you are one cold son of a bitch. Nicely played."

"You think I got his attention?"

Hunter nodded to the window where they could see Raymond's ashen face sweating and his hands trembling. "Oh, I think so."

"Good. I'm going to take a leak and get some coffee." His voice was casual. "You need anything?"

"I'm good. I'm going to check in with Sanders and Stacy."

* * * *

Twenty minutes later Barkley strolled back in as if he was coming back from a trip to the spa. "I don't know about you Paul, but I feel much better."

"Fuck you."

"Now is that any way to talk to the guy who's going to be able to protect your daughter from Bronson?" Barkley tsked as Raymond just glared. Barkley set his phone down on the table, tapped a couple of times to bring up the digital recorder and hit record. "Okay Paul, start talking. You know Bronson. Where is he holding up?"

Raymond's eyes were glazed over, almost catatonic. When he spoke, his voice sounded hollow and distant. "There's a lake house on

Eagle Mountain. Owned by a dummy corporation…"

Chapter 58

"All right, gather round guys. Let's talk about how this is going to go down." Hunter nodded to Zeke. "Thanks for coming."

"Should be fun Cowboy." Zeke leaned against a table.

Hunter checked the time, almost eight P.M. "By the time we get rolling, we're going to be working in the dark so I want to make sure everyone understands the plan."

He turned toward the whiteboard and pointed to a picture of Garret Bronson. "This is our guy. He won't go quietly. His second in command, Paul Raymond, opened fire on Barkley and me this afternoon at their company offices."

Stacy stared at the picture, absorbing every feature of Bronson's face.

Hunter continued. "According to Raymond, Bronson is most likely at a home near Eagle Mountain Lake. It's in a heavily wooded area at the end of a court. We will have to approach quietly and I expect it to be poorly lit."

Sanders raised his hand. "How sure is he on this location?"

Hunter walked to the map. "Raymond indicated that no one but he and Bronson know about the lake house. It's where Bronson liked to... sample the goods." He circled three other locations on the map. "These are three other holding centers, all of which are supposedly empty. There is an outside chance he's at one of these sites, but odds are with the lake house."

"How do we know he hasn't already made a run for the border?"

"He's a planner who doesn't spook easily. Bolting for a foreign country without nailing down logistics isn't his style. Besides, he wouldn't expect Raymond to talk." Hunter pointed to Barkley. "Detective Barkley has amazing persuasion skills." Barkley took a bow as Hunter continued.

Hunter drew a mockup of the court and house layout on the whiteboard and they started planning. By shortly after nine, Hunter stood back from the board. "Looks like a plan."

"Works for me." Zeke nodded.

Hunter glanced at his watch, looked around the room. "Load up in fifteen minutes. It's a thirty minute drive to the staging area. We'll be there by ten P.M."

"What about me?" Stacy had resumed staring at the picture of Bronson.

"I'll call you as soon as we have him in custody and you can be on scene with Evans' team." Hunter put his hand on her shoulder and leaned in close to her ear. "We're going to get this bastard."

* * * *

"Alejandro, *como estas?* This is Garret Bronson. Yes, yes it's been a while. Hope the family is well." He nodded and listened as he fed documents into the shredder. "It turns out I'm going to be in Monterrey tomorrow. My jet will leave Fort Worth at six A.M. tomorrow. I'll touch down just before nine. Can we get together for lunch?"

He moved from the office to the master bedroom as he continued his conversation for another ten minutes. "*Hasta manana.*" He hung up, went to the closet and packed his suitcase with extra clothes. He had checked his phone multiple times throughout the day but had not heard from Raymond.

They've got him.

He shook off the thought, zipped up the suitcase and headed back to the office.

He won't talk. He knows better.

When he got back to the office, he opened the cabinet housing the flat screen and punched up the multi-view of the security cameras.

All quiet.

He sat at his laptop, pulled up the security controls and turned on all the sensors. He dimmed the lights and glanced out the window that gave him a view to the front entrance and down the court.

Can't be too careful.

* * * *

"I'm pulling into the Exxon just past Wells Burnett Road. We'll do our final prep there." Hunter clicked the mic on his radio.

"Roger that." Sanders responded from his car.

"Ten four." Zeke and the SWAT team followed behind Sanders

The team exited the vehicles and Hunter spread his map out on the hood. "Okay, I'll lead." He pointed to the map. "There's a long, tight bend where the road follows the shoreline and then his street is on the right. It's a long court with only a handful of houses. Our target is at the end."

Zeke pointed to a bend midway down the street. "We'll block the road here and go the rest of the way on foot. The only light we'll have is the moon."

Hunter looked at Zeke. "I want you and two of your guys with Barkley, Sanders and me as the assault team. Your other three guys will man the roadblock." He looked at the rest of the team. "Lock and load. Get your vests on and let's roll."

Within minutes they were turning into the neighborhood. "Damn it's dark in this neighborhood." Barkley craned his neck to see around one of the curves as Hunter slowed looking for the turn. Another hundred yards, they found it and turned right. Sanders and the SWAT truck followed close behind.

Hunter killed his headlights and crept to a stop at the point Zeke had mapped. He angled his car sideways blocking one half of the road. Sanders followed his lead and blocked the other half.

Barkley dropped his Stetson into the seat as he stepped out of the car. The three detectives, Zeke and two of his team fanned out across the width of the road, drew their weapons and started moving south toward the target house.

"Place looks deserted." Hunter spoke quietly.

"Hell, the whole street looks deserted. I can barely see the outline of the house in the trees." Sanders squinted.

The house sat back off the road about a hundred feet in a thick stand of oak trees and heavy landscaping. The quiet of the neighborhood was punctuated by crickets and early June bugs. The distant sound of a motorboat buzzing across the lake mixed with their footsteps as they came to the entrance of the driveway.

Hunter stepped past the rock mailbox and signaled for the team to fan out as planned, Zeke and his guys taking the back, Hunter, Barkley and Sanders taking the front.

* * * *

Bronson jerked his head around at the beeping from his laptop. He looked at the flat screen and his heart jumped. Six shadowy figures stood by the mailbox. He slammed his laptop shut out of habit, grabbed his forty-five, doused the light completely and ran out of his office.

Shit. They're here. No time for anything. Got to go.

He weaved through the darkness, moving like a cat. The door to the garage came up fast and he almost ran into it. He grabbed his keys, opened the door and bolted down the steps.

* * * *

The sound didn't register until the bright light hit them and the roar of the engine was on top of them. Zeke and his team were too far back to have seen it. All three detectives swung and tried to sight in on the blinding light, but it was moving fast.

Hunter heard the motorcycle engine rev, fired twice but dove to the ground as the light roared past him. He felt the heat from the exhaust brush past his face and heard gunshots ringing out from different directions.

By the time he rolled over and got to his knee, the red tail light was rounding the bend toward the roadblock and he could hear the footsteps of Zeke and his guys coming up behind him.

"Go! Go!" Hunter waved them on and grabbed his radio. "He's coming your..."

The eruption of gunfire cut him off and made the quiet night sound like the Fourth of July. The revving of the motorcycle engine didn't stop. It cycled up and down but continued to fade into the distance as the sound of shots stopped.

* * * *

He hadn't expected the roadblock and swerved off the road and into the trees as he blew past it. The muzzle flashes left him seeing spots.

Oh shit.

Something stung his side.

Damn that hurts. Can't stop. Got to go.

He gunned the Ducati high performance bike out of the trees, over the curb, back onto the pavement and almost laid it down as he turned left off Valley View onto Timberlake. He was moving so fast, his headlight could barely light enough road for him to see. It felt like a video game on warp speed but he was winning because all the cops were behind him.

His hand twisted the throttle back harder as he leaned hard left into the curve.

* * * *

"Turn left on Timberlake Drive." Stacy reached up and turned off the GPS so she could focus on the winding road ahead. She'd studied the map enough to know that she was just down the road from where they were.

I'll stop at the entrance to the court and wait for Cowboy to call.

She followed Timberlake as it followed the contours of the shoreline, squinting into the darkness.

Stacy steered right around the bend, heard a sound and reached to turn down the radio. She flinched when the light hit her eyes. She slammed on the brake, but her world disintegrated before it got there.

Her arms flew out and her head snapped back as it seemed like all of her internal organs squished against her sternum. Sound exploded around her, metal tearing, glass shattering. She was shoved back against her seat and it felt like someone had punched her in the mouth.

For a moment, all she could see was white as things flew all around her. Then everything stopped. A hissing sound filled her ears as the airbag deflated. Smoke and the smell of gasoline filled her lungs.

She opened her eyes and screamed when she saw a man's shredded face inches from hers, his head and shoulders protruding through the front windshield, his eyes open and distant. Her reaction was to jerk back but there was no place to go.

Her hands fumbled for the door handle to no avail as she stared at the dead man in front of her. When her brain caught up with her, she stopped her hands and looked closer. She shuddered with satisfaction as she realized who it was.

Chapter 59

"Oow, that looks like it hurts." Anne Robinson of Emancipation Texas, looked at Stacy's matching black eyes as she reached over and squeezed her hand. She nodded to the rest of the team as she joined their table at the Swamp Donkey Saloon.

"It's not as bad as it looks." Stacy grimaced. "It only hurts when I smile."

"It's better now than it was yesterday. It's had a couple of days for the swelling to go down." Hunter frowned. "Maybe it will teach her to listen to me next time."

"Yeah, right." Stacy rolled her eyes. "If I had listened to you, Bronson would be in Mexico by now."

"I like him better in the morgue." Sanders grinned.

"I'll drink to that." Barkley held up his beer and the team followed suit.

Anne glanced around the table. "All right, so Colt filled me in on the highlights. Garret Bronson and Paul Raymond were the big dogs. What else did I miss?"

Hunter finished chewing a fry. "Well, after we scraped what was left of Bronson off Stacy's windshield…"

Sanders and Barkley both scrunched their faces. Stacy slapped him on the shoulder. "Do you have to be so disgusting?"

He shrugged. "We spent the rest of the night raiding the three locations that Raymond identified. As he'd said, they were all empty but Barkley's CSI team has spent the last two days scouring them and we expect to be able to combine all the fingerprint and DNA profiles from all six locations to build a victim's log."

"I spoke with Preston earlier today and it looks like that list is going to top two hundred profiles." Barkley pursed his lips. "He also told me that they matched prints to three other known felons, one of which was Mark Cooper. We've put out statewide APB's for all of them."

"Well, I want to thank each of you for what you've done on this case." Anne looked from face to face. "There are countless victims that you've saved by taking these guys down."

Everyone nodded, but Stacy's expression was solemn. Hunter noticed. "What's with the long face, Stace? We got the bad guys."

She blinked fast a couple of times and cleared her throat. "What about Kristi Quinn and Hallie Boyer... and all the others we don't even know about? What about those two hundred names on that list?" Her expression was pleading as she looked up. "What about them and their families?"

Barkley furrowed his brow. "We found contact information for a number of Saudi businessmen in Bronson's records. There were also details on additional..." He swallowed. "Transactions involving other girls." He took a sip of beer. "I had an initial meeting with the FBI this morning and we will be turning over all of our information to them and briefing them as we go forward."

"That doesn't sound very optimistic."

He opened his palms. "I think we have some legitimate leads for them to follow." He shook his head. "But it's out of our control and they're going to be dealing with several foreign governments, none of which value human freedom as we do." His voice went hoarse. "I wish I had a better answer for you."

The table went silent for a moment until Anne chimed in, her voice low but resolute. "Well, this team did a great job and my organization will continue the fight. Every life we save is important."

The mood lifted as that thought sank in. Hunter rubbed Stacy's shoulder and smiled before he turned to Barkley and tipped his beer. "Colt, it's been fun working with you." He shrugged. "But since we don't exactly get involved with human trafficking very often, I guess the chances of us working together again are fairly slim."

"Not so fast my friend." Barkley raised his eyebrows. "There's a little news on that front." He picked at the label on his beer bottle. "I've known for a while that after this case I was going to transfer out of human trafficking. Doing this kind of work when you have a young daughter causes too many sleepless nights. I wasn't sure of my next assignment until a couple of days ago. As it turns out, I'm going to be working with the MJSHU."

Hunter grinned. "The what?"

"Multiple Jurisdictions Serial Homicides Unit… Serial killers."

"And that's going to make you sleep better?" Sanders shook his head.

Barkley opened his palm and shrugged. "So if you run across something in that area, I might get to visit again."

"We'll keep that in mind." Hunter looked to Barkley. "So, are you heading back home tonight?"

"Just for the weekend. I'll be back on Monday." He smiled. "Seems I've got a loose end to tie up."

Sanders and Stacy both stopped and shot him questioning looks. Hunter cocked his head. "Loose end?"

Barkley smiled. "Yeah, you remember your connect-the-dot game?" Hunter nodded and Barkley continued. "Well, after we carted Garret Bronson off Wednesday night, my team spent all day yesterday and today doing a detailed search of his place which included having my computer forensics guy scour his laptop."

When Barkley paused, Hunter prompted him. "And?"

"And we found one more really strong connection."

Sanders perked up. "Really? To who?"

Barkley's eyes seemed to glow and a cocky grin crept across his face as he shrugged. "Lance Sledge."

Afterword

As a parent, I can't imagine a more painful scenario than for a child to simply disappear with no understanding of whether they are dead, alive, safe, abused, happy or sad. The inability to have any closure would lead to a torture that would surely take years off a parent's life. Those thoughts often crept into my mind as I wrote Stolen Innocence. One of my objectives was to shine a spotlight on this issue and if not truly educate on the topic, at least bring enough information to the table to make the reader think. Hopefully, I succeeded.

The world of modern day slavery, euphemistically called human trafficking, is one that affects an estimated 27 million people worldwide. Over 800,000 people are trafficked across international borders each year. This crime does not discriminate based on race or gender or nationality, however, the poor, undereducated and minority communities are disproportionally impacted. Half of the victims are children and 80% are female, most of those are trafficked into the commercial sex trade.

Slavery generates $32B a year in profits and occurs in almost every country on the planet. In the U.S., there are almost 20,000 foreign nationals trafficked into the country every year. There are an equal number of U.S. citizens who become victims each year.

While human trafficking is predominantly focused on the commercial sex industry, there are millions of victims globally who are forced laborers working in inhumane conditions. This crime has the potential to affect anyone from the girl next door to the busboy at the local restaurant.

There are a number of organizations focused on combating human trafficking. They range from intervention to education and include groups like Traffick911, Polaris Project, Global Freedom Center and Shared Hope. Do a web search to see how you can help.

Acknowledgements

As I continue to hone the craft of writing fiction, I realize each day that there is so much more to a good book than just coming up with an idea and writing a bunch of words to tell the story. It seems that the further I go on this journey, instead of my circle of support shrinking, it's actually expanding.

I continue to leverage the talents of the Greater Fort Worth Writers group. Susan Sheehey played the role of chief critic and editor. Scot Morgan and Bryan Grubbs relentlessly answered my non-stop questions about everything from grammar to cover art to formatting. Jeff Bacot, Kimberly Packard, Bethany Spotts and Chrissy Szarek provided insight into writing through their well thought out critiques of the work submitted by group members at our meetings. Kimberly also provided advice and guidance on any number of topics.

Clover Autrey provided an amazingly comprehensive guide to independent publishing.

With publishing comes marketing and my friend Terri Zelasko provided invaluable insight and guidance.

As with my first novel, the passion to write is fired by reading great work by other authors including David Baldacci, Robert Crais, Dean Koontz and Jodie Piccoult. I will continue to be an avid reader.

Finally, for the folks who continue to suffer as I chase the next idea or go to the next writer's meeting. My wife Greta, who is always my first editor and sounding board, now also gets to review cover art, marketing ideas and schedules. My two wonderful daughters, Caitlin and Aubrey, continue to put up with their dad constantly daydreaming about plots and characters and dragging his laptop everywhere. I love you dearly. You are why I'm on this earth.

Made in the USA
Charleston, SC
16 May 2016